The Key
to the
Last House
Before
the Sea

BOOKS BY LIZ EELES

LIZ EELES

The Key
to the
Last House
Before
the Sea

bookouture

Published by Bookouture in 2022

An imprint of Storyfire Ltd.
Carmelite House
50 Victoria Embankment
London EC4Y 0DZ

www.bookouture.com

ISBN: 978-1-80314-703-1
eBook ISBN: 978-1-80314-702-4

For everyone who likes to escape into a book

PROLOGUE

20 MARCH 1946

The girl wrenched open the front door and gasped as the fierce wind whipped away her breath. Tiles from surrounding cottage roofs were clattering to the floor and the navy sky was tinged with yellow, like a spreading bruise.

'Mum,' she yelled into the roar of the gale. 'Mummy, come back.'

But her mother didn't hear. She was running towards the sea, the black sea that was bucking and rearing as it smashed into the land.

Sorrel Cove was never like this. The girl dragged a hand across her eyes, wiping away sharp needles of rain. Sorrel Cove, nestled at the foot of the headland, was supposed to be calm and beautiful and safe.

But today, the village was at the heart of a maelstrom that roared and howled. Today, it reminded her of an old picture painted on the wall of the local church. She tried never to look at that painting, with its dark skies, licking fires of hell and figures writhing in agony.

Terrified now, the girl drew in a deep breath and yelled again. 'Mum, you have to come back. Please.'

'Ruth, come away from the door.' Her grandmother was suddenly at her side, putting an arm around her shoulders. 'It's not safe out there.'

The older woman flinched as a metal bucket, twisting in the wind, flew into the wall of a cottage nearby. Then, Ruth felt her body stiffen beside her. 'Where's your mother?'

She couldn't say it. She pointed instead, towards the sea that was flooding across the land and swirling around the cottages closest to the shore.

'Dear God.' Her grandmother clapped a hand to her mouth before yelling over her shoulder. 'Seth, Mariana's gone outside. She must be looking for his boat.'

Ruth had never heard her grandmother sound frightened before. Nor her grandfather, who rushed into the room and shoved his feet into his big boots that were heavy with mud.

'Stupid,' he muttered over and over again while his fingers fumbled with the laces. Then, not stopping for his coat, he rushed out into the storm.

Ruth watched as he ran towards her mother.

'Mum!' she yelled again. 'Please come back to me.'

For a second, the world was bright with lightning that forked into the water, and her mother turned. She looked at Ruth while thunder crashed overhead and a huge dark wave of water towered behind her. She raised her hand and seemed to smile as the wave curled above her head, like the jaws of a wild beast. And then it came crashing down, devouring her.

ONE

NESSA

The sea was calm today. Water was washing against the shoreline with a gentle slap, and gulls seemed to float overhead. Nessa breathed in deeply and tasted salt on the roof of her mouth as she looked around her.

This place, so long abandoned, was a familiar sight. Her family's derelict cottage stood to her right. In front of her were tumbledown walls and scattered stones – the ruins of the rest of the settlement that had once stood here. The village that had disappeared on a day the sea turned. When the water was whipped by storm winds into a malevolent force. It was hard to believe on a peaceful day like today.

Nessa walked to the edge of the land and looked across the rocky shoreline towards the horizon. The sun was rising in a pale blue sky scudded with wisps of white cloud, and boats were bobbing far out to sea. It was just the kind of summer day that her grandmother had loved. And would never see again.

Nessa swallowed and opened the plain box she was carrying. It was surprisingly heavy and had weighed down her arms, as well as her heart, on her walk here, to this forgotten village filled with ghosts.

Suddenly, she was desperate for company. She didn't have to be alone today.

Rosie, such a good friend, had offered to come with her more than once. But she was always busy, and was already doing more than her fair share to help. And Lily... Nessa smiled at the thought of her five-year-old daughter, who'd skipped into school half an hour earlier.

Lily was too young to handle what Nessa had to do today and she'd had enough to cope with recently. In the space of one month, she'd lost her beloved great-granny and her home. Only Rosie's offer of a room at her bed and breakfast place, Driftwood House, had saved them from who knew what fate.

Nessa shielded her eyes against the glare of the sun and looked along the coast. The village of Heaven's Cove nearby was huddled close to the shore and there was Driftwood House, standing on top of the cliff that rose above the quaint cottages.

It was a wonderful old building, with magnificent views of the sea to one side and a sweep of land towards Dartmoor on the other. But she and Lily couldn't stay there for long. It wouldn't be fair on kind-hearted Rosie, who had a guesthouse business to run and couldn't afford to take in waifs and strays.

Nessa shivered before turning her attention back to the task in hand. This was going to be hard, but it was what her grand-mother had wanted. It was what she'd asked of Nessa, as she lay in a hospital bed, her white hair fanned out across the pillow.

'My final request,' was how she'd described it, with the ghost of a smile.

It was strange, thought Nessa, slowly tipping the box she was carrying into the soft breeze. Her gran had refused to set foot in this place for seventy-five years, yet it seemed she'd always planned to come home eventually.

'Goodbye, my darling gran,' she whispered as a stream of ash fell from the box and was caught by the wind. It danced out across the ocean. 'Goodbye, Ruth Mariana Paulson. Rest in peace, you wonderful woman.'

Some of the ash fell onto the stones around her. But most rained down into the water that Nessa knew covered the ruins of homes swallowed by the sea one night long ago – the night of the big storm that had changed her family's fortunes forever.

Her grandmother had been left motherless and homeless by that storm. And now, decades on, here was Nessa in the same predicament.

Stifling a sob, she tipped out the remainder of the ash, all that was left of the grandmother she adored, as sunlight sparked on the golden bangle around her wrist.

She ran her fingers across the unusual bracelet – an overlapping circle of gold with a snake's head at one end and its tail at the other. She'd been fascinated by the bracelet as a child and loved hearing the story of how her great-grandmother had found it here, at Sorrel Cove.

But there would be no more stories of the old days now.

'I'll miss you so much, Gran,' gulped Nessa, above the screeching of the seagulls wheeling overhead. 'I'll look after Lily and keep her safe, I promise you. So you can rest now. You can rest with your mum.'

She bowed her head for a moment, overcome with sadness. Then she wiped away her tears and turned to the cottage that had once been her family's home.

It was easy to imagine her young grandmother standing in the doorway, snuggled against the leg of her mother. The mother she would lose only a few years later when the weather turned.

Five people had died here that night, as the wind howled and the black sea rose up. No wonder the village's name was rarely used and most locals called this place 'the Ghost Village'.

Children never came here, scared that the ruins truly were haunted. But Nessa, in spite of her grandmother's tales, had always found it a place of comfort. Especially on days like this when life seemed almost too much to bear.

She ran her hand along the rough stone wall of the cottage that her grandmother had once called home. Farthest back from the sea, and sheltered by land rising behind it, the building had fared better than its neighbours over the years. Its walls and roof were still intact but years of abandonment and neglect had taken their toll. The front door was swollen shut and windows were boarded up.

There was a gap in one board and Nessa peered through into what must once have been the main living room. Beams of sunshine had found chinks in the wood and were throwing light across a flagstone floor and brick fireplace. A wooden ladder lay abandoned against one wall, and Nessa could make out a stone staircase in one corner.

Once, this cottage had echoed with adult conversation and children's laughter. But now it was gloomy and empty.

Nessa could understand why her grandmother had never wanted to come back here. She'd listened, wide-eyed, to her gran's tale of fleeing the sea that engulfed everything in its path. And she'd realised Sorrel Cove held too many memories of what young Ruth had lost.

But at least her grandmother had returned in the end. And Nessa knew that the old lady's presence in this quiet place would be of comfort to her in the months ahead.

'Bye, Gran,' she said one final time, wiping away more tears. Then she began to walk away from the Ghost Village, away from memories of the past towards her current life, with all its problems.

TWO

NESSA

'How did it go?' Rosie nodded towards the kitchen. 'Cup of tea? Or maybe you'd like something stronger?'

'At ten thirty in the morning?' Nessa grimaced and pushed her dark hair over her shoulder. 'That would make me the kind of mother Valerie is convinced I am.'

She thought for a moment of her ex mother-in-law, Lily's grandmother – the woman who was convinced that Nessa was a rubbish mother.

'Valerie would never know,' said Rosie with a grin.

'She'd find out somehow. That woman has ESP when it comes to my mothering skills. So I'll pass on the alcohol, but tea would be an absolute life-saver.'

She followed Rosie into a large, bright kitchen and sat at the table while the kettle boiled.

Nessa loved this room with its worn quarry tiles and salt-streaked windows that looked out across the clifftop. It felt like the heart of the house that was currently a refuge for her and Lily.

'Did Lily go into school all right?' asked Rosie, placing a steaming mug in front of her. She slid into the seat opposite.

Nessa nodded. 'She was fine once we got there but she was a bit clingy on the walk down the cliff path. It's not surprising, with everything that's been going on lately.' She reached across the table and put her hand on Rosie's arm. 'I know I've said it already but I do appreciate you putting a roof over our heads. I promise we won't stay long.'

Rosie shrugged. 'I couldn't bear to think of you and Lily moving into some grotty bedsit miles away. Honestly, I don't know what's wrong with that Mr Aston bloke. He must have known that you and Lily were living with your gran, so selling the house straightaway is just mean.'

'It's business,' said Nessa resignedly. 'To be fair, we never got proper permission to move in with Gran. I don't think he cared as long as the rent was paid. And he's going to make a mint selling the place to some outsider who'll turn it into a holiday let.'

'Probably. But I still think that turfing you and Lily out so quickly was out of order.'

'He doesn't know that I'm skint and could only afford to move into a hovel.'

'Hmm.' Rosie narrowed her eyes. 'You wouldn't be so skint if Jake stopped being such a useless dad and started paying regular maintenance for Lily. Free spirit, my arse.'

Nessa nodded and sipped her tea. She appreciated Rosie's annoyance on her behalf but she'd gone past the stage of feeling angry at her ex. She'd had four years to get used to his excuses and no-shows, ever since he'd walked out on her and Lily, claiming he was a free spirit who couldn't be 'tied down'. He'd moved two hundred and fifty miles away and now seemed to spend his time flitting from job to job and volunteering with various protest groups.

'Anyway,' said Rosie, giving Nessa a bright smile, 'I love having you and Lily here so you can stay as long as you like.'

And Nessa smiled back, even though she knew that their stay here, high above Heaven's Cove, was temporary.

It had to be. Rosie was running a guesthouse and, with summer getting into full swing, she'd soon need every bedroom for paying guests. She couldn't afford to give up one room to Nessa and Lily for much longer. They'd have to move on to some soulless bedsit in God knows where, and Nessa would have to get her life back on track.

Nessa felt her bottom lip wobble but fortunately Rosie was distracted by the front doorbell ringing. And when she got up to answer it, she didn't see the tears that plopped onto the varnished wood.

Nessa scrubbed at her eyes but the tears kept falling. Not only was she homeless and mourning the loss of her gran, but she was also without a job. With appalling timing, Desmond Scaglin, who ran Shelley's, the hardware store where Nessa worked, had decided to shut the shop and retire.

Nessa wasn't normally one for self-pity. She'd always worked hard at being upbeat, even in those raw first weeks after Jake had moved out.

But life was starting to take the mick, she decided, dabbing at her wet cheeks with a tissue. There was only so much one thirty-year-old could take, but giving up wasn't an option, because of Lily.

Picturing her daughter's trusting face stemmed Nessa's tears. Crying wouldn't help and she couldn't let her daughter down.

With a sigh, Nessa got to her feet. She'd go to her bedroom and do something useful, like apply for jobs – though the long summer holiday from school was starting in six weeks' time and childcare would be an issue.

It was one problem after another, Nessa decided, shoving her soggy tissue into her pocket and opening the kitchen door.

She stopped. Rosie was standing in the sunny hallway talking to a tall man in a grey suit.

'Well, if that's the case, can you suggest anywhere else in the village?' he asked, pushing his horn-rimmed glasses further up his nose.

'Have you tried the B&B opposite the pub?'

'I have. I've tried every B&B in Heaven's Cove and they're all full. I was told you might have a room free, which is why I took a walk up here. But it seems I've wasted my time.' He groaned with frustration.

'The village is always popular at this time of year so it's best to book ahead,' said Rosie gently. 'I am sorry.'

Nessa's heart sank. Rosie was turning down paying business because of her. When she cleared her throat, Rosie and the man turned and looked at her.

'Sorry to interrupt but could I have a quick word, Rosie, about the... um, the room situation? Please,' she added when Rosie hesitated. Nessa addressed the man directly as Rosie walked towards her. 'Could you hang on there for a minute? Thanks.'

The man stared at her for a moment, his face flushed after walking up the cliff in the sunshine. Then he shrugged. 'OK, but I haven't got all day.'

Unnecessarily rude, thought Nessa, pulling Rosie into the kitchen and closing the door behind her.

'I know what you're going to say,' said Rosie, 'and the answer is no. I'm not prepared to throw you and Lily out.'

'Which is lovely. You're lovely – possibly the nicest person on the planet. But I'm not prepared to see you throw away the chance of a paying guest because of us. He can have our room.'

Rosie shook her head. 'Absolutely not. I said I'd help you and Lily and I will. Where would you go at a minute's notice? To Valerie's?'

Nessa shuddered at the thought. Valerie would love having

Lily to stay. For good, probably. But Nessa? Not so much. She'd never approved of her precious son's wife, who worked in a local hardware store and had a grandmother who lived in a rented cottage.

Valerie was a doting mother to Jake and a bit of a snob to boot. Nessa would never measure up to her high standards. She'd never forget the look of barely concealed horror on Valerie's face the first time Jake had taken her home to meet his family. Of all the women her beloved Jacob could have chosen, he'd picked Nessa-with-no-prospects from the village.

Though, Nessa had since realised, she was *exactly* the kind of woman Jake would always choose – someone slightly battered by life who was unlikely to demand too much of him.

Rosie made to go back into the hall but Nessa grabbed her arm. Rosie was right that she and Lily had nowhere to go, but they couldn't take up valuable space for paying guests.

'What about the box room?' she asked.

'What about it?' Rosie frowned. 'The clue's in the name, Ness. It's tiny and crammed full of boxes. And spiders.'

Nessa ignored the spiders comment. She'd rather not think about them.

'It's cluttered, that's for sure. But I could make space for us and it would be fine for me and Lily until I can find somewhere else to go.'

When Rosie hesitated, Nessa took hold of her hand.

'You've been brilliant, Rosie, to me and my daughter. But you're running a business and you're saving up for your wedding. Plus, where is that man going to sleep tonight? He'll end up dossing down on the beach and Belinda will freak out and call the police.'

Rosie grinned at the thought of Belinda, Heaven's Cove's resident busybody, sticking her oar in.

'But are you sure you'll be OK in that little room? I've got a couple of camp beds somewhere but I doubt they're very comfortable.'

'We'll be fine. Honestly. So go and tell that man he can stay before he combusts in the heat. Fancy wearing a suit on a hot day like today!'

Rosie grinned. 'Not the best sartorial choice in the circumstances.' Her face fell. 'But are you quite sure, Nessa?'

'Absolutely.'

'Well, if you don't mind, thank you.'

Nessa gave a mock bow. 'You're very welcome, and it should be me thanking you.'

She followed Rosie back into the hall, where the man was studying the grandfather clock while he waited. He turned, impatience written across his face.

'Sorry about the delay.' Rosie smiled at him. 'Actually, a room has become available, if you'd still like to stay, Mr...?'

'Gantwich,' said the man, perspiring gently in his shirt and tie. 'Gabriel Gantwich. In that case, I'll walk down and collect my car. Is there another road up to this place? I walked up because I didn't want to risk my car's suspension.'

Rosie shook her head. 'I'm afraid not. We're exposed to the elements up here and as fast as we repair the track, it disintegrates back into potholes. But it should be fine if you drive slowly.'

Mr Gantwich raised an eyebrow at that but he left without another word.

While Rosie dealt with the paperwork, Nessa rushed upstairs to expunge any trace of her and Lily's existence from the sunny bedroom that overlooked the sea.

It didn't take long. Nessa hadn't fully unpacked the large suitcase that was shoved under the bed. She hadn't wanted to get too settled in Rosie's comfortable guesthouse. That would make moving on even harder to bear.

She tidied away their few belongings and then stripped the

double bed, put on new sheets from the airing cupboard on the landing, and opened the window to let in a fresh breeze.

After ten minutes' hard work, she stood back with her hands on her hips. The room was guest-ready. No one would know that she and Lily had ever been here at all, sharing a bed.

She dragged her case along the landing to a room at the very back of the house. Opening the door, she clicked on the light and went inside.

Rosie hadn't been joking when she'd said the room was tiny, and crammed full. Cardboard boxes lined the walls and had spilled into the centre of the room.

It was a storeroom for all the clutter that Rosie didn't want on show but couldn't bear to throw away. Nessa ran her hand across an old photo album on a dusty shelf, and a pile of books about Devon folklore. They'd probably belonged to Rosie's late mother, Sofia, who'd always been into the weird and wonderful.

That was what had sparked the friendship between Nessa and Rosie – the sad fact they'd both lost their mums. Nessa when she was a teenager, still at school, and Rosie more recently. They were both unwilling members of the Motherless Club.

Nessa shook her head. There was no point in feeling sorry for herself. This was a storeroom all right but, with a little work, there would be enough space for her and Lily to move in.

It would certainly do for a few nights while she did her best to find somewhere else. Wherever it was, it would have to be halfway decent. Living in a grotty place was OK for Nessa, but she couldn't take Lily anywhere too bleak and there was so little available, particularly at this time of year.

Most local places were rented out to holidaymakers, private landlords weren't keen on single mums without jobs, and the social housing waiting list was depressingly long. So this would do for now.

Nessa got to work, moving boxes and setting up the camp

beds that she'd fetched down from the attic. Lily would have the more comfortable bed, she decided, sitting on both to test them. And she fished Lily's *Frozen* duvet cover out of her case to make it look more inviting.

By the time she'd finished, the room looked much better and the only two spiders she'd found had been trapped under a glass and put out through the window onto the roof. It would definitely do for a little while.

When she went downstairs, Rosie was sitting at the kitchen table with a book open in front of her.

'My accounts,' she said, glancing up as Nessa came into the room. 'I'm beginning to think I really can make a go of this place, if guest numbers stay up and nothing else drops off the building. That storm last month cost me a fortune in roof tiles, but I'm still making a decent profit.' She winced. 'Sorry, Nessa. It's insensitive of me to go on about things going well when—'

'When my life is a total shambles?' Nessa laughed. 'I don't begrudge you a moment of your happiness, Rosie. You deserve it.'

'So do you. I just wish...' She shook her head.

'Me, too. But hey, something will come up,' Nessa butted in, trying to sound upbeat. 'And in the meantime, let me help you out around here to help earn my keep. What needs doing?'

'I can find you a few jobs, if you're sure, before you have to go and get Lily from school.'

'Valerie's picking her up and taking her home for tea so I'm all yours for the rest of the day.'

'OK.' Rosie narrowed her eyes. 'Maybe you should take it easy though, after saying goodbye to your gran. Put your feet up for a while and enjoy some peace?'

'No, I'm fine. And honestly, it's better if I keep busy and distract myself from thinking too much about... everything.'

Nessa paused, overwhelmed by a rush of grief – for the loss of her grandmother and for losing her way. This wasn't the life she'd always assumed she'd be living by now. Where were the fulfilling career, comfortable home and loving partner?

But I have Lily, she told herself sternly, *and Lily will always be more than enough. So stop feeling sorry for yourself.*

'Are you sure you're all right?' asked Rosie, her voice laced with sympathy.

Nessa forced a smile. 'Yeah, you know me. I'm always all right, and I'm raring to go. So, find me some jobs and put me to work.'

THREE

NESSA

Nessa peeled off her rubber gloves and fetched a teapot and cup and saucer from the kitchen cupboard. For the last few hours, she'd been outside painting the conservatory window frames and now she was inside helping Rosie with housework and making late-afternoon snacks for guests.

Rosie was very grateful for the support. And Nessa was grateful that keeping busy and active had helped to ease her grief and smother her worries about the future. There was something soothing about the rhythmic strokes of a paintbrush or polishing a kitchen worktop until it gleamed.

She'd only stopped for half an hour at lunchtime, to job-search online. But that had proved fruitless and she'd needed to clean a bathroom from top to bottom to shake off feelings of despair.

'What am I going to do, Gran?' she asked, switching on the kettle.

But Ruth Mariana Paulson didn't answer. She never would again.

Nessa blinked furiously to ward off tears and concentrated on making a cup of tea for Mr Gantwich, the new arrival, who'd come down from his bedroom and was currently in the guests' sitting room.

Soon Lily would be home, and her smiling face would be a tonic, as always.

Nessa put a jug of milk on the tray, next to the teapot and cup, and plastered on a smile before carrying it through to the latest guest at Driftwood House.

Mr Gantwich was sitting near the window, ignoring the view across the ocean as he flicked through a pile of papers.

He was still in his suit and looked out of place in the sunny sitting room. He didn't notice Nessa come in so she had a chance to have a proper look at him.

The man who had, albeit unwittingly, booted her and her five-year-old out of their bedroom was about mid-thirties. No. Nessa revised her estimate of his age. The grey suit, neat brown hairstyle and glasses made him look older than he probably was. Thirty, Nessa decided. Early thirties at most. He had long fingers that were rifling through a cardboard folder, and pale skin that looked as if he spent most of his life in an office.

He glanced up and nodded towards the small table next to him.

'Just leave it there,' he said gruffly before pulling some papers from the folder.

Still rude, Nessa decided, putting the tray down. As she straightened up, a name on the top piece of paper leaped out at her: *Sorrel Cove*. She craned her neck, trying to read more over his shoulder.

'Can I help you?' he asked sharply, turning the page face down in his lap.

'No, no. Rosie thought you might like a cup of tea so I... um...' She tailed off, feeling awkward.

'Right. Well, thanks, I suppose.'

I suppose? He really was charmless.

'You're welcome,' said Nessa as icily as she could.

Gabriel sighed and settled back in his chair. 'Do you work here?' he asked, sounding as though he couldn't care less.

'Not really. I'm helping Rosie out. Rosie owns the place. She's a friend of mine.'

Gabriel pushed his papers back into the folder and dropped it into the briefcase at his feet. 'Are you local to Heaven's Cove, then?' he asked.

'I've lived here all my life.'

Gabriel sat up straighter in his chair. 'That's interesting.'

Was it? Nessa narrowed her eyes. Was he being sarcastic? It was hard to tell.

'Where are you from?' she asked.

'London. Have you been?'

Now he *was* being sarcastic. Nessa flushed and brushed her hands across her ancient Seal Rescue T-shirt. She might look like a country bumpkin but of course she'd been to London.

Only a few times, admittedly, and she'd found the pace of the place intimidating. But she'd never say as much to Gabriel, who had the look of a man who thrived in the cut and thrust of a busy city.

'I have been to London but I prefer to live by the sea.'

'Really?' he said, wrinkling his nose.

'Really,' answered Nessa firmly. 'Well, enjoy your tea.'

She walked to the door, inwardly fuming. Snooty Gabriel Gantwich made preferring fresh, salty air to traffic fumes sound like a character flaw. So what on earth was he doing in Heaven's Cove in his suit, reading about Sorrel Cove?

Nessa should go back to the kitchen and wait for Lily to arrive. She should leave this annoying guest in peace to read his important papers. But Sorrel Cove held a special place in Nessa's heart. So she stopped and asked him: 'Are you here on holiday?'

He looked up from the cup of tea he'd just poured, seemingly surprised that she was still in the room. 'Not exactly.'

'Are you here because of Sorrel Cove?'

Gabriel took a sip of his tea before answering. 'What makes you think that?'

Nessa felt her face colouring again. 'I wasn't snooping but I happened to see the name on the papers you were reading.'

'And you know Sorrel Cove, do you?'

'Yes. I know it very well.'

'Hmm.' Gabriel caught her eye, for the first time since she'd come into the room, and held her gaze until she felt uncomfortable. Then he said, 'I'm interested in seeing the place.'

'Why?'

Gabriel raised an eyebrow. 'Do I need a reason? I'm interested in its history and I'm told it's worth a visit.'

'It's a very special place.'

'I'm sure.' Gabriel carefully placed his cup back into its saucer. 'I'm interested in the whole of Heaven's Cove, actually.' He picked up his pen and tapped it against his mouth for a moment, as though he was thinking. 'And I need someone to show me around.'

'It's not that big. There's a tourist information place at the village hall, where you can get a map.'

'A map isn't the same as being with someone with local knowledge though, is it?' He tapped his pen some more, then said, 'I'll probably regret this, but do you fancy being my tour guide tomorrow?'

Nessa hadn't been expecting that. She opened her mouth and closed it again. No, she didn't fancy being his tour guide tomorrow. *I'll probably regret this*, he'd said. She definitely would.

Gabriel stared at her. 'I suppose you'll be working here tomorrow.'

'I don't really work here. I'm between jobs at the moment,' said Nessa before mentally kicking herself. Why was she telling this man anything about herself?

'So can you show me around tomorrow or not?' he asked, a hint of irritation in his voice.

Nessa paused, thinking of the new shoes Lily needed that she couldn't afford. 'Will I be paid for my time?'

He shrugged. 'Of course. What do you charge?'

Nessa bit her lip. Spending time in this man's company would be a pain, but she knew the local area like the back of her hand – and she was totally skint right now.

'I charge fifteen pounds an hour,' she told him, trying to keep her voice level. That was more than she'd earned per hour at the hardware store, but Gabriel Gantwich, in his beautifully cut suit, looked like he could afford it.

Her suspicions were confirmed when he nodded straightaway.

'All right.'

Nessa made some mental calculations. A tour round Heaven's Cove would take at least an hour, if she showed him all the sights. And then there was the walk across the headland to the Ghost Village, and she could spend a while telling him the history of the place, in great detail.

She could probably make forty quid, which would buy the shoes and some new T-shirts for Lily. She was growing out of everything, and Jake's promise of new clothes for his daughter had never materialised.

'OK, then,' Nessa told Gabriel, before she could change her mind. 'What time tomorrow?'

'Nine o'clock prompt.'

'Can we make it quarter past nine?' she asked, thinking of the school run.

He gave an almost imperceptible eye-roll. 'Yes. Whatever. What's your name, by the way?'

'Nessa. Nessa Paulson.'

'Right.'

He frowned when there was a sudden thundering of feet in the hallway. Lily, who always made her presence felt, was home. She darted into the room and flung her arms around Nessa's waist.

'Hello!' she squealed, squeezing tight.

Nessa smoothed down her daughter's dark hair. 'Hello, sweetheart. Did you have a good day at school?'

'It was fun. Marcus got a nosebleed and his shirt went all red and spotty.'

'Eek, poor Marcus. Is he all right now?'

'Yeah. Miss Jones gave him extra fruit at break time and let him read his book instead of going in the playground.'

'That sounds very wise of Miss Jones. And did you have a nice time with Granny?'

Lily nodded happily while Nessa looked over the top of her head at Valerie, her ex mother-in-law, who'd followed Lily inside and was standing in the doorway.

'Thank you very much for giving Lily tea and bringing her back,' she said politely.

Valerie gave the slightest of nods. 'You're welcome. I love spending time with Lily, and it's no problem bringing her... home.'

There was a slight gap before the word 'home', as though Valerie couldn't believe that a guesthouse was a suitable home for her precious granddaughter.

She probably had a point, thought Nessa wearily. Though even if she and her daughter lived in a manor house, she didn't suppose that Valerie would approve of her.

But at least she'd done one thing right in Valerie's eyes. Nessa looked down at Lily and hugged her tightly. Whatever Valerie thought of her, they would always be united in their shared love for this child.

When she glanced up, Gabriel was staring at her.

'Yours, I presume,' was all he said.

'Yes, very definitely mine,' Nessa replied, giving her precious daughter an extra squeeze.

An expression flashed across Gabriel's face, so swiftly Nessa found it hard to read. Was it sorrow? Irritation? Indifference?

He'd probably realised that Lily was the reason why his local tour couldn't begin tomorrow at nine, and he was annoyed, thought Nessa, deciding he was probably the type of man who disapproved of single mothers while doing everything he could to avoid paying his taxes.

She looked away so he wouldn't spot any hostility in her eyes. However rude Gabriel Gantwich was, and however much she didn't want to spend time in his company, she needed the money from tomorrow's tour.

So she would smile and be nice, for Lily's sake.

'Thanks again, for collecting Lily,' she said to Valerie, who was still standing in the doorway and showing no sign of leaving. 'Would you, um... would you like a cup of tea before you go?'

She would continue to be nice to Valerie as well, however poorly the older woman treated her. And that, too, was for Lily's sake.

However hard life got, thought Nessa, pulling in a deep breath, she could cope so long as her precious daughter was by her side.

FOUR
VALERIE

Rosie had done a good job of turning Driftwood House from a family home into a guesthouse. Valerie had to admit that. Everywhere had a fresh coat of paint and the place smelled of fresh coffee, and cakes in the oven.

But it was still a shame that she had to take in paying guests to make ends meet after her mother died. Though at least she owned the business. Not like Nessa, who'd worked at that cluttered little hardware store in the village, before losing even that job.

The shop had closed down because its owner, Mr Scaglin, had moved closer to his family in Tiverton. But Valerie couldn't help feeling that Nessa was somehow to blame for her own joblessness.

'You're being ridiculous,' had been Alan's verdict when she'd told him what she thought. 'Old Scaglin's ancient. It's amazing he kept that shop going for as long as he did.'

But once Valerie took against someone it was hard for her to feel kindly towards them. And she had every reason to have taken against Nessa.

'Thanks again, for collecting Lily,' Nessa said. 'Would you, um... would you like a cup of tea before you go?'

Valerie shook her head but, when Nessa smiled at her, she felt obliged to smile back. She didn't want to appear unfriendly or wash her dirty linen in public. Certainly not in front of the man, sitting by the window, who was watching them.

He was young, good-looking and, Valerie noted approvingly, wearing a suit – obviously a businessman in the area to seal some deal or other. He reminded her of Alan when she'd first met him, when he was setting up the estate agency that he'd run until taking early retirement last year. Before he'd changed.

Valerie stood waiting until Nessa found her manners and introduced her to the stranger.

'Oh, this is Mr Gantwich, who's just arrived at Driftwood House, and this is Valerie, my, um...'

Valerie waited to see how Nessa would introduce her. *The mother of the man I chased from Heaven's Cove,* perhaps?

Nessa's freckled cheeks grew pink. 'She's the grandmother of my daughter, Lily.'

Lily, whom Valerie loved with all of her heart. Lily, who shouldn't be living in this place with guests coming and going.

'Are you here for business or pleasure, Mr Gantwich?' she asked, taking in the expensive cut and cloth of his charcoal suit.

'A little of both. Your... Lily's mother has agreed to show me around the village tomorrow.'

Valerie bet she had. She tried to maintain her smile as she felt her face collapsing into a sour expression. At least this man looked too sensible to be fooled by Nessa.

Not that her son, Jacob, wasn't a sensible man. But he was a sensitive and trusting soul, which had made him more open to Nessa's manipulation. And now Nessa was living in Heaven's Cove and Jacob wasn't. Valerie's smile was definitely slipping.

Manchester wasn't that far away. Not really. And Jacob seemed to have made a good enough life there. But it was too far away for frequent weekend visits and Valerie felt her son's absence keenly. Only Lily could warm her heart in the same way.

She suddenly realised she was finding it hard to breathe.

'I'd best be off,' she said curtly, running a hand through her greying hair. 'I'll see you soon, Lily. Goodbye, Mr Gantwich.' She ignored Nessa completely.

On her way back down the cliff, Valerie breathed in the smell of the sea and enjoyed the early evening sun on her face.

She regretted fleeing from Driftwood House now. Nessa had given her a strange look when she'd rushed off. But sometimes, recently, Valerie had an overwhelming urge to escape – though what she was escaping *from*, she wasn't sure. It was all very strange.

Valerie stopped to pull a stone from her sandal and looked out across the ocean. The water was shimmering orange and gold as the sun slipped closer to the horizon.

It looked so beautiful that tears prickled at the corners of her eyes, but Valerie ignored them and walked on. She'd never been a crier and, if she started now, she'd be late getting Alan's tea.

She should have brought her car up to Driftwood House, but she'd left it in the lane at the bottom of the cliff because she hadn't fancied driving up the cliff road.

It was stupid but she felt anxious these days as the car bumped its way higher. As though it might lose traction and plummet back towards the village far below.

She never used to be so nervous about life, but sometimes these days she hardly felt like herself at all. Perhaps it was hitting her mid-fifties and starting to feel the pull of old age. Perhaps that was why she veered between feeling murderous towards Alan and so sad that she could hardly get out of bed some mornings. Thank heavens for Lily, the one bright spot in her life.

Her thoughts turned again towards getting home and cooking for Alan, who was expecting grilled mackerel and roasted vegetables this evening.

She dreamed of the day she'd arrive home to find Alan cooking for her. But he never had in thirty-five years of marriage so was unlikely to start now. Not unless Valerie was struck down with some dreadful disease. Though, if that happened, he'd no doubt plead ignorance in the kitchen and Valerie would have to drag herself from her sick bed.

'I don't know where you keep the mixed herbs,' he'd say, heading back to his newspaper and comfy chair, even though they'd lived in the same house, on the edge of Heaven's Cove, for the last ten years.

Valerie glanced again across the shining sea and tried to think more positively. Things would be different when Lily moved in. Alan wouldn't be keen at first but it was the only solution.

Nessa couldn't keep a five-year-old in a guesthouse full of strangers, or a dingy bedsit somewhere. She'd come round eventually and see that Valerie's plan was the only way forward.

Valerie smiled and quickened her pace, suddenly feeling more cheerful. Lily would bring joy and chatter and life back into her house. She would make Valerie's life worth living again.

FIVE
GABRIEL

Gabriel stood in front of the wardrobe that took up a corner of the bedroom. His father, if he were here, would insist that he wear a suit, shirt and tie today – after all, he was, to all intents and purposes, working.

But being shown around Heaven's Cove in his suit was a bit over the top. Especially when the day promised to be hot and sunny. Not that he had much choice because all he'd packed was an extra suit, underwear, and a few shirts and ties. He wasn't a 'casuals' sort of person.

He walked to the window and stood there in his underpants, gazing at the sea. It was choppy today, but the most beautiful shade of azure. He hadn't seen an ocean that colour since his fateful trip to Tobago with Seraphina.

The trip during which it had finally slapped him full in the face that he couldn't face the rest of his life with a woman who spent two hours getting ready to lie on a beach, and then did nothing but complain about it being too sandy when she got there.

Seraphina had seemed equally irritated by him, so he'd been

surprised that she'd taken their split so badly. His father's ire, on
the other hand, had been expected.

Gabriel could still hear his voice in his head. *What do you
mean, you've broken off your relationship? What are you playing
at? Seraphina is the perfect wife for you.*

Gabriel was sure Seraphina would have played the role of
wealthy corporate wife to perfection – hosting dinner parties,
making small talk with his clients, spending a fortune on
making their home look amazing.

His father knew that too, which was why he'd welcomed
her with open arms. The fact that she and Gabriel would have
ended up making each other thoroughly miserable didn't regis-
ter. Nothing did with Billy Gantwich, other than the company
that he'd turned over the years into a multi-million-pound
concern.

All that mattered in his eyes was that Seraphina was the
perfect trophy wife for a man set to take over the family
business.

Gabriel pushed down the niggling question that edged its
way into his brain occasionally: *Do I actually want to take over
the family business?*

Of course he did. He'd be an ungrateful idiot to feel otherwise. Thousands would kill to have his prospects and privileges.
This was his destiny, and he needed to man up and make it
work.

Gabriel stretched out his arms and yawned. He'd get his
business here sorted out quickly so he could go back to
London and the luxury he was used to. There was nothing
wrong with this guesthouse – the room was comfortable and
the views were magnificent. But he missed his power shower
and underfloor heating. He grinned. He'd gone soft over the
years.

Gabriel's attention was suddenly caught by a flash of pink
and he realised, with horror, that the woman he'd hired to show

him around today had just appeared at the top of the cliff – and she was looking directly at him, in all his half-naked glory.

He stepped quickly to the side so he was hidden by the curtain. Great. That had got the day off to an awkward start. He wasn't a prude in the bedroom, but he wasn't one for flashing at strangers. Especially not bolshie women living in the back of beyond with their kids.

An image of Nessa and Lily locked in an embrace floated into Gabriel's mind. And breath caught in his throat. He shook his head and started getting dressed. He needed to stay focused on what he was here to do, and then get the hell out.

Five minutes later, Gabriel was looking smart in his grey suit but already uncomfortably hot. Feeling rebellious, he loosened his tie, slipped it over his head and threw it onto the bed. His father wasn't here, so he'd never know.

A breeze was blowing through an open window when he went out onto the landing and somewhere a door was banging, the sound echoing through the house.

He'd reached the foot of the stairs when he heard the beep of his mobile phone. It was a text from his father. Gabriel felt a shiver go down his back. Did he somehow know about his minor act of rebellion?

'Don't be ridiculous,' he muttered, opening the message which said: *Don't hang about, Gabriel. Have a look, get it sorted pronto and get back here. Lots to do at HQ.*

There was always lots to do back at HQ, a gleaming office block near the Thames. But would it kill his father to say good morning once in a while?

He pushed the phone back into his trouser pocket and went into the conservatory dining room, to nab some breakfast before the day's business began.

One very decent cooked breakfast later, Gabriel stood on the doorstep of Driftwood House, waiting for Nessa and wondering if she'd spotted him at the window this morning.

Oh well, what if she had? He'd be away from here soon enough.

He glanced at his watch. She was irritatingly late, but at least it gave him a few moments to fully appreciate the location of this unusual house. His father would kill to own this building, in such a beautiful, isolated spot – though he'd immediately raze it to the ground and build several luxury apartments.

That would be a shame, Gabriel acknowledged, admiring the house's impressive architecture. This home had stood here for decades and been weathered by fierce winter storms and blazing hot summers. It had character.

He had a sudden urge to paint the scene before him: the house with its stark white walls and russet roof, the china-blue sky streaked with vapour trails, the azure sea swelling against the cliff. But it was a stupid notion. He hadn't painted in years and wasn't about to start now. He had far more important things to do today.

'Good morning.' Nessa appeared behind him, making him jump. 'Sorry I'm late. Let's get going, shall we? Where would you like to go first?'

She didn't catch his eye, because she was rude or because she'd seen him half naked. Gabriel, tie-less but still too hot, realised he didn't much care either way.

'Maybe you could start by giving me a whistle-stop tour of Heaven's Cove,' he said, undoing a second button on his shirt.

'Sure. Let's walk down into the village.'

Nessa walked off and he followed. She picked her way confidently down the steep cliff path, in blue shorts and a pink halter-neck top that showed off the tan on her shoulders. The gold bracelet coiled around her arm caught the morning sun.

Gabriel supposed he should make polite conversation, but he didn't know what to say and she didn't seem that bothered, so they walked into Heaven's Cove in silence.

An hour later, he'd been shown the village church, which

faced a pretty green edged with trees and old cottages. He'd also been to the quayside – which smelled of fish – and to the castle ruins, which were also crying out to be captured on canvas.

Gabriel mentally shook himself again. What was it about this place that made him want to break open the oil paints?

But time was pressing on, and his father kept texting for updates. So, when Nessa suggested going to the beach, he shook his head.

'Maybe I can get to the beach another time. I'd really like to visit Sorrel Cove, if you could show me the way.'

Nessa, who'd been civil enough and had chatted on about Heaven's Cove, stopped walking and gave him a straight stare.

'Why are you interested in it?' she asked directly. 'Most people give it a miss because there's nothing much there to see. It hasn't been inhabited for decades and most of it's in ruins.'

'I know all that, but I read about it and the place sounds interesting.'

Nessa stared at him a moment longer, then puffed out her cheeks. 'Sure. It's your tour. We can get there by walking over the headland, if you're up to that.'

'Oh, I think I can manage it,' he said, raising an eyebrow and hoping he sounded suitably sarcastic.

He might not look like one of the rugged local fishermen he'd seen at the quay, with their weathered skin and muscles, but he wasn't a total wimp. The swish London gym he went to three times a week cost him a fortune.

But Nessa simply said 'OK' and led him to the edge of the village, to a piece of land that jutted out into the blue sea. He followed her up a path that wound through trees on the flanks of the headland.

Gabriel watched her as they climbed, the sun dappling through the branches and casting her face into shadow.

She was young – a little younger than him, he'd guess – and pretty, with long, dark hair that she twisted into a ponytail as the temperature rose. But there was something about her, a weariness or cynicism, that had forged a faint line between her eyebrows.

She was a tired single mother, he supposed. There was no ring on her left hand and po-faced Valerie had referred to Driftwood House as 'home' when she'd brought the child back yesterday. There was also no sign of a partner, and surely Nessa and her daughter wouldn't be living at the guesthouse if she was in a supportive relationship?

I don't work hard and pay an exorbitant amount in taxes to support single parents.

Gabriel could hear his father's voice in his head. He often did, even when he tried to drown it out with alcohol. He drank rather too much these days – a habit which had led to deeply unsatisfying one-night stands with friends of friends he'd been set up with on blind dates.

'Have you ever lived anywhere other than round here, even for a short while?' he asked Nessa, who was striding ahead. He supposed he ought to be polite and feign some interest in her life.

'Nope,' she said over her shoulder, still climbing. 'Bit boring, huh?'

'I wouldn't say that,' he replied, as they emerged from the trees at the top of the headland. To be honest, it did sound rather unenterprising but, looking at the view from up here, perhaps not surprising. Why would anyone want to live anywhere else?

The sun, temporarily veiled by wisps of cloud, was casting gauzy beams of light onto the ocean, which rolled towards the village. Seagulls were dots of white, skimming the waves and calling mournfully to one another.

It was truly beautiful. An artist's delight – only he was a property developer who never painted.

He pursed his lips and squinted along the coast. 'So where's Sorrel Cove?'

'You can't see it from here,' said Nessa, brushing a strand of hair from her eyes. 'It's in a sheltered spot on the other side of the headland. Follow me.'

They walked on, past tourists spreading picnic blankets on the grass, and descended a steep slope until they were almost at sea level. And there, tucked away, Gabriel spotted the ruins of a small community.

So this was Sorrel Cove. Gabriel stopped and shielded his eyes against the glaring sun.

A couple of the cottages were roofless, gaping and open to the elements. But the rest had collapsed entirely and were nothing more than mounds of stone scattered about the site.

Only one building remained relatively intact, at the back of the village, sheltered by rising land. Its stone walls and roof looked sound, but its windows were boarded up and tall grasses and wild flowers twisted around its foundations.

'I thought the village would be bigger,' he said to Nessa, who was standing watching him with a thoughtful look on her face.

'It was, once. Come with me.'

He followed as she picked her way down the slope, into the heart of the destroyed hamlet, and walked to the edge of the land. She pointed at a tumbledown wall that was so close to the water, it glistened with sea spray.

'That house was once at the centre of the village.'

'So, where are the others?' He followed her gaze to the waves washing over the rocks near them.

'Several were submerged in the storm that wrecked Sorrel Cove on the twentieth of March, 1946. Five people died here when the storm hit unexpectedly. It was expected to hit inland France but it veered off course and struck this coast instead. I guess weather forecasting wasn't as precise as it is now.'

'That's tragic.' Gabriel peered into the water, wondering what ruined buildings lay just below the shoreline. What bodies had been swept out to sea? He shivered. 'I read that the other villagers moved out soon afterwards.'

Nessa nodded, her face solemn. 'There was so much sorrow here, and the rest of the village wasn't safe. Other buildings that escaped being washed away that night have fallen into the sea since.'

'I hear that new sea defences farther along the coast are helping to protect this area now.'

Nessa narrowed her eyes. 'That's right. It's a welcome by-product of the work that's been done. How do you know about that?'

'I told you. I was reading up about the village,' said Gabriel, looking around him.

His father was right: this was a beautiful spot, with the headland rising up high behind the ruins and the sea in front. And the land was less steep to the left of the village and would take a decent road. There was a tidy profit to be made here.

'Don't you think?'

Gabriel stopped counting pound signs and looked at Nessa. What had she just said?

Nessa gave a tight smile. 'You were miles away. I said, this is a very peaceful place.'

Gabriel nodded, though it wouldn't be so peaceful once the excavators and dumper trucks he had planned arrived. Maybe some of the original stone from the surviving cottages could be used. That would be a nice touch when it came to marketing.

They'd stopped outside the best-preserved cottage, and Nessa ran her hand across the bumpy stone wall.

'My grandmother lived here when she was a child.'

That caught Gabriel's attention. He blinked. 'Really? Was she here when the storm hit?'

Nessa nodded. 'She was. Her mum died that night. She'd

gone out to look for her husband's boat, which hadn't come back into harbour, and she was washed away by a huge wave.'

'Gosh. I'm sorry,' said Gabriel, imagining what it must have been like that night, with the wind howling and towering waves. 'Was her husband... I mean, did he...'

'No, my great-grandfather survived, thankfully. His boat had put into harbour farther along the coast when the weather turned. But he and his daughter – my gran –moved out after that, along with his in-laws, who'd been living at Sorrel Cove with them, and everyone else in the village. Gran told me they were all too scared and heartbroken to stay.'

'Does your grandmother still live around here?'

'She did, but she died recently.'

'I'm sorry,' said Gabriel, as Nessa swallowed as though she might cry. Without thinking, he reached out and touched her arm, before pulling his hand back.

What was he thinking? The two of them were alone in a secluded place after he'd very possibly flashed her in his under-pants. What happened if she got spooked and thought he was coming on to her? It wouldn't look good for the business, and his father would hit the roof.

You've got to think ahead and be prepared for every even-tuality.

There was his father's voice in his head again. Gabriel took a deep breath and glanced at Nessa, who was staring out to sea.

'Shall we head back?' he asked, but she didn't move.

'I love it here in the Ghost Village,' she said quietly. 'It's a place of peace and history, family history. My gran told me stories about the people who used to live here. The men who went out on their boats to catch mackerel, bream and cod, the women who sewed by gaslight to bring in extra money, the chil-dren who played hide and seek as the sun went down. There was a close community here.'

'The Ghost Village?'

'That's what the locals call this place. Only outsiders call it Sorrel Cove.'

For some reason, although the term was accurate, Gabriel took offence at being classed an outsider.

He sniffed. 'I'm surprised there aren't more people here. Living people, I mean.'

'Being known as the Ghost Village tends to put local kids off. And it's not the easiest place to get to either, which keeps most tourists away. There's a dirt track that runs from the nearest lane, but it doesn't have a decent road.'

It would soon, thought Gabriel, bringing in more people than Nessa could ever imagine. And her beautiful, peaceful place would disappear.

For a moment, he felt sad but then he hardened his heart. This was a business decision, and one that would earn him lots of brownie points with his father – if he could pull it off without a hitch. His father had found and secured the land and now it was his job to get the project moving.

'Why *are* you here?' asked Nessa suddenly. 'You seem more interested in this place than Heaven's Cove.'

Gabriel momentarily considered telling her the truth. But it was probably best to keep things under wraps for as long as possible.

'Like you,' he said, 'I love the history of this place.'

'Hmm.'

Nessa gave him a straight stare as she ran her fingers over the gold bangle at her wrist. She clearly wasn't stupid and had picked up that there was more to his interest.

'I love art, too,' he said, to distract her. 'And this place is crying out to be painted, don't you think?'

She smiled. 'My great-grandmother loved arts and crafts. Gran said her mum often sketched the village and the sea, and they made collages together, using driftwood and shells from the beach.' She turned her soulful brown eyes on Gabriel. 'Do you do much painting, then?'

He swallowed, wrong-footed by the question. 'No, not now, though I had a place at art college once.'

Too much information. Gabriel cursed under his breath, wishing he hadn't told her anything so personal.

'But you didn't go?'

'I decided it wasn't for me,' he said briskly. 'Right, let's leave this place to its ghosts and get back to Heaven's Cove, shall we? We've been out a while and I'm very aware that I'm on the clock.'

Nessa's smile disappeared and she glanced at her watch. 'Don't worry. It won't take us long to get back.'

Then, without looking back, she began to climb again towards the top of the headland. Gabriel followed, gently sweating in his suit, and wondering why he felt so rattled.

He stopped halfway up the slope and looked over his shoulder at Sorrel Cove. The wind was picking up and blowing through the tall grasses that grew around the mounds of stone. A gust suddenly swirled around him. It sounded like a sigh and sent a shiver down his back.

SIX
NESSA

It was no good. Nessa couldn't stop thinking about Gabriel's interest in Sorrel Cove. She couldn't put her finger on what was bothering her particularly. But she had a bad feeling about it. A hunch.

'So who do you work for?' she asked, trying to sound nonchalant as she led Gabriel up the cliff path towards Drift-wood House.

Gabriel stopped walking and put his hands on his hips. He had a piercing stare that made her feel uncomfortable.

'I work for my father,' he said in his low, deep voice. 'I work for the family firm.'

She would have left it there, if it weren't for The Flutters. That's what Lily had dubbed the unease she felt when her dad was due for one of his infrequent visits. And Nessa's stomach was chock-full of flutters right now.

She took a deep breath. 'So, what exactly does your father do?'

'He identifies—' He hesitated. '*We* identify possibilities and turn them into investment opportunities.'

Well, that was as clear as mud. Nessa sighed.

'Would I have heard of your business?'

Gabriel turned his gaze to the blue sea sparkling nearby. 'Possibly.'

'Is it doing well?' asked Nessa. This was turning into Twenty Questions.

'Yes, it's doing extremely well.'

'Congratulations.'

Gabriel raised an eyebrow, unsure if she was being sincere. She wasn't. 'Thank you. I think.'

He wiped a bead of sweat from his forehead. But it was his own fault, thought Nessa, for dressing so inappropriately.

'Is your wife involved in the family firm too?' she asked, fed up with being fobbed off.

Gabriel shot her a look that said she was asking too many personal questions but Nessa was unfazed. After all, she'd seen him half naked this morning.

He'd been hard to miss, standing there with his arms outstretched, like a half-naked Adonis. And it was hard to find him intimidating when she'd clocked an eyeful of him in his underpants, which were, at least, black and tight, rather than the baggy off-white boxers that Jake used to slob around in.

'I don't have a wife,' answered Gabriel. 'My girlfriend, Seraphina, and I broke up a while ago.'

He frowned, presumably annoyed with himself for saying too much, while Nessa tried not to giggle. Of course an uptight businessman like Gabriel Gantwich would have a girlfriend called Seraphina.

She doubted that Seraphina was a single mum living in a friend's box room. Seraphina probably lived in Chelsea and had a swish apartment large enough for a king-size bed and a walk-in wardrobe.

She suddenly had an image of Gabriel and blonde Seraphina – she was bound to be honey-blonde – entangled in the king-size bed, and frowned. Gabriel was attractive, but in a squeaky-clean, well-groomed, expensive kind of a way, which wasn't her thing at all.

Jake, for all his many faults, had a sexy grunge vibe going on. This man wouldn't know grunge if it walked up and slapped him in the face.

'Is it tricky, working with your dad?' she asked, to distract herself from thinking of Gabriel in bed.

'No,' he replied quickly and then added, 'Not really. My cousin works in the company too so there are three of us to keep it going. Plus lots of other staff, of course.'

'Do you, your dad and cousin all get on well together?'

'Well enough. Why?'

'No reason. So is your interest in Sorrel Cove personal or professional?'

It was a tactic Nessa used when trying to get information out of Lily about her day at school. Talk about something else and casually drop in the question that you really wanted answered.

Gabriel scowled and Nessa could see him thinking: *She's not going to let this drop.*

When he stared at her without saying a word, the flutters in Nessa's stomach intensified.

'My company is interested in Sorrel Cove, yes,' he said, finally.

'As an investment opportunity?' asked Nessa, feeling ice slide down her spine.

'That's right.'

'What sort of investment opportunity?'

'Development,' said Gabriel curtly, folding his arms. 'Bijou, bespoke development.'

Nessa opened her mouth but no sound came out.

'It's all hush-hush at the moment,' continued Gabriel, 'but you'll find out soon enough, I suppose. My father runs a property development business and we're interested in developing Sorrel Cove.'

'But you can't,' blurted out Nessa.

'Yes, we can.' He sounded calm – bored, even. 'We've acquired the land and are looking to build there. It's a beautiful location, you said so yourself. And the new sea defences mean the area is more protected and suitable for commercial ventures.'

'So you own the land?'

'Yes. We bought it a while ago.'

Nessa let that sink in. She hadn't known, and she bet no one in Heaven's Cove did either. The Ghost Village belonged to this man and his 'investment opportunity' business.

'But what about the old houses?' she managed.

'They'll be demolished. Though, let's be honest, they've been half demolished by the sea and weather already. The site will be cleared and we'll build a small number of luxury apartments for people looking for weekend escapes from the city.'

Nessa felt like she couldn't breathe. Gabriel was planning to destroy the Ghost Village, and she'd just collaborated in his scheme by showing him around.

'Maybe your father won't agree,' she muttered.

'He's the person who sent me here to start finalising arrangements. He's visited Sorrel Cove already and wants to go ahead.'

'But you can't destroy the Ghost Village. It's a monument to all the people who lived and loved and died there.'

Gabriel sighed. 'I know it has a particular significance to you because of your family history, and I'm sorry about that. But at the end of the day, it's just stones.'

'Just *stones*?' uttered Nessa, finding it hard to breathe.

She had an overwhelming urge to shove Gabriel Gantwich off the path and into the sparkling sea. When she took a step towards him, he stepped back, as though he could read her mind.

'Look, we'll have to move the stones when we prepare the site for new construction. But maybe we could incorporate some of the old stone into the new building.' He shrugged. 'At the end of the day, it's a business decision and those are made by one's head, rather than one's heart.'

Did the man in front of her even have a heart? Nessa doubted it as he droned on about the logistics of what was planned. It seemed to involve dozens of lorries clogging up Heaven's Cove's narrow roads so outsiders could waltz in for occasional weekends before disappearing back to their real lives.

His 'bijou, bespoke development' would destroy the place that she loved. The place that was a last link to her beloved grandmother, whose ashes still nestled amongst the stones.

It was another kick in the teeth in an awful year. No family, no home, no job, and now, if this man had his way, no Ghost Village where she always found peace among the dead.

'Are you listening to me?' he asked, running his hands through his hair.

'No, I've listened to enough of your lies already.'

'Lies?' His face reddened. 'I've just told you exactly what's planned for Sorrel Cove. I shouldn't be telling you all these details but—'

'But you didn't at first. You got me to show you the Ghost Village and told me you were interested in history and art.'

'I didn't want to trumpet what's planned until I'd seen the site for myself. And I *am* interested in history and art.'

'No, you're not. If you were, you wouldn't be plotting to destroy such a precious village.'

Gabriel took a deep breath and, when he spoke, his voice was low and controlled. 'Don't you think you're over-reacting?'

Nessa glared at him, so furious she didn't trust herself to

speak. Maybe she *was* over-reacting, but he'd do the same if he had no family, no home, no job, and now the only place where he found real peace was about to be flattened.

She pushed past him and marched towards Driftwood House without looking back.

SEVEN

NESSA

Nessa stomped across the clifftop, straight past Driftwood House, and kept on going.

She hardly noticed the wildflowers carpeting the grass, the gulls wheeling above her, or the fresh smell of the sea. Although she had somewhere important to be, her mind was firmly fixed on Gabriel's bombshell.

What an arrogant, uncaring man! He acted as if he could do whatever he wanted. *He's got money so he probably can*, said a little voice in Nessa's brain, but she ignored it and carried on stomping.

How could he contemplate destroying a place that was so steeped in local history? The man was a complete philistine.

By the time her destination, Heaven's Brook, came into sight, Nessa was all stomped out and feeling drained. The adrenaline spike prompted by Gabriel's news had worn off. And she started wondering why she'd been summoned by her grandmother's ex-landlord to this tiny hamlet, nestled between the coast and woodland.

She glanced at the text she'd received from Mr Aston earlier that week: *I'd be grateful if you could meet me at the cottage sometime. Shall we say Friday at 1 pm? I have something of your grandmother's to return.*

Nessa had no idea what that 'something' was, and she was early for her appointment with him. But it would be good to get this over with. She didn't want to spend any longer here than was necessary.

It wasn't that there was anything wrong with Heaven's Brook. Far from it. Thatched cottages lined the lanes, and an ancient Celtic cross sat on the miniscule patch of grass that was grandly known as the village green. Everything was peaceful and pretty, and her grandmother had been very happy here.

But the hamlet held too many memories. Nessa could picture her gran sitting in her whitewashed cottage, or waiting at the bus stop for the one bus a day, or walking to and from the stone cross 'to stretch my legs so they don't stop working'.

Maybe, in the future, Nessa would find comfort in reminders of her grandmother, but for now they simply made her feel sad.

She could understand why many of the displaced people of Sorrel Cove had moved out of the area after the storm, needing a fresh start away from the tragedy. But the grieving Paulson family – Nessa's family – hadn't moved away. They'd stayed living locally, and motherless Ruth had grown up and made her life in Heaven's Cove. She'd only moved out here to Heaven's Brook five years ago, after her husband had died.

The thatched cottage she'd rented from Mr Aston was perfectly proportioned for one person. But it had become Nessa and Lily's home too, after she'd stepped in to help them out.

Ruth couldn't afford to make up the rent on Nessa's Heaven's Cove flat – the rent that sometimes fell short thanks to Jake's irregular maintenance payments. But she could offer a roof above their heads, and they'd got on well, all squeezed in together for the last year. But now she was gone.

Nessa's throat tightened as she walked past a 'For Sale' sign and up the garden path towards the cottage. Her grandmother would often be waiting at the front door for her, white hair pinned into a bun. She would smile, looking so much like Nessa's mum, and ask how her day had been and hug Lily tight.

The thought of never seeing her again was almost too much to bear.

Nessa swallowed and raised her hand but the door was pulled open by Mr Aston before she could knock.

He'd turned a blind eye to Nessa and Lily moving in. But now his official tenant was gone, he couldn't wait to sell the cottage and make a tidy profit. And even though that was bad news for her and Lily, Nessa couldn't really blame him. Cottages around here were being snapped up by buyers.

'I saw you coming down the path. How are you?' he boomed, looking ill at ease. 'You're early. I thought we said one o'clock?'

'Yes. Sorry. I came over without stopping for lunch. Is now convenient or would you like me to come back?'

'No, now is fine. Would you like to come in?' When he tilted his head to gesture her inside, a blizzard of dandruff dropped onto his collar.

Nessa looked over his shoulder into the sitting room. It was empty. Her grandmother's ancient sofa and two wingback chairs were currently being stored in a local barn that belonged to Liam – Rosie's farmer fiancé – and the rug had gone to a charity shop. The floorboards that her gran had polished were dusty and the hearth was cold.

She shook her head. 'Thank you, but I've got a few things to do in Heaven's Cove before I pick up Lily.'

'Ah, yes, your daughter.' Mr Aston tilted his head, concern in his eyes. 'Where are you both living now?'

'We're staying with a friend at Driftwood House.'

'That magnificent house up on the cliffs?' He smiled, his

conscience eased. 'Marvellous! You'll have a much better view from up there.'

He was right. The sweeping vista of sea and sky was more picturesque than the lane that ran past this cottage. But Nessa would gladly trade any view to be back here with her grandmother.

She dug her nails into her palm, determined not to cry. 'When you rang and said to come over, you mentioned that you'd found something that belonged to my gran?'

'Oh, yes. I found it at the back of the cupboard in the front bedroom. It was shoved behind an offcut of old carpet, so I'm not surprised you missed it.' He reached to the side of the door and picked up a battered leather case, hardly bigger than a shoebox. Two buckled straps held it closed. 'Here you go. It looks very old.'

He handed the box over. The tan leather was cracked as though someone had taken to it with a hammer. She'd never seen it before.

'Thank you,' said Nessa, stroking her fingers across the rough leather and wondering what the box held. She'd been expecting a lost earring or mislaid paperwork, not this.

'I thought it might be important. I didn't look inside, obviously.'

Mr Aston cleared his throat and stared at his feet. He had looked inside, realised Nessa, clasping the box to her chest. And somehow that seemed worse than turfing her and Lily out of the cottage. He'd snooped into something that her grandmother had kept private.

'Obviously,' said Nessa levelly. 'I appreciate you returning it to me.'

'You're welcome.' He was still staring at the floor. 'And if I come across any other hidden treasures, I'll be in touch. Anyway, I'm terribly sorry about your grandmother. She was a nice woman and a good tenant, and I'm sure you'll miss her.'

'I will,' gulped Nessa. 'Lily, too.'

'Hmm.' He pushed a finger beneath the collar of his polo shirt and pulled it away from his neck. 'I have to sell the place, you know. Well, I don't *have* to, obviously, but the housing market has gone crazy around here and selling makes more sense than renting right now. I have to think of my pension. Maybe you'd be interested in purchasing the place?'

'I'd love to but I'm not in a position to buy right now.'

Not now. Not ever. Nessa knew there was no way she'd be able to afford to buy locally. Even renting was proving impossible, but she couldn't impose on Rosie and stay at Driftwood House for much longer.

Mr Aston tilted his head again, sympathetically. 'I see.' He shuffled his feet as though he had somewhere else to be. 'Well, I wish you and your daughter the best of luck.'

'Thank you,' said Nessa. They were going to need it.

After Mr Aston had shut the door, Nessa walked briskly to the garden gate, keen to be away. She'd never come back to this cottage or to Heaven's Brook. The last vestige of her grandmother's life in this hamlet – a mysterious leather box – was under her arm, and there was nothing left for her here.

EIGHT
NESSA

Nessa walked along the lane, cut across the field and started climbing back up over the clifftop towards Driftwood House, which was a smudge in the distance.

She'd folded the battered leather box into the crook of her arm and it pressed against her side as she moved. The weight of it felt like her grandmother's hand on her waist. If only it was. If only her gran was here to give advice on how to do the best for Lily when Nessa's life was such a muddle.

But Nessa had learned long ago that *if onlys* were pointless. If only her mum hadn't died so young, if only she hadn't been too busy as a carer to pass her exams at school, if only Jake hadn't turned out to be such a mistake.

Nessa shook her head as she marched on up the steep slope. No. Jake would never be a mistake because, without him, she'd never have had Lily. And however hard life got, her daughter was nothing but a blessing.

She stopped when she got to the top of the cliff, hands on her hips and puffing. She'd missed lunch and her stomach was grumbling. She'd make herself a sandwich at Driftwood House, as long as Gabriel wasn't about. But first she had to find out what was in her grandmother's mysterious box.

Nessa walked to the edge of the cliff and looked down. It was a dizzying drop. Hundreds of feet below, the sea was pounding into rock and, a little farther along the coast, there was Heaven's Cove. Tourists were thronging the narrow lanes, and flags were flying from the ancient church that stood at its centre. The faint toot of car horns was caught on the breeze. The village was gridlocked as people, taking advantage of the heatwave, flooded into the area.

It would have been a good day for Shelley's to sell the inflatable toys, windbreaks, buckets and spades that tourists lapped up at this time of year.

But Shelley's would likely be turned into flats that locals couldn't afford to buy, and Mr Scaglin was now miles away, living near his daughter. Nessa would take Lily to visit him, when she got a new job and could spare money for the bus fare.

She sat down on the tinder-dry grass and pulled her knees up to her chin. The box was beside her and she eyed it nervously. What was inside?

There was only one way to find out. Nessa pushed her gold bangle up her arm and unbuckled the straps around the box. Then she opened it slowly, as seagulls wheeled and screeched overhead and sunshine warmed her skin.

Inside lay a pile of black and white photos and yellowing papers. Nessa pulled out the top piece of paper, which was a local newspaper cutting announcing the engagement of Nessa's mum and dad.

The printed announcement seemed quaint – from a time before social media allowed everyone to trumpet their news, good and bad, at the touch of a button.

She ran her fingers across the fading newsprint, feeling almost unbearably sad. There were her mother's and father's names. They must have been so excited and blissfully unaware of the heartache to come.

First, Mark, her father, had died of an undiagnosed heart condition when Nessa was four years old. And then her lovely mum, who'd already suffered so much, developed a degenerative nerve disease eight years later.

People said lightning never struck twice, but it had in her family, leaving her orphaned at the age of seventeen.

Perhaps that was why she'd fallen for Jake's charms so easily and had wanted to have a child of her own – to make her own family whom she could love and protect.

Nessa shivered as she thought of Lily squeezed into Rosie's box room, with no home to call her own. Loving her daughter was easy, but protecting her? That was proving harder.

Nessa pushed her hand further into the box of treasures from her gran. There were black and white photos of her gran and gramp as a young couple, photos of Nessa as a child and more recent photos of Lily.

Nessa was touched to find some of her old school reports, pictures she'd drawn twenty years ago, and a copy of her antenatal scan when pregnant with Lily.

Nessa ran her fingers across the shadowy image of her daughter before she was born. She'd known from Jake's reaction to the image that he wasn't going to find fatherhood easy. He'd been keen to try for a child but, when faced with evidence that a baby was on the way, he'd become irritable and withdrawn, his insistence that he was a 'free spirit' not sitting well with the ties and responsibilities of parenthood.

And then, when Lily was only a baby, he'd had a one-night stand with Gemma, a tourist he met in the pub. He'd told Nessa all about it on the day he'd walked out for good.

Nessa pushed that memory from her mind and pulled a black and white photo from the box. It was of three men, sitting side by side, wearing tin hats. One looked familiar and, when she turned the picture over, she saw written on the back: *Seth, G. Rider and ?, France 1918*.

Seth, her great-great grandfather. She recognised his face from the photo of him and his wife that her gran had kept propped up on her bedside table. Her gran had been so proud of him for being a wartime hero.

'He saved the life of his captain, George Rider, during a great battle in France,' she'd tell open-mouthed Nessa, who lapped up stories of his courage. 'His army unit was awarded the Croix de Guerre for its bravery and your great-great-gramp was the bravest of the brave.'

Nessa doubted Seth Paulson had ever insisted he was a 'free spirit' unable to cope with responsibility. He'd have been too busy fighting for his life.

She took another look at the photo, noticing the army uniform, the exhaustion etched across the men's faces, and the wall of mud behind them. They were in a trench. And the man sitting next to Seth, G. Rider, must presumably be the comrade he'd saved. The man whose family had once lived in this area too, before they'd upped sticks in the 1920s and moved to Cheshire. 'The posh part,' her gran had once told her. 'They were loaded.'

Nessa put the precious photo back into the box for safe-keeping and pulled out another drawing. This one, unlike her childish sketches, had obviously been done by an adult. An intricate pattern had been drawn in pencil, its irregular shapes shaded in with jewel colours – ruby red, emerald green, sapphire blue. It was beautiful, like a mosaic.

Nessa squinted at the faded words written beneath the picture. It was her grandmother's writing.

We left it behind, Mama's art,
And with it forever a piece of my heart.

Nessa smiled. It was poignant, but her gran had always been the first to admit she was a better artist than poet.

Glancing back into the box, she recognised her grandmother's writing again. This time her words were scrawled across a manila envelope: *I was never brave enough to return. Maybe one day you will be.*

Intrigued, Nessa opened the envelope and pulled out the papers inside. There was something else in the envelope and, when she tipped it up, a large key fell into her hand.

The key was almost the length of her palm and had rusted with age. Nessa peered at it curiously. Thin strands of metal at the top of the key had been twisted together into the shape of a heart. What on earth did this unlock? And why had her grandmother never mentioned it?

She picked up the papers that had come from the envelope and, squinting in the sun, began to read. It seemed to be an old legal document relating to the cottage at Sorrel Cove. Perhaps that was where the key belonged.

She read on, ploughing through the old-fashioned style of writing, and realised with a start that the papers were some sort of lease. And if she was reading it correctly, this lease appeared to give the Paulson family the right to live in the cottage.

She skimmed through the legal language again and noticed a signature at the bottom of the document, next to the date: sixteenth of February 1919. She peered at the tiny, looped handwriting, just able to make out the name: *Seth Paulson.*

Another name was nudging at the edges of her brain. The name she'd just seen on the first page of the lease. She flicked back and gasped. *Rider.* This agreement was between her great-great-grandfather and Mr Edward Rider – George's grateful father, perhaps? It seemed he had thanked the hero who had saved his son by granting him and his family a home for life.

It was pure supposition but it made sense, thought Nessa, wishing her grandmother was here so she could ask her about it.

Her gran had never mentioned this document or the story behind it. But, traumatised by witnessing the death of her mother, she'd never much wanted to talk about the Ghost Village or the cottage – even though she knew how peaceful Nessa found the place. The few stories she had told had focused on her neighbours in Sorrel Cove rather than her own family.

Nessa gently traced her fingers across Seth's faded signature. She loved touching where his hand had rested as he'd written his name. She loved the feeling of connection across the years, because even long-dead ancestors were comforting when your current family was so small.

Nessa suddenly felt the absence of a loving, supportive family acutely. Sometimes, in spite of great friends like Rosie, she felt terribly alone and scared as she tried to do the best for Lily.

Taking a deep breath to ward off a spiral of self-pity, she went through the legal agreement again. It seemed to remain in effect for 125 years, which meant – Nessa did the maths in her head – it was still valid for another twenty-two years.

A sudden thought hit her like a sledge hammer. Did that mean, as a member of the Paulson family, that she could move into the cottage? Twenty-two years would give Lily a 'forever home' for the rest of her childhood and beyond.

Nessa gazed across the ocean, to where the sea disappeared and became sky, and tried to figure out what this all meant.

If only she and Lily *could* live in beautiful Sorrel Cove, in their own home with its ties to her family.

If only the house wasn't in such a state.

If only it wasn't going to be demolished by Gabriel Gantwich and his father.

She was drowning again in *if onlys*. Nessa lay back on the grass to calm her jumbled thoughts.

But as the sun warmed her body and a light aircraft droned

gently overhead, she couldn't stop her mind from racing. Images of the mum she still missed so much and the grandmother she'd miss forever drifted through her head, along with Lily's upturned, trusting face, and Jake running off into the distance.

I was never brave enough to return. Maybe one day you will be.

Nessa sat bolt upright and rubbed her eyes. She was fed up with being a victim in her own life. She was tired of things happening to her – people dying, partners abandoning her, jobs ending. Surely, it was about time she made things happen for herself.

She had no money, no job, no prospects. But maybe she could secure a home for Lily. How hard would it be to do up the cottage and make it habitable? There was just one fly in the ointment.

Picking up the lease again, she read the clause that had leapt out at her: *Said property shall remain available to the Paulson family as their primary dwelling so long as a family member occupies said property for thirty days and nights continuously.*

If she understood it correctly, it meant that to activate the agreement again, she'd have to move in for a whole month. Thirty days would be OK, but nights? Nessa shivered, imagining her family's derelict cottage in the small hours. The Ghost Village wasn't spooky in daylight but what about when the sun dipped below the horizon and shadows lengthened?

'I can do it,' muttered Nessa, getting to her feet and standing with her hands on her hips and her chest pushed forward. She'd read that this was a power pose. Something to do with superheroes and boosting your confidence. Was it working?

As a circling seagull flew out across the ocean, squawking mournfully, Nessa pushed aside the doubts that started crowding her mind.

Of course she could do it. She could move in for thirty days – and thirty nights – and even if she and Lily couldn't live in the cottage long term, maybe the prospect of a sitting tenant would stop it from being demolished.

And that, in turn, might save the Ghost Village, and preserve some of Lily's heritage into the bargain.

'It's a crazy idea,' shouted Nessa into the wind, holding the lease tightly in her hand.

It *was* crazy. Completely off-the-scale bonkers. And, as well as being hugely difficult to pull off, it would put her on a collision course with Gabriel Gantwich and his father.

But she'd done difficult things before. She'd truanted from school to care for her dying mother, and being a single parent was no walk in the park. However, she didn't regret either of those things for a moment.

Nessa swallowed hard. Maybe she'd live to regret this one, but she had to try. Gabriel wouldn't like it. But she didn't much like him, so who cared?

He was blind to the beauty and significance of Sorrel Cove. It was nothing more to him than an investment opportunity. So why couldn't he invest somewhere else and allow the souls of the Ghost Village to rest in peace?

'I'm not sure I am brave enough, Gran,' said Nessa into the salt-laced air. 'But I'll give it a go.'

NINE

GABRIEL

'Hello. Do you like living in my room?'

Gabriel jumped as he pulled a towel from the airing cupboard. Nessa's daughter had appeared seemingly out of nowhere and was leaning against the wall on the landing, watching him.

'I'm helping myself to a new towel because I dropped mine in the shower and it got soaked. I saw the lady who runs this place putting towels in here yesterday and didn't want to bother her.'

Why was he explaining himself to a child? he wondered, willing himself to shut up. For some reason, he felt vaguely guilty, as though he'd been caught pilfering.

The girl folded her arms and nodded. Her jeans were a bit too short, he noticed, and there were ketchup stains on her T-shirt, which sported the slogan: *I'm a little angel.*

She did look like an angel, with her pink cheeks and huge brown eyes. She looked a lot like her mother, thought Gabriel, though he certainly wouldn't describe *her* as angelic. She'd been horrified yesterday by his plans for Sorrel Cove and, if looks could kill, he'd be six feet under right now. He should never have told her about the development, and he still wasn't quite sure why he had.

'So *do* you like living in my room?' asked the girl again, still staring. What was her name? Lola? Layla? 'I could see the sea from our big bed, but Mummy said we had to move.'

'Is that right?' asked Gabriel, feeling a flicker of unease. 'So where did you move to?'

'Right here,' said the girl, pointing at the closed door behind her. 'Do you want to have a look?'

'I was just going down to breakfast,' said Gabriel. The smell of fried bacon was wafting up the stairs and teasing his taste buds. But the girl was having none of it.

'Mummy says it's our den,' she told him, flinging the door open. 'Look,' she called, disappearing inside. 'Elsa's on my duvet.'

Elsa? Did that Nessa woman have another child she hadn't mentioned?

Gabriel walked to the door and poked his head into what appeared to be a box room. The girl had jumped onto one of two camp beds set up in the middle, and the rest of the space was filled with boxes and piles of books. Pale sunlight was peeping in through a tiny window.

There was no sign of Nessa, which was just as well. Gabriel didn't fancy round two with her this early in the morning.

'Did you and your mum move here?' he asked, noticing a large spider scuttle behind a box in a corner. He shivered. It was pathetic but he'd never been great with them.

When Lola – Layla? – nodded, Gabriel briefly closed his eyes. Had she and her mother moved into this gloomy, spidery room because of him? He'd spent last night stretched out comfortably across a double bed while they were squashed in here.

The guilt flooding through him was swiftly followed by irritation. He was a paying guest, and no one had told him what was going on when they'd said there was a room here for him. No one had mentioned that he'd be displacing a mother and her child. Trust that annoying woman to make an altruistic gesture that put him on the back foot.

He rubbed a hand across his eyes, still feeling guilty at the thought of a child sleeping in here. More than one child, perhaps.

'Where does Elsa sleep?' he asked.

The girl opened her eyes wide and giggled. 'On my bed, silly.' She pointed at the picture of a girl with a long white plait which was printed on her duvet cover. 'Princess Elsa.'

'Ah, I see.' Gabriel smiled in spite of his bad mood. 'So, this is your den, is it?'

The girl nodded. 'I didn't like it at first. It's scary in the dark, but Mummy lets me get in bed with her.'

'That's good.'

Gabriel eyed Nessa's bed, which was hardly wide enough for one person, let alone two. Annoying guilt began to prickle again.

The girl picked up a comic on her pillow and started to leaf through the pages. Then she paused, her fingers ready to turn another page. 'Who are you again?'

She was direct, just like her mother.

'I'm Mr Gantwich, but you can call me Gabriel,' he said, deciding now wasn't a time for formality. 'What's your name again?'

'I'm Lily.' That was it! 'I'm five, and my daddy doesn't live here,' she added.

Gabriel was wrong-footed by the conversation's shift in direction. He wasn't used to children.

'So, where does your daddy live?' he asked.

Lily thought for a moment, her brow furrowed.

'I'm not 'xactly sure. I don't see him very much, but sometimes he stays with Granny Val. I'm staying with Granny tonight and Daddy's coming.'

When she grinned, her eyes sparkling, Gabriel wondered why he and Nessa had split up. Probably because Nessa was supremely annoying, though she appeared to be a loving mother, at least – more than his own had been.

Gabriel was suddenly overcome with emotions that he worked so hard to suppress.

'I'm off to have breakfast,' he said in a fake cheery voice, backing away from the box room. 'Have fun with your dad.'

He threw the clean towel onto his big, comfy bed and rushed down the stairs, faintly appalled that he felt so rattled by a conversation with a five-year-old. *I'm a mature, successful businessman,* he told himself, *and the sooner I get back to London and my normal life, the better.*

He stood in the hall for a moment, until all of his inconvenient emotions had been shoved back into their box, and noticed that the row of walking boots belonging to other guests was gone.

The whole house was quiet, and when Gabriel glanced at the grandfather clock he did a double-take because it was quarter past nine.

He never normally slept this late. He was usually up, breakfasted and out of his Hampstead apartment by eight o'clock at the latest.

But here, high above Heaven's Cove, he'd slept in – perhaps because of the fresh sea air or, more likely, because he'd had trouble dropping off last night. It must have been two a.m. before the rhythmic boom of waves hitting rock had finally lulled him to sleep.

Gabriel yawned and poked his head into the dining room. No one was sitting at the table, which was worrying. Had he missed breakfast altogether?

Muttering to himself about provincial guest houses, he

made his way to the kitchen, pushed open the door, and stopped dead. The place was in uproar. Surfaces were covered with the detritus of several breakfasts – cereal bowls lined up on the worktop above the dishwasher, two large frying pans in the sink, and empty coffee mugs on the table at the centre of the room.

He was expecting to spot Rosie, who'd said last night that she'd see him at breakfast. But Nessa was at the centre of the chaos, bending over the dishwasher. She was loading it with plates smeared with traces of egg and beans.

He stood still in the doorway, not relishing any further discussion about the fate of her 'Ghost Village'. And now there was the added complication of her giving up her room for him.

But beating a hasty retreat would be absurd. He was thirty-one, for goodness' sake. And he was also very hungry.

He watched for a second as she rearranged a couple of plates, her dark hair falling across her face and her gold bracelet clinking against the china. She had no idea he was there, and standing watching her suddenly felt inappropriate. He gave a small cough.

She straightened up, her face flushed.

'Oh, I didn't see you there,' she said, without a smile. 'Are you here for breakfast?'

'I was hoping for something but I'm rather late, so don't worry. Maybe I could grab a piece of toast?'

He'd need more than that to get him through the morning but hopefully one of the cafés in the village served croissants and a decent cup of coffee.

'I assumed you'd already gone out. Everyone else staying has already eaten and left. They're heading to Dartmoor, to go walking.'

'Good for them.' Gabriel swallowed. That sounded brusque and Nessa was staring at him. 'What I mean is, it's good they've gone out walking. Good for their health – physical and mental – or so I've read. I had a lie-in instead.'

Gabriel stopped talking, annoyed with himself for burbling on and almost apologising for not getting up at the crack of dawn on a Saturday.

He'd just decided to give breakfast at Driftwood House a miss when Nessa said, 'Go and take a seat in the conservatory and I'll cook you something.'

'You really don't have to.'

Nessa pushed a strand of hair from her hot face. 'I know that, but you're a guest and I'm helping Rosie out by cooking today's breakfasts. She's had to go out early. Would you like bacon and egg? Or would you prefer toast and muesli?'

'Don't you need to be with your daughter?'

Nessa raised an eyebrow. Did she think he was criticising her parenting skills? This woman was too touchy for her own good.

'Lily's great at occupying herself when I'm busy,' she said, frostily. 'So what will it be?'

Gabriel hesitated for only a fraction of a second. He should choose the healthier option. He always did at home, but what the hell.

'I'll have bacon and egg, if that's OK.'

'Of course. Would you like to take your coffee with you?'

'If you don't mind.'

Nessa gave the slightest of shrugs before fetching him a cup of strong cafetière coffee, and fishing two more frying pans from a cupboard.

Gabriel took his drink into the conservatory, sat at the head of the table and stared out of the window. Driftwood House might be a provincial B&B but it had the most wonderful views, even facing away from the sea. The vibrant clifftop was covered in wild flowers, and the land beyond stretched in swathes of green towards Dartmoor.

He sipped his coffee, which tasted surprisingly good, feeling relieved that Sorrel Cove hadn't been mentioned, and that

Nessa – though hardly friendly – was being polite. Perhaps she'd accepted the inevitable.

Nessa cut into his thoughts by sliding a plate onto the table. It held an egg and a pile of crispy bacon, along with two grilled tomatoes scattered with herbs, a fat sausage and a mound of baked beans.

She caught his eye. 'Just leave what you don't want.'

Gabriel started eating, trying not to shovel the food in too fast. It was so long since he'd enjoyed a British fry-up. Seraphina would never let anything fried within fifty feet of him. She was into 'clean eating', which meant Gabriel had had to be the same. He still watched his diet, but this... this tasted wonderful.

He bit into another piece of salty bacon and closed his eyes briefly, picturing all the bacon rolls he'd missed during his three years with Seraphina.

She was tall and so slim she seemed almost brittle. Nessa, in contrast, was shorter and more curvaceous in her blue jeans, and an emerald-green sweatshirt that contrasted with her dark, shiny hair – hair such a dark brown it was almost black.

Seraphina always looked beautifully turned out and wealthy, in her carefully chosen designer clothes, whereas Nessa looked thrown together, with egg stains on her top and her cheeks flushed from the heat of the cooker. She looked harassed and worn down by life, mused Gabriel, noticing her bare feet on the tiled floor.

And utterly beautiful.

Where had that thought come from? Gabriel speedily shoved a forkful of beans into his mouth.

'Is it all right?' asked Nessa, giving him a sideways look. And when he nodded, unable to speak with his mouth full, she wandered back to the kitchen.

He ate the rest of his breakfast as quickly as he dared and had finished his food by the time she returned with more coffee.

'I thought you might like a refill of your—'

'No, thank you,' he interrupted her, pushing his chair back. 'I need to get on with my day.'

'Of course.'

Nessa bit her lip, still hovering with the coffee. Was she going to force him to drink another cup? Or pour it into his lap?

'So...' She shuffled from foot to foot. 'What are your plans for the day?'

It would be an innocuous question from most people, but not from her. He rolled his shoulders, feeling ill at ease. He'd dealt with people opposed to his family firm's plans before, but they were usually tough-nosed corporate types, rather than single parents down on their luck. Her vulnerability, he realised, put him at a disadvantage emotionally.

'I didn't realise you and your daughter moved out of my bedroom so I could stay here,' he said, changing the subject.

'How do you know that?'

'Your daughter ambushed me when I was on the landing.'

'Ah, yeah.' The faintest flicker of a smile played across Nessa's face. 'Lily does that.' She put the coffee pot down on the table. 'It's no big deal. Rosie's letting us stay here as a favour and I'm helping out in lieu of rent. So I didn't want to deprive her of a paying customer.'

'Even one who's interested in the Ghost Village?'

'I didn't realise that when I made my altruistic gesture.' Nessa folded her arms while Gabriel mentally kicked himself for bringing up the sore topic of Sorrel Cove. 'I'm going to fight you, you know.'

Gabriel blinked at Nessa's words.

'You're going to fight me, for the bedroom?'

Nessa shook her head. 'I'm going to fight your plans to destroy the Ghost Village.'

He sighed. Of course she hadn't accepted the inevitable.

'You can try,' he told her, 'but I'm afraid you won't succeed.'

'It can't be right to obliterate all that history.'

'So what's the alternative? Leave the place to gradually fall down by itself?'

'It's a monument to the people who lost their lives.'

'And our new apartments there will be a monument to the fact that life goes on and people need homes in which to live. You can't be Canute and hold back the tide of change.'

That sounded pompous, even to his own ears, and he wished he hadn't said it. He was making a hash of talking to this woman who was now standing with her hands on her hips and her lips pursed, as if she wanted to punch him or cry and hadn't quite made up her mind which.

'Your new homes are a monument to your desire to be even richer, in your ivory tower in London,' she retorted.

She was being ridiculous now. The company HQ was hardly an ivory tower. It was in a pleasant enough part of London but it was still a nondescript office block on a busy street.

'These new houses you want to build,' Nessa continued, 'are they homes that local people like me can afford?'

'Probably,' said Gabriel, getting to his feet and wishing that he had given breakfast a miss. He pictured the four luxury apartments planned, their balconies complete with hot tubs overlooking the ocean, and shook his head. 'Probably not. But they'll bring money into the area.'

'Only at weekends, when the homeowners aren't in London or wherever they usually live. Or they'll be let as holiday homes.' She took a deep breath as though she'd rehearsed what she was going to say. 'Do you realise that people like me can't find places to live locally because we can't compete with the huge sums people will pay to stay here for a week or two?'

'I'm sure that's difficult but—'

'*Difficult?* You have no idea. All I want is a decent place that Lily and I can call our own.'

She *was* almost crying now and Gabriel had a bizarre urge to step forward and put his arms around her. Though he had no doubt that she'd punch him if he tried.

'I'm sure you do, but the situation round here isn't my fault.' He felt a rush of irritation. This woman's problems weren't his and her attempt to guilt-trip him wasn't going to work. 'Anyway, this conversation is getting us nowhere and I really must get on,' he said curtly. 'I think you'll find that it's better to accept the inevitable in life rather than pointlessly rail against it.' Then, he added: 'Thank you for the breakfast,' because, however infuriating this woman was, he'd been brought up to have good manners.

But he walked out of the conservatory without saying goodbye. He was glad to see the back of Nessa and, from the look on her face, the feeling was mutual.

TEN

VALERIE

Valerie shoved the long tube of the vacuum cleaner under the chair, bashing into her husband's feet. He grumbled and turned another page of the newspaper he'd been reading for the last half hour.

It was somewhat passive-aggressive, Valerie realised, assaulting her husband with the Dyson. But he'd done nothing but spend the morning faffing about with a crossword and being no help whatsoever.

'What time is Lily arriving?' shouted Alan, raising his feet a fraction.

'Whenever her mother deigns to bring her over.' Valerie turned the vacuum cleaner off and sniffed. 'She said this afternoon so I expect it'll be around two-ish.'

'Lily's stayed here before, you know. The place doesn't have to be scrubbed clean. I read it's good for youngsters to come into contact with germs.'

'She comes into contact with who knows what at that guest house, so the least I can do is make this place clean and tidy. A guesthouse is no place for a child.'

Valerie switched the machine back on, wondering if she'd

have time to wash down the paintwork. Though Alan would only make fun of her if she did, which would feed Valerie's fears that she was becoming obsessive about germs.

But she felt safe in her sparkling clean home. Safe, but bored, and sometimes in the silence – Alan wasn't the most loquacious of people – she felt as if the walls were closing in on her.

If only Jacob were here, but he wouldn't be home – she checked her watch – for a good few hours. He was coming on the train from Manchester, and he worked hard so she didn't expect him to get up too early on a Saturday.

Why on earth had he moved so far from Heaven's Cove? If only he'd never met that woman and been driven away by her demands.

Valerie stopped herself from gnawing at the inside of her cheek. She had to look on the bright side. Nessa was a pain but at least she'd produced Lily, who was the love of Valerie's life – along with Jacob, of course. She was very fond of her husband, too, but he'd slid down the pecking order since he'd started picking his feet in the sitting room.

She turned the vacuum cleaner back on and did another sweep of the rug, just in case any of his dead skin was lurking in the pile.

'Phone!' yelled Alan over the top of his paper.

Valerie switched off the machine for the second time and picked up the phone that was within reach of her husband.

'Hey, Mum.'

A smile spread across Valerie's face. 'Jacob! Are you on your way already? We're not expecting you for ages but that's no problem. The house will be ready for you whenever you arrive.'

'That's what I'm ringing about. I'm sorry but I'm not going to make it this weekend, after all.'

Valerie felt her heart sink but tried to keep her voice upbeat. 'Not at all?'

'I'm afraid not. I'm so busy at work right now, I've had to come into the office to catch up.'

'Your boss sounds like a slave driver. Do you have to work all weekend?'

'Well, not *all* weekend, obviously. But it's a new job, and good impressions and all that... So it's going to be too tricky to get down to see you. It's a bit of a trek. And the eco group I belong to has got a protest planned next week and I said I'd make some placards.'

Valerie took a deep breath. It wouldn't do to sound too needy. 'That's a shame,' she said levelly. 'You won't get to see Lily.'

'Nah, I'm gutted about that, obviously, but I did see her a few weeks ago.'

'It was at least four months ago and she changes all the time. You're missing such a lot, Jacob.'

'I know. Don't try to make me feel guilty, Mum.' His voice had taken on the sulky tone that Valerie remembered from his childhood. 'I do have to work, you know. And fight for the planet. We can't all swan about being retired, like you.'

Swan about? Valerie had left her admin job at a building merchant's in the spring, soon after her fifty-fifth birthday. But constantly clearing up after Alan didn't feel much like swanning about.

She sometimes regretted leaving work, but Alan had encouraged her to join him in early retirement. And she'd thought it would be different from this endless... nothingness.

When she stayed quiet, Jacob filled the silence.

'Look, I'm really sorry, Mum.'

'Won't you lose lots of money on your train ticket?'

'No, I hadn't got round to booking one. I was going to buy it at the station today, so it would have cost a fortune.' He paused. 'Look, I'll see you and Dad soon, and I'll text Ness to let her know I can't make this weekend.'

'No, don't,' said Valerie quickly. 'I can tell her.'

Lily might not come to stay if her father wasn't here, and Valerie wasn't sure she could cope with another quiet weekend with only Alan for company.

'If you're sure.' There was a hint of relief in Jacob's voice. 'She'll only go off on one if *I* tell her. Oops, gotta go. The boss is calling me.'

Valerie hadn't heard anyone calling, but Jacob had an important role at work, apparently, so no doubt was in demand. She said goodbye, adding a fervent wish that he was eating well, but he'd already ended the call.

'What was that?' asked Alan as Valerie replaced the phone in its cradle. 'Jacob not coming after all?'

'No, he's too busy at work.'

'Ah, well. Never mind.'

Never mind? When Alan went back to his crossword, Valerie experienced an unsettling urge to snatch his newspaper, roll it into a tight tube and hit him round the head with it.

Instead, she breathed out slowly, vowing to up her intake of the herbal tea she'd bought online. The tea was supposed to promote calm and serenity, especially in middle-aged women like herself.

So far, all it had done was give her a mild stomach ache, but it was worth persevering because she couldn't go on like this.

Honestly, if it wasn't for Lily brightening up her life, she sometimes felt she couldn't go on at all. What was the point? But that was a ridiculous idea and not something she was willing to explore any further.

Valerie switched the vacuum back on and went back to cleaning the spotless rug.

ELEVEN
NESSA

'Come on in, Nessa, and take a seat.'

Jackson Porter, Heaven's Cove's resident solicitor – now retired – moved a pile of newspapers off his sofa and dumped them on the floor. 'Sorry about the mess. It's usually neat as a pin in here but I've—'

Nessa never found out the reason for the clutter in Jackson's front room because his golden retriever bounded in from the kitchen and started leaping over the furniture.

'Terry, get down!' shouted Jackson, his rotund face growing redder by the second. Grabbing hold of Terry's collar, he half led, half dragged him back into the kitchen and firmly closed the door.

'Sorry about that. I was assured he'd calm down once he was past the puppy stage but that hasn't happened. At least he keeps me on my toes. And he's company.'

He gave a sad smile that made Nessa's heart hurt. Jackson had lots of friends in the village but there was an air of loneliness about him.

'I bet a dog is great company,' she told him. 'Lily would love one.'

'I'm sure she would, but I dare say you'd be the person taking him for walks and picking up poo.'

Jackson gave a rueful grin and gestured for Nessa to take a seat, while he closed the window. The temperature had dropped today and a chilly breeze was blowing in off the sea.

'Where is your daughter?' he asked over his shoulder, banging the ill-fitting window shut.

'Rosie's looking after her for me. We're staying at Driftwood House for a while.'

Nessa sat down in an armchair near the fireplace and looked around her. Jackson had lived in Heaven's Cove for as long as she could remember but she'd never known him to have a partner.

Local gossip Belinda reckoned he'd been sweet on Rosie's mum, Sofia, back in the day, and heartbroken forever when she chose another man. But whether that was right or not, Nessa didn't know. All she did know was that Jackson was a kind man who, with any luck, wouldn't mind giving her some advice for free. There was no way she could afford to pay.

'So, Nessa.' Jackson sank onto the sofa, his unruly grey hair in dire need of a comb. 'What brings you to my door on a Saturday morning? Is everything all right?'

'Yes, thank you,' said Nessa, deciding to ignore being strapped for cash, jobless, and currently sharing Driftwood House with an arrogant property developer who was driving her to distraction.

'So what's going on?'

'It's a matter of life and death,' Nessa blurted out, then blushed. 'Well, it is, for a building.'

'A matter of life and death regarding a building?' Jackson smiled. 'That sounds intriguing. You'd better tell me more. Off you go.'

So Nessa gave him a brief version of Gabriel's plans, how she came by the lease, and her idea for the cottage, trying hard to be matter-of-fact and not let her antipathy towards Gabriel show.

Then, she handed Jackson the document but he rested it on his lap and looked at her over the half-moon glasses balanced on the end of his nose.

'First of all, can I say how sorry I was to hear about the death of your grandmother. I didn't know her well but she seemed like a lovely woman.'

'Thank you.' Nessa swallowed, willing herself not to cry. 'She was.'

'And secondly, you do know that I've retired now and I'm no expert on leases?'

'Yes, but I'm still interested in what you think of it. I'm sure you know more than me. But if you'd rather not give your opinion, I'll understand.'

'Oh, I don't mind.' Jackson grinned. 'You'd be surprised how many people ask for my opinion on leases and other documents – from wills and pre-nups to passport applications. I'm happy to have a quick look.'

With that, he picked up the old, yellowing pieces of paper and started reading through them carefully.

'What do you think?' Nessa asked after a while. She pulled the key, found in her grandmother's leather box, from her pocket and turned it over in her hands. 'Does the lease stand up or am I crazy?'

'Hmm. It's an unusual agreement.' Jackson handed the lease back to Nessa. 'But my opinion, after a quick read through, is *probably*, and *yes*. Probably, because I don't see why the agreement wouldn't still be in force, and yes, you are crazy to think you can stop the Ghost Village being levelled by doing up the cottage. But...' He took off his glasses and peered at her. 'I do like it when ordinary people do crazy things in a bid to thwart big business. You might not believe it but I was a bit of a rebel in my youth. Up the revolution!'

He punched the air while Nessa decided that she did find it hard to believe. Jackson, a lawyer going to work in his suit and carrying a briefcase, had always looked the sort of man who would stick to the rules.

He put his hands together in his lap, his face suddenly serious. 'You do realise, though, that the lease stipulates you would need to spend at least thirty consecutive days and nights at the property? It certainly won't be valid unless that clause is fulfilled.'

Nessa nodded. 'Yes, I saw that bit.'

'And I doubt the cottage would be an appropriate environment for a child.'

'It's definitely not. But I expect Lily could stay with Valerie. I'm sure she'd love having her granddaughter to stay for a month. They have a close relationship.'

'That's good.' Jackson's bushy eyebrows knitted into a frown. 'I presume you've lost your job now that Shelley's has closed down?'

'That's right. I'm looking for something else that fits in with Lily's school hours.'

'Which must be tricky with the school summer holidays fast approaching.' Jackson made a 'tsk' sound between his teeth. 'Troubles tend to come together, don't they? Well, I wish you good luck with your job search.'

'Thank you. I appreciate that.'

Jackson puffed out his florid cheeks. 'I was so sorry to see Mr Scaglin's shop close. The village isn't the same without a decent hardware store. There's almost nothing else that's practically useful for local people in Heaven's Cove. It's all gift shops and ice-cream parlours and over-priced clothing boutiques. Do you know what's happening to the building? The last time I peeked inside, the place still needed a final clear-out.'

'Most of the stock's been sold off but there are a few odds

and ends left that Mr Scaglin has to sort out. As for the building? I expect it'll be turned into another gift shop.'

Jackson gave a mock shudder. 'Probably. More tat and trinkets for tourists. Ah, well. That's a cross we bear for living in such a beautiful place.'

There was a lull in the conversation when he stared out of the window, and Nessa got to her feet. She'd already taken up too much of this man's time.

'I'll head off and leave you in peace,' she told him. 'But thank you so much for seeing me on a Saturday morning and for giving me your opinion.'

Jackson waved his hand. 'You're welcome. You've brightened up my rather boring day, and I wish you the very best of luck with your endeavours.'

TWELVE
NESSA

Nessa hurried down the track to the Ghost Village and picked her way through the ruins to her grandmother's old home.

She couldn't be long. Rosie had offered to look after Lily while she visited Jackson, but she couldn't take advantage of her friend's good nature. And Valerie was expecting Lily in a couple of hours for an overnight stay.

Lily was excited at the thought of seeing her father after all this time. Nessa was less so, but she'd grin and bear it for her daughter's sake because family was important. That was one reason why this cottage, standing amid the ruins, felt so significant.

Nessa stood in the doorway, gazing across the ocean, the lease stuffed into the bag over her shoulder. Clouds scudded across the sky as she imagined her grandmother standing in this very spot, watching as her mother was swallowed by the sea.

Sorrel Cove should be a sad place. A place of pain and sorrow. But, over the years, it had mellowed into a place of comfort and remembrance as its tragedy had faded – for Nessa at least, though not for her grandmother.

How sad then that the Ghost Village now faced a new tragedy. The sea hadn't destroyed it completely, but Gabriel and his family business would. Was Nessa brave enough to stop that from happening? Jackson was right that she would need the very best of luck.

Nessa drew back her shoulders and pulled the key from her pocket. It felt heavy in her hand as she pushed it into the lock on the front door. And she felt a sense of excitement as the key slid perfectly into place.

She twisted it impatiently, desperate to open the door after all these years. But the key stopped halfway round, the lock damaged by decades of sea spray and rust.

Nessa used her shoulder to push the heavy wooden door, but it remained wedged shut.

So that's that, said the little voice in her head. The little voice that sometimes told her she hadn't been good enough for Jake, and she wasn't good enough for Lily

Nessa ran her hand across the stone wall of the cottage. 'I'm not giving up so easily, Gran,' she muttered, before pushing the key back into her pocket.

She circled the building, knowing there were chinks in the boards covering the ground-floor windows, and she found one at the back of the cottage that might do.

With a look round to make sure no one was in sight, she pushed her fingers into the gap in the wood and began to pull. Splinters speared the flesh under her nails but she kept on pulling until the rotting board gave way and fell onto the grass at her feet.

She smelled damp earth and dust as she pushed her face closer to the window. A small pane of glass was missing and she managed to open the window after sliding her hand inside and unfastening the metal clasp.

'This is not sensible,' she told herself. Did it amount to breaking and entering? But she knew she couldn't stop now.

She clambered inside, swearing as her arm scraped across the stone windowsill, and looked around her.

The room was grubby and there were signs of squatters over the years – an old mattress in one corner, rusting empty cans of soup, and ashes in the brick fireplace.

But the room seemed fairly watertight and there were few signs of damp on the plastered walls.

This was where her family had lived and talked and argued and loved. Nessa swallowed, feeling prickles of the past settle on her shoulders. And then she saw it.

Something was embedded in the wall above the mantelpiece. Sunlight was falling on the plaster and an indentation was casting a faint shadow.

When Nessa got closer, she could see a rectangular shape covered in a layer of dirt and dust. She rubbed at it, firstly with a tissue and then with the sleeve of her sweatshirt. There was definitely something beneath the grime. It was a collage, she realised, made of stone and glass.

As Nessa continued cleaning, nuggets of ruby and emerald sea glass began to glow in the light from the board-free window. And tiny squares of coloured stone – orange, yellow, black and cream – became more vivid as years of dirt were rubbed away.

Nessa stepped back, hardly able to believe what was in front of her. This was her great-grandmother's artwork. It was unmistakeably the same abstract, intricate pattern that her grandmother had drawn and placed in her leather box of treasures – the artwork, according to her gran's poignant poem, that her family had had to leave behind when they fled.

The beautiful richness of it hinted at the vibrancy of the woman lost in the storm. Her great-grandmother, for so long merely a ghost in her grandmother's stories, became more real with every glint of light on stone and glass. It was beautiful.

A gust of wind sighed around the cottage and brought Nessa back to the present. She didn't have much time.

Quickly, she climbed the stairs to the first floor of the building. The stairs were made of stone and seemed safe, though the handrail attached to the wall was rotten. Huge flakes of desiccated wood rained down onto the steps as she climbed.

At the top, Nessa stepped onto the landing and stood still. Everywhere was silent, save for a faint wash of the sea in the distance.

She inched forward carefully over the dark floorboards, which looked sound enough. Some of the windows up here weren't covered so at least she could see where she was going.

Nessa poked her head into a bedroom and jumped back in alarm when a large bird flew at her.

'Woah!'

Her voice echoed through the cottage as she steadied herself against the wall, her heart hammering.

This was foolish. She couldn't bring Lily to live in a place like this. Not even to stop Gabriel from knocking it down and building fancy homes that Nessa could never hope to afford.

'I don't think I am brave enough, Gran,' Nessa whispered, all bravado deserting her as she thought back to the key and the lease, and her grandmother's words scrawled across the envelope that had contained them. She slid down the wall until she was sitting on the floor. 'I'm sorry.'

She sat there for a while, feeling as alone as she'd ever felt in her life and wondering what to do next. One thing was for sure. She couldn't impose on Rosie for much longer. It wasn't fair.

Nessa pulled out her phone, opened her notes and started to make an action plan. Having a plan, however outlandish, always made her feel more in control. And she'd always had one on the go, ever since her mother had first fallen ill.

Her brow furrowed as she typed into her phone.

1. *Chase local landlords/social housing again to see if anything suitable/affordable/available.*

Nessa bit her lip. The waiting list for social housing was long, and all she'd been offered by private landlords so far was either damp, grotty or miles from Lily's school. Lily loved her school and the friends she'd made there. Changing schools would break her heart.

2. *Find a job that fits around Lily's childcare needs.*

That was proving to be easier said than done, especially with the long summer holiday approaching. Frantic job-searching had come to nothing, and while Valerie was always keen to look after Lily, she couldn't be expected to provide huge amounts of childcare.

3. *Improve my relationship with Jake.*

Nessa thought a moment before deleting her words. She was already doing all she could to maintain a decent relation-ship, for Lily's sake. But it was hard when he was so unreliable. It might help, of course, if Valerie was more supportive and didn't think her son was a faultless human being.

Nessa raised a hand to shield her eyes as sunlight pierced a salt-streaked windowpane and dappled around her. Sunbeams caught the snake bracelet on her arm, scattering rainbow colours across the walls.

Her grandmother had rarely worn the bracelet. She'd been the sort of woman who saved good clothes for best, so hardly ever got them out of the wardrobe. But Nessa had learned in her relatively short life that good things rarely last. So, she'd worn the piece of jewellery constantly since it became hers.

But one day – maybe one day soon if she couldn't find a suitable job and Lily needed new shoes – she might have to pawn her precious bracelet, or even sell it. The thought of being so desperate made Nessa feel unutterably sad.

She moved her arm and watched the colours – red and green, blue and violet – dance across the landing. They brought life and movement back to this cottage, which had been silent and empty for far too long.

Nessa switched off her phone and shoved it into her pocket. What was the point in making action plans if she didn't take action when the answer was right in front of her?

She got to her feet, brushing dust and dirt from the backside of her jeans.

Doing up this cottage was a crazy idea. Jackson thought so, even though he'd been supportive overall, and everyone else would think so too. But maybe she could make it work, for her and for Lily.

She walked to the window and looked out across the tumbled stones towards the churning sea. She had to make it work because she, just like the Ghost Village, was out of other options.

THIRTEEN

GABRIEL

Gabriel took another bite of his scone and licked thick clotted cream from his lips. Nessa had been right when she'd recommended this café during her tour of the village.

Of course, he should be nibbling a healthy sandwich right now, after his full English breakfast. If he was at his desk in London, he'd be eating sushi or a mixed salad.

But outdoors, with the smell of sun cream in his nostrils, he felt more free and rebellious. Here in Devon, he was free of his father's expectations, free of work obligations, free to wreck his arteries if he so chose.

Though his father's latest terse text – *Following receipt of your report, demolition team organised to join you on Monday* – had served as a reminder that this was an illusion.

Gabriel took another large bite of scone and watched the people passing by from his pavement table. They strolled along as if they were without a care in the world – aside from the parents dragging recalcitrant toddlers, looking stressed and knackered.

It couldn't be easy being a parent, especially ones juggling child-rearing on their own.

Gabriel's thoughts turned again to Nessa, for the second time in as many minutes, which was annoying. For a waspish woman who couldn't abide him, she was taking up far too much headspace.

But the only thing she had going for her – apart, Gabriel had to admit, for her beautiful eyes – were her parenting skills. She was obviously a good mother.

He'd watched from his bedroom window yesterday evening as she'd chased Lily outdoors, whooping and cheering. She'd caught her daughter in the end and the two of them had fallen into a giggling heap, with Nessa cradling her daughter in her lap.

Gabriel had stepped back from the window at that point, partly because it felt like intruding on a private family event, but mostly due to the pain in his heart.

He couldn't remember his mum ever chasing him like that, or cradling him in her arms. Perhaps she had, before she'd divorced his dad and married a banker with bad breath and a posh house in the Cotswolds. A banker who didn't want to take on someone else's kid.

So Gabriel had stayed with his father and been brought up by a succession of au pairs who never stayed for long. He'd learned, as a child, not to get attached to any of them.

His father's girlfriends had also come and gone. The latest, Collette, was young enough to be Gabriel's sister, and she took no interest in his family. Her main interest seemed to be his father's impressive investments.

Gabriel shook his head. What did he know? Maybe Collette was madly in love with his father, who looked rakish in a well-cut suit.

Gabriel glanced down at his white shirt and suit trousers. Was he turning into his father, who wouldn't be seen dead in shorts, even in a tiny seaside village in the middle of nowhere?

He picked up the last piece of scone and was about to shove

it into his mouth when, to his horror, he noticed Nessa walking past.

He abruptly dropped it onto his plate, and wiped a paper serviette across his mouth, preparing for verbal combat. With any luck, Nessa would pretend she hadn't seen him and walk on. He desperately wanted her to walk on because she wouldn't like his latest news.

But it wasn't his lucky day. Nessa stopped when she spotted him, walked on a few more paces and then retraced her steps. She was striding directly towards him now, her brow knitted and sun glinting on the golden snake bangle that encircled her wrist.

She stopped in front of him but said nothing. Then she swallowed as though she was building up to something. Gabriel sat back in his chair, waiting for whatever was to come.

'Hello,' she said finally, using her hand to shield her eyes from the glare. 'What do you think of our famous Devon cream tea?'

That threw him. Her body language – fists clenched, jaw tight – screamed stress and dislike. But here she was, making small talk.

'It's very nice, though I've got far too much of it,' he said woodenly. He gestured at the second scone he hadn't yet touched. 'I think the woman who runs the café is trying to feed me up.'

'Pauline takes it as a personal affront if people don't order a mountain of food.'

Her shoulders dropped slightly as she smiled at the woman who'd served him. She looked very different when she smiled – younger, less intense, prettier. Gabriel realised he was staring at the freckles on her nose. He looked away and pushed his plate across the table. He didn't want any more carbohydrates.

'So, can I help you?' he asked, trying to sound languid but realising too late that he sounded bored instead.

Nessa stared at him then dropped into the seat opposite. 'I need to have a word, if you've got a minute.'

'Yeah, sure,' he said, turning his palms to the sky in what he hoped was a conciliatory gesture. He paused. 'Would you like the other scone?'

That put her on the back foot. Surprise sparked in her deep brown eyes and she shook her head. 'No, thank you. I'm not here to eat. I wanted to ask, when will work start at Sorrel Cove?'

Gabriel sighed quietly but there was no point in sugar-coating it. He got the feeling that Nessa would see through any obfuscation.

'I've just heard that preparatory work will be starting next week. We'll make the site ready while planning permission's being finalised because my father's been assured it'll get the green light. The new sea defences are spurring investment in this area, and the local council's keen to support projects like ours.'

'I could fight your application.'

More fighting talk? Gabriel sighed again. Much as he admired Nessa's determination, she had no idea what his father was like.

'You could, but my father will bring in experts and he'll win. He always wins.'

Nessa's cheeks coloured at that and she folded her arms. 'What will you do to make the site ready?'

He hesitated, annoyed with himself for not wanting to tell her of the destruction that the diggers would wreak. This was a big deal for him. A big deal that would put him in his father's good books, for once. And Sorrel Cove, he told himself, was just a pile of old stones at the end of the day, whatever Nessa's senti-mental views.

'What will the work entail?' she asked again, leaning forward.

He took a deep breath. 'We'll demolish any standing struc-
tures, take away the stone and prepare for new foundations to
be laid.'

'Will you demolish my family's cottage immediately?'

He held her gaze. 'Yes, we will.'

'What if you can't?'

'We can and I'm sorry but there's nothing that can stop it.'

'Yes, there is.' She pushed her hands into her bag and
brought out some papers. 'What if there's someone already
living on the site?'

He shook his head. 'Squatters can be evicted.'

'What if they have a right to live there?'

Gabriel narrowed his eyes. What was she getting at? 'I don't
understand,' he said slowly.

Nessa swallowed. 'The cottage at the back of the village,
where my family used to live – it belongs to me.'

Gabriel folded his arms, unsure where this bizarre conversation was going. 'I know your family lived there a long time ago.
But that doesn't mean it belongs to you.'

'Well, not belongs exactly, but I have a right to live there.'

'Says who?'

'Says this lease.'

She thrust the papers at him and sat back in her chair, biting her
lip. He pushed his sunglasses up into his hair and started reading.

What the hell? In his line of work he'd seen plenty of leases
and agreements involving property – and this one, though old,
looked legitimate enough at first glance.

'Where did you get this?' he demanded sharply as he
reached the end of the document.

'It was amongst my grandmother's possessions.' Nessa tilted
up her chin and stared at him defiantly. 'It says that the Paulson
family – my family – have a right to live in that cottage for 125
years, which means it's mine for another twenty-two years.'

'I assumed that Paulson was your married name.'

'I kept my maiden name, just like my gran and her mother before her.'

Of course she had, thought Gabriel. During their short acquaintance, he'd already gleaned that Nessa wasn't always inclined to take the conventional approach. And it was obviously a family trait.

He skimmed through the lease again, his sense of unease growing until his eyes settled on a very important clause she must have missed. He smiled with relief.

'It says here that the cottage is only yours if you stay there for at least a month, day and night. So this lease is null and void because you don't live there.'

'Not yet,' said Nessa, her face deadly serious. 'But I'm about to move in.'

'Don't be ridiculous. You can't live there. The place is falling down.'

'It's not. The roof is on, there's glass in most of the windows, and the place is watertight, more or less. I think squatters lived there a while back and did some repairs.'

What self-respecting squatters would make home improvements? Sorrel Cove would be the death of him. Gabriel sat back in his seat, feeling more hot and bothered than at any other time during his stay in Devon.

'You can't live there,' he told her. 'The place has been empty for ages.'

'I'm going to do it up.'

'While you're living there? That's crazy.'

Nessa's determined expression faltered but she shot back, 'Maybe, but sometimes you have to do something crazy to change your life for the better.'

This was getting them nowhere. Gabriel changed tack. 'How can you think of moving in with a small child in tow?

You'd have to live there day and night for thirty days. That's no place for your daughter.'

He'd struck a nerve. He knew it when Nessa bristled and pushed her face towards his.

'I think I know better than you what's best for my daughter,' she said, her words clipped. 'And what she needs is somewhere long term that she can call home. I'm sure I can make the cottage habitable enough for her in a month, and in the meantime she can stay with her grandmother. It's all arranged.'

'And what happens after the thirty days?'

'The cottage will be ours, I can finish doing it up and we can live there, happily ever after.'

Happily ever after? The deluded woman was living in some kind of fairy tale.

Gabriel folded his arms and gave her his best icy stare.

'So what you're saying is you'll be a sitting tenant on the land, which means our plans will be severely affected?'

'That's right.'

She sat back and held his gaze, only the tightness of her jaw betraying her strong emotions.

Gabriel breathed out slowly, torn between anger at this woman's attempts to thwart his plans and grudging admiration that she wasn't rolling over and letting the diggers move in. Most people did.

'You can build your posh apartments somewhere else,' added Nessa, her lips pursed. 'That's the only solution.'

When she continued eyeballing him across the table, Gabriel's admiration for her began to fade. This woman was attempting to scupper his plans. And if the lease held up, she might just manage it.

But the cottage had to go. The footprint of the new apartments included where it currently stood. And redrawing the project to avoid demolishing the cottage wasn't the answer –

people paying a fortune for luxury homes wouldn't want a tumbledown house left on the site.

If the project didn't go ahead, he'd never live it down with his father. Or with his cousin, James, who, Gabriel knew in his heart of hearts, was far more suited to corporate life than he was.

'I need a copy of this lease,' he said coldly.

Nessa reached over and pulled it from his hands. 'Of course. I'll get you one, but right now I have to go.'

She stood up, pushing her chair back so hard, it wobbled and almost fell into the table behind her. Then, she shoved the lease into her bag and, with a curt nod, hurried off.

He watched her go, a sick feeling in the pit of his stomach. He'd badly misjudged single mum Nessa. She looked vulnerable and unthreatening, but she was proving to be a real thorn in his side. And his father would be furious at any delay.

Gabriel picked up a teaspoon, pushed it into the pot of thick cream and shoved the sickly sweet spoonful into his mouth. He was going to need lots of energy for the phone call he was about to make.

FOURTEEN
NESSA

What had she done? Nessa hurried through the village, hand in hand with Lily, replaying the conversation she'd had with Gabriel an hour earlier.

She turned into Sheep Lane, deliberately avoiding the road that led past Pauline's café, just in case he was still there, shovelling scones into his mouth.

Telling him about the lease hadn't been the plan. Not yet, anyway. First, she'd wanted to discuss everything with Rosie and square Lily's stay with Valerie.

But she'd been all fired up after going into the cottage and discovering her great-grandmother's artwork. And she'd snapped when she'd spotted Gabriel lolling at the café, as though he didn't have a care in the world. She'd wanted to wipe that rich-boy, arrogant expression off his face.

'Mummy, slow down,' urged Lily, pulling on her mother's hand.

'Sorry, sweetheart.'

Nessa slowed her pace and deliberately calmed her breathing. Gabriel Gantwich was on her mind far too much, and it was time to think about something else – anything else – for a while. It was time to focus on her daughter and make sure that she had a good time with her father.

Valerie's 1980s house, tucked away on the edge of Heaven's Cove, looked pristine as ever when Nessa and Lily approached the front door.

Two topiary boxwoods in pots stood either side of the front step and the brass door knocker gleamed. Most windows in Heaven's Cove were streaked with salt, but Valerie's windows sparkled in the sunshine.

Before Nessa could knock, Alan opened the door and ushered them into the hall.

'Hello, ladies. Come on into the sitting room,' he said gruffly before disappearing into the room, which overlooked the castle ruins.

Nessa slipped off her shoes before undoing the buckles on Lily's sandals and taking them off too.

Lily could get away with tracking dirt into her grandmother's house but Nessa knew it would never be tolerated from her – the scheming hussy who'd stolen Valerie's son before banishing him to the North.

That wasn't what had happened, of course. The truth was that Jake had relentlessly chased her until she'd agreed that he might make a suitable boyfriend after all. Her initial doubts – that being a self-proclaimed 'free spirit' meant, in reality, that he was an eejit – had been proven true. But he could still do no wrong in his mother's eyes and she always made excuses for him, even when he left for Manchester.

But at least he was coming back this weekend, and Lily was both excited and apprehensive because she didn't know Jake very well these days.

Nessa hoped this weekend would go towards changing that. Jake had turned out to be a rubbish partner, but she still held out hope he'd step up to the plate when it came to fatherhood –

although those hopes were fading as the years went on. It had been months since Jake had last seen Lily.

'Good afternoon, Nessa,' said Valerie when Nessa walked into the sitting room. 'You're later than I expected. Are you all right? You're looking a little peaky.'

Nessa blinked, used to Valerie's passive-aggressive greetings. 'I'm fine, thank you. How are you?'

Valerie wrinkled her nose. 'Not too bad.'

Would it kill Jake's mother to crack a smile? She was staring at Nessa's big toe, which was poking through a hole in her sock, and raising an eyebrow.

Nessa sighed quietly. *Quite honestly, Valerie, I've got bigger fish to fry than finding a pair of hole-less socks that meet with your approval.*

But she bit back the tart retort and gave her ex mother-in-law a wide, bright smile. She was trying to be the grown-up in this relationship and, if that failed, maybe she'd end up killing Valerie with kindness. Silver linings, and all that...

Valerie's sour face lit up as Lily pushed past her mum and ran towards her.

'Granny!' Lily squealed, throwing her arms around her grandmother's waist.

Valerie hugged her back, her face totally transformed. She might be a tricky ex mother-in-law, but she was a loving granny, and Nessa was grateful for that. Lily had such a small family and unsettled life right now, she needed as much love and stability as she could get.

Alan, who'd sunk into his favourite chair near the window, looked up from his iPad.

'I hear you're staying overnight, Lily.'

Lily grinned. 'Yes and I'm very 'cited, Grampy.'

When Alan harrumphed quietly, Nessa suppressed a smile because Grumpy would be more appropriate. He was narked because he'd prefer Lily to call him Alan, but this was a move that Lily had strongly rejected.

'Can I play in the garden, Gran?' asked Lily, eyeing up the swing and slide that Jake and Alan had put up together. Jake had expected a World's Best Dad award afterwards, Nessa remembered. He was good at putting up play equipment – just not great at being around for broken nights, bumped knees, and first days at school.

But at least he'd be here this weekend to build his relationship with his daughter. Nessa watched as Lily ran back into the hall to retrieve her sandals and headed through the open French windows into the garden. She could go outside on her own here and run around, with no cliff edges to worry about.

Nessa turned to Valerie. 'What time does Jake—' She caught herself. 'I mean *Jacob* plan on arriving? Presumably he's on the train from London already?'

'Well...'

Nessa had a sinking feeling when Valerie wouldn't catch her eye.

'There's been a slight change of plan because Jacob is so busy in his new job. They really can't do without him. Not even for a weekend. So I'm afraid he's had to postpone his trip.'

'A slight change of plan?' said Nessa, feeling angry but resigned. Of course Jake wasn't coming; she'd been an idiot to think he was. But what about her daughter? Their daughter? 'Lily's looking forward to seeing him.'

'I'm well aware of that.' Valerie's mouth had set in a thin line. 'He can't help being in demand at work and he was very apologetic, wasn't he, Alan?'

'What?' Alan looked up from his iPad. 'Oh, yeah. Very apologetic. Very upset.'

When Nessa raised an eyebrow, Valerie had the good grace to look embarrassed. Nessa doubted that Jake had been upset at the thought of not seeing his daughter. If he cared so much about Lily, he'd pay maintenance more regularly.

Nessa looked into the garden, at Lily hurtling down the slide.

I'm so sorry, darling girl, that I landed you with such a hopeless father.

'She can still stay for the weekend,' said Valerie, pushing a strand of ash-blonde hair behind her ear. 'It would be a shame to cancel that too.'

Nessa was so disappointed on her daughter's behalf, she was tempted to whisk Lily away. But that wouldn't be fair on Lily. Or on Valerie, whose hands, Nessa noticed, were shaking slightly. Valerie spotted her staring and folded her fingers together, as if she was praying.

Nessa looked more closely at the older woman's pale face. Actually, she was the one who looked peaky and not her usual self.

'So what do you say?' urged Valerie. 'I've got Lily's favourite food in, which will go to waste, otherwise. And I was going to take her to the mini-zoo tomorrow. She'll love it.'

She would adore the zoo, and Nessa didn't have the transport or spare cash to take her there herself. Cancelling the whole weekend because Jake had let Lily down would be mean, especially as Valerie must feel let down by her son too. Even though she'd never admit it.

Nessa nodded. 'Of course Lily can stay. But I'll have to go and break the news that she won't be seeing her father.'

'I can do that, if you like.'

Valerie glanced at the photo of her son, on the mantelpiece. He was standing on top of a high granite tor on Dartmoor and laughing, as though he didn't have a care in the world.

'Thank you, but I think it's probably best coming from me.'

Valerie nodded. 'Please make sure you tell her how disappointed her father is not to see her this weekend.'

'That's exactly what I was planning on telling her,' said Nessa.

Lily would form her own opinion of her father in her own time. Let her have a lovely weekend being spoiled rotten by Valerie. It was more than Nessa could give her at the moment.

Ten minutes later, Nessa had told Lily that she wouldn't be seeing her father after all – a blow considerably lessened by news of the zoo visit the next day – and she was standing at the front door, slipping her feet back into her ancient trainers.

'You don't have to worry about Lily,' said Valerie stiffly, opening the front door. 'I'll look after her.'

'I know you will,' said Nessa, building up to asking her ex mother-in-law a very big favour. 'Um.' She paused at the door. 'I wanted to talk to you about something. I know you're having Lily to stay overnight but I wondered if you might be willing to let her stay here for a bit longer?'

'Of course. I'd love Lily to stay for longer, and we can tell Jacob so he can come down to see her.'

Nessa nodded, unconvinced that Jake would manage to make it down from Manchester any time soon.

'When are you thinking of and for how long?'

'Quite soon, for a few days,' said Nessa, being deliberately vague because a thought had just struck her.

It was all very well declaring to Gabriel that she was going to do up the cottage, but she didn't have the money to improve anything right now. She couldn't afford paint and other supplies, which meant her crazy plan would fall at the first hurdle, unless...

'Are you all right?' asked Valerie, peering into her face. 'You seem very odd today. Why do you need Lily to stay for longer? Have you got a new job?'

'Not yet,' answered Nessa, deciding to keep her plans quiet for now. What was the point in broadcasting them, if they might not happen?

All she'd do was give Valerie ammunition for the future. *'Do you remember when you entertained the idea of taking Lily to live in a derelict cottage?'* She'd spread it around the village, using it as proof that Nessa was a terrible mother.

Did it mean she *was* a terrible mother?

Valerie frowned. 'Are you quite sure you're all right?'

'Absolutely. Anyway, I must go. Perhaps we can talk about you having Lily for longer some other time? Thank you so much for having her tonight. I do appreciate you looking after her so well.'

Nessa stopped gabbling, having done nothing to dispel the impression that she was being 'odd' this afternoon.

Valerie sniffed. 'I look after her so well because she's my granddaughter and I care a great deal about her welfare. Drift-wood House isn't the best place to bring up a child, with all the comings and goings. So, however long you'd like Lily to stay here will be fine, for us and for her.'

However long you'd like Lily to stay here. Cold dread clutched at Nessa's heart.

This wasn't the first time Valerie had intimated that Lily would be better off living with her. And sometimes, in the dead of night, with Lily gently snoring nearby, Nessa wondered if it might be best for her beloved daughter. Especially now she'd lost her job and the two of them were sleeping in a tiny room filled with boxes.

But the thought of losing Lily was too much to bear. She was the reason Nessa dragged herself out of bed in the morning and was fighting for a better life.

'Thank you,' said Nessa. 'Our stay at Driftwood House is only temporary. I'm sorting out something more permanent at the moment. Anyway, I'm not sure Alan would be keen on having Lily in the house too much.'

'You don't need to worry about Alan,' said Valerie, holding the front door open wide. 'I doubt he'd even notice.'

. . .

That hadn't gone swimmingly, Nessa thought wryly, walking through the village. Valerie's opinion of her was low to begin with and now the woman had her marked down as odd into the bargain. She so wished that things were different.

She'd been excited about marrying into Jake's family. It was small, but bigger than hers, and the prospect of being a daughter-in-law had seemed wonderful at first.

Nessa had even secretly hoped that Valerie, though never taking the place of her own mother, might step into the void her mum had left behind.

But it wasn't to be. Valerie had never been particularly welcoming and their relationship had deteriorated in parallel with Jake's growing desire to be shot of his new wife and child.

'Where do you think he gets it from?' her gran had muttered while consoling a heartbroken Nessa after their split. 'That damn woman has indulged him and turned him into a selfish young man.'

It was the only time Nessa ever heard her gran speak badly of Valerie. Ruth had had a sunny nature and rarely spoke ill of anyone. She usually gave people the benefit of the doubt – and Nessa had been the same once, before life became overwhelming.

Nessa missed who she once was. Now, her trust in people had all but disappeared and she wasn't sure she liked the person she'd become. Sometimes, she worried that she was becoming too hard and uncompromising.

For example, should she be giving Gabriel the benefit of the doubt? After all, he was only doing his job and there was no reason why he should care hugely about the Ghost Village.

Nessa squashed down the treacherous thought before, heaven forbid, she started feeling any sympathy for him. Being tough was necessary when life threw curveballs, and she needed to stay strong and focused if her plan had any chance of succeeding.

She also needed the help of a person who'd walked out of her life more recently than Jake.

Nessa stopped in front of the village's ancient church and pushed open the gate to the churchyard. She'd sit here in peace and make the call that would either propel her crazy scheme forward or put the kybosh on it before it had even begun.

FIFTEEN
GABRIEL

Gabriel paced his bedroom at Driftwood House and picked up his mobile. Then he put it down again. This was ridiculous. He was going to have to tell his father sometime.

Taking a deep breath, he grabbed the phone and rang his father's number. It was picked up after two rings.

'Gabriel. I hope you're calling with good news.'

His father's voice was clipped, with a hint of irritation at being disturbed. Around him, Gabriel could hear the sounds of the office, even though it was a Saturday – a low hum of conversation, phones ringing and doors closing. His father was busy. His father was always busy.

'I have good news and bad news,' said Gabriel, fiddling with the buttons on his shirt and feeling grateful that it wasn't a Zoom call. He'd caught the sun and his nose was pink.

'I don't like bad news,' said his father, in a low tone.

The sounds of the open-plan office faded away. He'd obviously retreated to his own office for some privacy – though privacy in a glass-walled box was limited. Gabriel sometimes thought his father looked like a caged animal at his desk, staring out at his workforce, ready to pounce.

He cleared his throat, annoyed that he still felt like a child when talking to his father. He was over thirty, for goodness' sake.

'The good news,' he said, trying to sound as confident and adult as possible, 'is that you're right, and the site is perfect for the development that's planned... in many ways.'

'In *all* ways, surely?'

Gabriel stared out of the window and tried to focus on the sea, which, today, was as blue as he'd ever seen the Mediterranean.

'I'm afraid not because there's a slight problem.'

'What kind of a problem?'

'A young woman who has a lease on one of the properties on site.'

'I didn't think there were any properties. I thought they were all in ruins.'

'Most of them are. All of them, in fact, except for one cottage at the back of the site, which is more sheltered and has fared better over the years.'

'And let me guess, this woman has a lease for this particular cottage.'

'That's right.'

'And yet you've only just found this out now?'

There was silence after that from his father. A silence that Gabriel remembered from his school days. His father would read his school report and then stare at him for a few moments before launching into a litany of disappointments. It didn't matter how well Gabriel had done, he always managed to disappoint his father in some way or other.

'The lease is old and has only just come to light,' said Gabriel briskly. 'But I'm dealing with it.'

'It should have come to light when we were acquiring the site.'

'I know, but it didn't.'

His father breathed out loudly. 'Who dealt with the buy-up?'

'Barry in Acquisitions.'

'Then I want to see him in my office, immediately.'

'That might be a problem because you sacked him a month ago.' Gabriel waited for his father to speak but when he remained silent, added: 'It is unfortunate, but I'm aware of the lease now and I'm sorting the situation out.'

'I certainly hope so because the whole site must be cleared. I won't have some old wreck left in the corner, bringing down the asking price on my new apartments.' Billy Gantwich paused. 'So, is this lease watertight?'

'No. Well, maybe. I'm not completely sure. It's very old.' Gabriel swallowed. He was making a hash of this. He took a deep breath. 'I'm getting a copy of the lease and I'll take it from there.'

'This will all take time.'

Gabriel could hear his father tapping his pen on his desk.

'Sorting this out through the courts could be expensive but, more than that, it's bound to be time-consuming. And it will draw attention to what we're doing, and we don't want to stir up local antagonism. Locals can be a nuisance in these circumstances.'

'They don't seem to visit the site much so I don't think they'll be particularly bothered. Ness— I mean the woman who has the lease, has a family link to the site so she feels strongly about the planned development.'

'Strong feelings. They'll be the death of me.' His father groaned. 'So what do you propose?'

'The lease has a particular clause, a criterion that has to be met. The leaseholder has to live in the property for thirty days and nights continuously for it to be valid.'

'Well.' His father sounded more cheerful all of a sudden. 'In that case, I don't see what the problem is. You said the property is more sheltered but, presumably, it's still in a bad state of repair and she hasn't been living there.'

'She hasn't, but she's about to move in.'

'For goodness' sake!' All hint of cheer had vanished. 'Tell me more about this idiot woman.'

'She's about my age, a single parent who lives in Heaven's Cove.'

'And what's she like?'

Gabriel reviewed what he knew of Nessa – bossy, tired, opinionated, sad, a loving mum, quite pretty, and extremely annoying when it came to thwarting his plans to make himself look good in his father's eyes.

He said none of that. 'She's a regular single parent who's trying to get by, I guess.'

'Does she have much of a support network around her?'

'I don't think so.'

She certainly hadn't mentioned any family in the area, apart from her former mother-in-law. And there didn't seem to be any love lost in that relationship.

'So there's no partner around?'

'I don't believe so. Her ex-husband lives up north somewhere.'

And he was never around, from the little Gabriel had gleaned. But he didn't say that either.

'And her child is how old?'

'Five.'

'Well, that's fine. She won't want to move her child into a derelict property.'

'I believe the child will stay elsewhere for the month.'

There was another loaded silence and then his father spoke very quietly. Ironically, Gabriel knew that when his father was quiet, that was when he was at his most volatile. He'd seen business colleagues and competitors relax prematurely often enough.

'If this woman is causing problems, Gabriel, you have to solve them. That is your job and part of your role within this family. You do whatever it takes to nail the deal. She'll never stay thirty nights in an abandoned cottage in the middle of nowhere, and you need to catch her out when she sneaks back to her comfortable bed. Move in with her, if you have to.'

He paused to draw breath, before continuing. 'We'll query the lease, of course, but it will be far less problematic if you prove that she's not upholding the terms of the lease in the first place.'

'So you want me to spy on her?'

'Of course I do. Do you have a problem with that?'

'Well, yes. I can hardly barge my way into a secluded cottage with a young woman I hardly know. She'd certainly never agree to me moving in. Quite rightly.'

'Just get it sorted, Gabriel. I have every faith in your ability to make this problem go away.'

When his father ended the call without saying goodbye, Gabriel sat down heavily on the bed.

The problem was, his father didn't really have faith in his ability to sort this out, and he was probably wishing he'd sent his nephew James to Heaven's Cove instead.

This was supposed to be the deal that proved once and for all that Gabriel would be a worthy successor to his father's business one day. And Nessa was about to screw everything up.

He could hardly insist on moving in with her for a month. The lease seemed clear that she had the right to stay there alone. And in any case, he'd rather stick pins in his eyes than spend time with that disagreeable woman.

He'd hoped they could mostly avoid each other for the few days he'd be spending in Heaven's Cove. However, that was before she turned into some kind of lease-wielding ninja on a mission to save the Ghost Village, and his stay here was extended.

Yet he had to make a success of this business deal or he'd never live it down.

His father was right. Gabriel got to his feet. He would do as much as he could to catch Nessa out in her hare-brained plan to spend a month living in the cottage. And if that meant staying on in Heaven's Cove for a while and working remotely from the sitting room at Driftwood House, so be it.

The good news was that Nessa would never last more than a few days roughing it at the cottage, so he wouldn't have to bear this place for long. Or her either, for that matter.

SIXTEEN
NESSA

Nessa wandered past the weathered gravestones, towards the church that had been at the heart of Heaven's Cove for centuries. She sat on a wooden bench that faced the sea – a flash of blue between cottages – and pulled her phone from her pocket.

A sparrow landed at her feet and pecked at breadcrumbs scattered across the ground as she tried to calm down.

Time was rushing by so she should make the call. But first she needed to slow her racing thoughts.

Her whole life seemed to be on fast-forward at the moment and filled with significant events that could shape the rest of her life with Lily: her grandmother's death; losing her job and her home; Gabriel's plans for the Ghost Village.

Her thoughts lingered on Gabriel and the way his demeanour had changed after he'd read the lease. He'd been perfectly civil up until that point, even offering her his spare scone. And he'd looked quite handsome, with the sun warming his office-pale face.

Nessa shook her head. He'd only been civil because he

hadn't believed her vow at breakfast to thwart his plans. But after reading the lease, he appeared to have changed his mind.

Gabriel was worried she could be a thorn in his side, and Jackson's opinion of the lease had been positive. But the only person who held the key to the whole crazy scheme right now was her former employer, Desmond Scaglin.

Nessa looked across the churchyard, at the tall grass being ruffled by the breeze snaking between the gravestones. Would Mr Scaglin ride to the rescue, metaphorically speaking?

It was something Jackson said that had given her the idea to ask him for help.

Do you know what's happening to Scaglin's building? The last time I peeked inside, the place still needed a final clear-out.

Nessa pulled her mobile from her bag, dialled a number and listened to a phone ringing many miles away.

Finally, when she was just about to ring off, a familiar voice said: 'Hello? Who is it?'

'Hello, Mr Scaglin.' Although Nessa had worked in his shop for years, he'd never invited her to call him by his first name. 'It's Nessa here. I hope it's OK to give you a call. How are you?'

'Nessa? How lovely to hear from you.'

He sounded delighted, though his voice was quivery. He sounded much older than the tired but fairly sprightly man who'd closed his store for the last time just a few weeks ago.

'How are you doing in Tiverton?'

'Oh, you know. It's good to be near my family but I do miss going into work every day.'

'Me too. But it must be nice for you to have a rest.'

'I suppose so, though the days seem very long. My daughter calls in every lunchtime but I miss my friends.' He paused. 'I'm not sure that moving from Heaven's Cove was the right thing at my age, but it's too late now. What's done is done.'

Nessa's heart broke for the man. He'd driven her bats with his inflexible attitude to punctuality and his eccentric stock-ordering – who in Heaven's Cove wanted plastic roses that played the national anthem or draught excluders shaped like dragons? But he'd taken a chance on employing her when she was a single mum with a young child, and she'd be forever grateful to him for that.

'Why don't Lily and I come over to Tiverton soon to see your new place and say hello?' she said, worrying where the money for the journey would come from but determined to make the trip.

'Oh.' He sounded taken aback. 'Would you do that? It would be lovely to see you and Lily, and to hear all about the goings-on in Heaven's Cove. How is Lily doing?'

'She's fine, thank you.'

'And have you found another job?'

'Not yet, but there are some possibilities,' lied Nessa, who'd spent the previous evening trawling through the latest job opportunities. She'd applied for a couple in retail but most jobs advertised were incompatible with being a single parent as the school holidays approached. And she couldn't rely on Valerie long term for childcare.

'Well, I wish you luck.' Mr Scaglin cleared his throat, as though he wasn't keen to ask the next question. 'Can you tell me what's happening with the shop? The landlord hasn't been very forthcoming.'

'It still says "Shelley's" outside and the stock you left hasn't been cleared. Maybe the landlord is having trouble finding someone to take over the premises.'

'At the rents he charges, I'm not surprised.'

'Actually...' Nessa hesitated. 'I'm taking on a DIY project and wondered if it would be OK if I nabbed some of the leftover stock that hasn't sold? I'm afraid I can't afford to pay for it right now but I could pay you back in instalments.'

Mr Scaglin thought for a moment, while Nessa crossed her fingers. If he said no, her plan to improve the cottage would be over, just like that. But his next words warmed her heart.

'I believe that would be acceptable. The landlord has been bleating about me not clearing the shop completely so he can't complain if you take some of it away. And there's no need to pay. There's not much left and it will end up in a skip otherwise.'

'That's so kind of you. Are you sure?'

'I'm very sure. I felt bad about having to let you go.'

'You shouldn't feel bad about that. You had to do what was best for you.'

'Yes, though I wonder now if it was best for me.' He sniffed. 'Anyway, I'll contact the landlord to let him know you need access. What's the DIY project you're tackling?'

Nothing much. Just moving into a derelict Ghost Village cottage for a month and making it habitable.

Nessa shook her head. 'It's a bit hard to explain but I'll tell you about it when Lily and I come to visit. Thank you so much, Mr Scaglin.'

'You're welcome, and I'll look forward to your visit. Oh, and Nessa...'

'Yes?'

'I think you should call me Desmond, don't you? Take care, dear.'

And with that he ended the call.

Nessa hadn't cried since she'd scattered her grandmother's ashes to the wind. Even though she'd since had to deal with a difficult ex mother-in-law, dwindling finances, a perpetually disappointing ex-husband, and a posh businessman from the city who wanted to destroy her family's heritage.

But being invited to call Mr Scaglin by his first name, after all these years, was the final straw. Tears filled her eyes and spilled down her cheeks.

SEVENTEEN

VALERIE

Valerie was washing up when she heard the garden gate click. The house had been so quiet since Jacob moved out, she heard most people approaching.

Lily had brought some life to the house, but she'd only stayed one night and had been picked up earlier this afternoon by her friend Olive's mum. Lily was going to tea with Olive and would no doubt have a lovely time, but Valerie wished she'd stayed for another hour or two.

To banish the silence, she'd turned the radio on for a while. The upbeat tones of Radio 2 were cheery but Alan had complained about the music being too loud and had switched over to a radio talk show. That had done nothing but depress Valerie, as it was full of people giving their opinion on things about which they knew very little.

Valerie took off her rubber gloves and laid them carefully on the drainer so they wouldn't drip onto the floor. She didn't want to make the floor slippery and cause an accident. Then, she stood leaning against the sink, trying to push down the disturbing feelings that sometimes threatened to overwhelm her.

She'd tried once to describe them to Alan. She'd attempted to explain the jumble of sadness, anger and desperation that made it hard to breathe. But Alan had looked at her as if she was mad, so she hadn't mentioned her feelings since. She did her best to keep them hidden from everyone, including herself.

'Get a grip, Valerie,' she muttered, pushing herself away from the sink and walking wearily into the hall. Someone was approaching, their shadow dark in the frosted glass of the front door.

When the bell rang, she waited a moment before pulling the door open. It wouldn't do to look as if she'd been waiting, with nothing else to do.

'Oh.'

To her surprise, Nessa was standing on the doorstep, and Valerie's heart started hammering.

'Is everything all right with Lily? Olive's mother picked her up as we'd arranged. That was right, wasn't it?' Her voice sounded high and panicky.

'She's fine, Valerie.'

'Only it can't be good for her, living with strangers all the time.'

It was a non-sequitur and Valerie knew it. She'd jumped from asking if it was OK that Olive's mum had collected Lily to condemning her grandchild's living arrangements. She couldn't help it. Her grandchild should be living somewhere more permanent.

'Driftwood House is very nice and, as I've said, it's only temporary.' Nessa wiped her hands across her eyes, as if she was weary too. 'Sorry to call unexpectedly but could I have a quick word please?'

'Yes, of course.'

Valerie stepped back and let Nessa into the hall, curious to find out why she was here. She never called round without Lily.

All childcare arrangements were made at arm's length, through phone calls or texts. It was better that way.

When Nessa sighed quietly, Valerie realised how exhausted she looked. And, for a moment, she felt sympathy for her. It must be hard for a young girl, being a single parent. But she'd chosen her path, thought Valerie, hardening her heart as she remembered her precious son far away.

When the kettle started whistling, Valerie jumped. Damn thing. Alan liked a peaceful house but he still insisted on having an old-fashioned kettle that sat on the hob.

'Come with me,' she ordered Nessa, going into the kitchen and turning off the flame. 'I'm making a cup of tea for Alan. Would you like one?'

Nessa shook her head, much to Valerie's relief.

'No, thank you. I have things to do but I wanted to ask you a favour while Lily wasn't here. A big one.'

She seemed nervous, Valerie realised, as she warmed the teapot and spooned in loose tea leaves. Tea bags were another modern invention that Alan didn't much approve of. Not that he ever seemed to make the tea himself.

When the spoon hit the side of the pot and leaves scattered across the worktop, Valerie had a bizarre urge to cry – over tea leaves, for goodness' sake. What on earth was wrong with her?

Nessa was suddenly at her side.

'Why don't you sit down, Valerie, and I can finish making the tea.'

And she sounded so concerned, so kind, Valerie was filled with gratitude, and irritation at herself. How silly must she seem when she couldn't even make a pot of tea without messing it up? Quite honestly, she felt like someone else these days.

'I'll be fine,' she said brusquely, adding 'thanks' for good measure because Nessa was being kind. 'What was the favour you wanted to ask?'

Nessa perched on one of the stools that lined the breakfast bar. 'First of all, thank you for having Lily to stay last night.'

'You're welcome. We had fun and she loved the mini-zoo this morning.'

'I'm sure she did. She always enjoys staying here and, actually, that's what my favour is all about.'

'Is this something to do with the mysterious additional stay you mentioned yesterday?' asked Valerie, concentrating as she poured hot water into the pot. It wouldn't do to scald herself in front of Nessa.

'Yes. Sorry if I was a bit mysterious but I wasn't sure that my plan would come off. But now it's all arranged and it's something that I feel I have to do, even if it doesn't come to anything in the end.'

Valerie looked up from the steaming teapot. What on earth was the girl talking about?

Nessa took a deep breath, her cheeks burning.

'What I want to ask is, would it be possible for Lily to stay here for longer than one night and—'

'Of course,' interrupted Valerie. 'You didn't need to come over to ask me that. You know I love having Lily here.'

'I know, but this isn't just for a couple of nights. This would be...' She hesitated. 'This would be for a month.'

'A *month*? Why? Are you going somewhere?'

'Kind of.' Nessa bit her lip before a torrent of words spilled out of her. 'I'm going to stay in the Ghost Village. Sorrel Cove. My grandmother left me a lease on the cottage there, where my family used to live. I'm trying to save it from demolition and maybe even do the place up. But, according to the terms of the lease, I need to stay there for thirty consecutive days *and* nights to lay claim to the house.'

'You're going to live in one of the Ghost Village cottages?' Valerie stood still, an empty teacup in her hands. 'I haven't been there for years. But I believe they're falling down.'

'This one isn't. Not really. It's been more protected from the elements than the others and, well, I think it could end up being a new home for me and Lily.'

Valerie felt her jaw drop. The girl had gone mad.

'I heard a rumour that the ruins are going to be knocked down,' she said, still trying to digest this information. Was Nessa truly contemplating taking her precious granddaughter to live in a derelict house that was under threat of demolition?

'Me taking on the cottage is one way of stopping the whole village from being demolished. And I think the cottage could be just what Lily and I need to get back on our feet, if I work really hard on it. It's peaceful and in such a beautiful spot. Lily will love it.'

Would she? It sounded as if Nessa was trying to convince herself. When Valerie said nothing, Nessa continued.

'I obviously can't stay in the cottage for thirty nights with Lily, not until I've had time to make the place more habitable.'

'What would Jacob think of you taking his daughter to live in a place like that?'

'If he sent his maintenance money on time, I'd be in a much better position to secure different accommodation that might meet with his approval,' said Nessa sharply.

Valerie scowled. Of course Jacob paid regularly for his daughter's upkeep. He was working his socks off hundreds of miles away while Nessa was swanning around with grand ideas about doing up totally unsuitable property.

Nessa folded her hands in her lap. 'I'm sorry, Valerie. Let's not talk about Jake right now. I realise you having Lily here for a whole month is asking a lot. I'd still be around to take her to and from school and the like. I just wouldn't be around overnight. But if you don't want to have Lily staying here for that long, I understand.'

Valerie spoke up quickly. 'Of course I want her to stay. That's no problem.'

The truth was, she desperately wanted Lily to stay for a month. If she had her way, Lily would stay forever, her energy and laughter bringing life back into this silent house.

And while enabling Nessa's crackpot plan wasn't ideal, the daft woman would soon come to her senses and realise that she couldn't provide what Lily needed – Valerie looked around her cosy kitchen – whereas she could.

Nessa would have time to think, sitting alone in her damp, derelict cottage, about how Lily would be far better off in her grandmother's care.

'I heard the kettle,' said Alan, ambling into the kitchen from the garden with a newspaper under his arm and his sunglasses pushed on top of his bald head. His nose was bright red. He should have been wearing a hat.

'Hello, Nessa,' he said, giving Valerie an enquiring glance. 'Is everything all right?'

'Everything's fine,' said Valerie. 'Nessa came to ask a favour and I said yes. So we're having Lily to stay for a month.'

'A month?' blustered Alan, panic in his eyes.

'I hope you don't mind,' said Nessa.

'He doesn't mind at all,' said Valerie quickly.

She cooked his meals, cleaned his house, and washed his underpants. So this was one thing he could do for her.

He glanced at Valerie, surprised by her firm tone of voice.

'Perhaps I ought to let you and Valerie have a chat about this,' said Nessa, getting to her feet. But Valerie was having none of it.

'We don't need to chat. I said it'll be fine and it will be.'

'Alan?' asked Nessa, turning to him.

'Well, it's lovely having my granddaughter here, obviously. She's just rather noisy.'

Of course she's noisy. She's a child! thought Valerie. As far as she was concerned, the more noise the better. At least there would be some joy in this house for a whole month. Maybe longer.

And Jacob could come to stay and spend time with his daughter and his parents. When Lily moved in for good, he'd come home lots to see her. Valerie was sure of it. Perhaps he'd even move down south again.

She glared at Alan, daring him to say anything that would make Nessa change her mind. Let her go and rough it in a falling-down building for a month. She would spoil Lily and feel useful, which would be a nice change.

Valerie smiled at Nessa. 'Just let me know when Lily will be coming and I'll make sure her bedroom is ready for her.'

Nessa swallowed. 'I was thinking, maybe tomorrow?'

'Tomorrow?' spluttered Alan, but Valerie silenced him with a glare.

'Tomorrow will be perfectly fine, and you don't need to worry about Lily. She and I are going to have such a wonderful time, she won't want to leave.'

It was a pointed remark and it hit home. Valerie could see it in Nessa's eyes, which were sparking with relief, and something else... probably resignation that Valerie was right and her daughter would be better off here.

She felt another twinge of sympathy for Nessa but stamped it out quickly. The most important person in all of this was Lily, and now Valerie had a chance to change her life for the better.

EIGHTEEN
NESSA

Nessa stood in the middle of the cold room, a pile of timber, paint pots and cleaning materials at her feet.

She'd loaded up Rosie's borrowed car three times with supplies from the hardware store and had driven to the Ghost Village, with paint pots clattering as she rounded corners.

But she was properly here at last, with her supplies, and Operation New Home could begin.

'Go, Nessa!' she said into the empty room, punching the air with her fist.

But her confidence faded almost immediately. She folded her arms, feeling foolish, and already missing Lily, although she'd dropped her at school only two hours earlier.

Valerie would pick her up later and take her home because that's where she'd be living for the next month. Lily thought it was a great adventure and Valerie seemed delighted. It was only Nessa whose heart hurt at the thought of thirty nights of separation.

'It's for the best of reasons,' Nessa told herself, picking up the old broom she'd found in a corner at Shelley's.

She'd used it often enough to sweep the hardware store and

now it would help her to spruce up this old cottage, so Lily could come home for good.

She started sweeping dust and dirt into piles, jumping as a gust of wind slammed the front door shut.

'Stop being such a wuss,' she muttered, glancing at her bedding roll and sleeping bag in the corner. What would it be like here on her own in the middle of the night?

She had access to water from a well behind the house. Rosie reckoned it would poison her though it looked clear enough – she'd boil it on her portable gas stove for safety's sake, until it could be checked. But there was no electricity supply as yet. So it would be flickering candlelight when the sun slid below the horizon.

A frisson of fear slid down Nessa's back. Sorrel Cove wasn't called the Ghost Village for nothing. Locals reckoned that the spirits of those lost in the great storm haunted the ruins and wailed a warning when a storm was brewing.

Nessa didn't want to wake up to wailing at three in the morning.

'Stop it!' she said, more loudly this time. 'Or you're not going to last one night, let alone thirty.'

Thirty long nights out here on her own. What on earth had she got herself into? The only comforting thought was that, even if ghosts did haunt the village, one of them would be her great-grandmother, who surely wouldn't let any harm come to her.

Nessa ran her hand across the mosaic above the fireplace. The sea glass and bright shards of stone set into the wall felt smooth beneath her fingers and she began to feel calmer. She should be here, continuing her family's story after it had been so cruelly halted.

Picking up the broom, she began to sweep the flagstones again but stopped when she heard the hum of a vehicle approaching. She glanced out of the window, sure it was Rosie bringing provisions in Liam's truck.

As well as worrying she'd be poisoned, Rosie was convinced that she'd starve, and reminding her that the nearest shop was only a thirty-minute walk away had done nothing to ease her fears.

But Nessa's visitor wasn't Rosie. A shiny blue car had parked next to Rosie's battered Mini. And Gabriel was getting out of it and stretching his long legs.

Nessa frowned when he tried the door handle to make sure that the car was locked. Who did he think was going to steal it when no one was in sight? He started walking down the narrow path that had been worn into the hillside.

He was still in a suit, Nessa noticed, and he looked faintly ridiculous, with his tie flapping in the breeze. Honestly, who wore a tie on a baking hot day to harangue someone in an abandoned village?

She started sweeping again, razing the floor with brisk, hard strokes. The sooner Mr Gantwich said what he had to say and left her in peace, the better.

A minute later, Gabriel's tall frame filled the doorway of the cottage, and he cleared his throat to attract her attention.

'Hello,' said Nessa, trying to sound unconcerned by his arrival. She brushed hair from her eyes as the dust she'd disturbed danced in the air.

'I see you're ready to get started,' said Gabriel, nodding at the paint pots.

'No time like the present,' answered Nessa, deliberately brightly. She wouldn't give this man any inkling of the apprehension she felt.

'Is it all right if I come in?'

Nessa shrugged. 'If you like.'

'How did you get in, in the first place?' he asked, stooping to avoid banging his head on the door lintel.

'Through the front door. My grandmother left me a key.'

That was true enough, this time, because copious amounts of WD40 squirted into the keyhole had freed up the lock. Nessa didn't mention clambering through the window on her first visit.

Gabriel looked around him. 'It's all a bit of a mess, isn't it?'

'That's not surprising. No one's lived here properly for decades, but a few hours of cleaning and painting will make all the difference.'

'If you say so.'

Gabriel brushed dirt from his trousers, while Nessa wondered if it was wise being on her own in such a lonely place with a man she hardly knew.

But, much as he annoyed the life out of her, she felt safe. He was arrogant at times, single-minded and hard-nosed, but she didn't sense any aggression behind his pomposity. According to Lily, he was 'a very nice man' but five-year-olds weren't always the best judge of character.

'What's this?' murmured Gabriel, walking to the mosaic on the wall.

'It was made by my great-grandmother.'

'Wow, it's beautiful. She had a rare talent.'

Gabriel stretched out his hand to touch the stones but drew his fingers back when Nessa said: 'If you've arrived to try and dissuade me from living here, you've had a wasted journey.'

Her words came out more sharply than she'd intended, but she didn't want him to touch the mosaic. Not when his wrecking ball would destroy it, along with the cottage.

He looked at her thoughtfully, dark hair falling across his forehead.

'Are you really going to live here for a whole month?'

'I am.'

Did that sound determined enough? Nessa squared her shoulders and pulled her mouth into a tight line.

'What about your daughter?'

'She's staying with her grandmother, like I said, until I've got the place more together.'

'And how long will that take?' He glanced around the derelict room and raised an eyebrow.

Nessa pulled herself up to her full height of five feet and two inches. 'Not long.'

'I'm not sure you appreciate the size of the challenge you've taken on. I've spoken to my father and he's not happy with the way things are going.'

'Oh well, if your father's not happy...'

'He's not a man to be trifled with.'

'So are you here to threaten me?'

'What? God, no.' Gabriel pushed a hand through his fringe. 'Of course not. I'm not some heavy out of *The Sopranos*. But you should know that my father will query the lease and fight it in the courts if need be. Can you afford that?'

Nessa's resolve began to falter and she instinctively reached for the bangle on her arm and smoothed her fingers across it. Gabriel's hectoring tone reminded her of Jake. But she'd had enough of being pushed around.

She folded her arms. 'I'll take my chances. I've moved in here for a month and then I'll take it from there.'

'There's no point in making the effort. My father never loses.'

'There's always a first time.'

When Gabriel stared at her, Nessa picked up the broom and began to sweep again, tears prickling at the corners of her eyes. She'd lost so much over the years – her parents, her husband, her grandmother and her home. She wasn't about to lose this chance of a new start too. Not without a good fight.

Gabriel started tapping his foot on the flagstones. 'All right. If that's the way you want to play it, I'll need to stay on here until this charade comes to an end.'

Nessa stopped and glared at him. 'What on earth are you talking about?'

'I need to make sure that you move in properly for thirty days and nights and don't break the terms of the lease.'

'And how do you intend to do that?'

Surely he wasn't going to suggest moving in with her? Nessa swallowed, watching him warily.

'My father suggested that I move in with you. But—' He raised his hand to stop the words that were about to spill from her mouth. 'I appreciate that would be inappropriate.'

'Totally inappropriate,' spluttered Nessa. 'And the lease is in my family's name, you have no right—'

'I agree and, believe me, I have no desire to move into this... place with you.' He looked around the cold, empty room and shook his head. 'The best compromise appears to be if I stay on in Heaven's Cove and work from Driftwood House, but come down first thing in the morning and last thing at night to make sure you're living here.'

'So you'd be spying on me, basically.'

'I don't see it as spying. I'd be helping you to prove to my father and others that you're upholding the terms of the lease, which would be to your benefit.'

'But you'd still be trying to catch me out.' Nessa shook her head. 'Why on earth would I agree to those terms?'

'Because if you don't agree to me verifying that conditions are being upheld, my father will immediately start legal proceedings over the lease and who knows what that could end up costing you?'

'Why isn't your father doing that already?'

'He doesn't see the point in wasting his time and money because he thinks you're going to fail.'

'And you'll be here to prove it.'

'That's right.'

When Nessa glared at Gabriel, he met her gaze and held it.

People like him knew that money would always win an argument, thought Nessa angrily. Especially when it came to people like her, without a penny to rub together.

'I *am* going to stay here for a whole month,' she told him defiantly.

'Then you need to prove it, and my...' He searched for the right word. '... checks will only strengthen your case. It's either that or my father will see you in court.'

Nessa paused and then nodded. 'It seems I have no choice, but you'll get fed up with coming back and forth to the Ghost Village long before I do.'

'That's not going to happen,' he told her, his eyes glittery hard. 'I suppose I'd better get back to Driftwood House to confirm with Ms Merchant that I am staying longer.'

He knew her name was Rosie and yet he still insisted on calling her Ms Merchant. Nessa bit back irritation at his pomposity and said instead: 'I'm sure she'll be glad of the business.'

'I'll call round at eight every morning and ten at night to make sure you're staying here.'

'You'd better make it seven in the morning because I'll be up early to get to Valerie's and take Lily to school.'

When Gabriel didn't blanch at losing beauty sleep, Nessa added: 'Aren't you worried that I might bunk off and sleep somewhere else between ten p.m. and seven a.m.?'

Gabriel tilted his head and stared at her until she felt uncomfortable. Then he said, gently, 'I don't believe you have anywhere else to go.'

The sad truth of it took Nessa's breath away. Even if she'd wanted to sleep elsewhere, Valerie wouldn't have her to stay, she couldn't sleep at Driftwood House because Gabriel might spot her, and no other friends could accommodate her every night for a whole month.

She pushed her shoulders back. 'I'll be staying here for

thirty nights and then the cottage will be mine. And if you're insisting on calling in twice a day, you could always change out of your suit and help me to clean the place up.'

'And why would I do that?'

Why, indeed? Nessa could hardly think straight. 'Because it might be good for you to do something positive for a change,' she retorted. 'And, despite evidence to the contrary, I don't believe you're a total arse.'

An emotion flitted across Gabriel's face at that – annoyance, acceptance, hurt? Nessa wasn't sure but wished she hadn't been so blunt and rude. Her grandmother wouldn't be happy with her.

'What I mean is—'

'Your meaning is crystal clear,' said Gabriel tartly.

He gave her a curt nod before stepping outside and walking up the hill towards his shiny, locked car.

* * *

Gabriel slid into his car, closed the door and sat there without moving. Had he just arranged to call at a derelict cottage twice a day to spy on a woman he hardly knew? A woman who couldn't stand him?

Not for the first time recently, Gabriel pondered his life choices.

He gazed at the seascape in front of him. It was one of those startlingly hot days that led to a heat haze shimmering over the land. But the sea, sparkling in the sunlight, made him feel cooler. He could imagine throwing off his suit and diving into its inky depths.

What he really wanted to do was set up an easel and capture this strange, ruined community on canvas. He thought of Nessa's great-grandmother, who had embedded a beautiful work of art into the plaster of her home. He had no experience of making mosaics and collages. But his brush strokes would capture the tumbled stones, streaked with lichen, that had become a part of the earth. And the cottage standing whole but isolated, the only survivor of the tragedy that had struck this place.

Unfortunately, his father didn't value his artistic talent, even when he was offered a place at art college. *Especially* when he was offered a place at art college, which his father deemed full of 'layabouts and wannabes'. And Gabriel didn't have time now for hobbies. When not in the office, he was either networking to further the business or catching up on sleep.

That was an excuse, of course. He opened the window to let some air into the stifling car. He could find time to paint if he really wanted, but what was the point?

He'd chosen the course of his life the day he'd turned down his college place. His future lay in property development, rather than slapping paint onto canvas and creating half-decent pictures.

Half decent wasn't acceptable in the Gantwich family. And, as his father had been quick to point out, 'mucking about with crayons' wouldn't bring in a fraction of the money that the family business generated each year.

Not that money was everything. Gabriel shook his head. Even thinking such a thing felt vaguely rebellious.

He watched as Nessa stepped outside the cottage and shook a dustpan into the wind. She'd looked so determined and full of hope when she'd told him she would beat his father. He hated that he would have to quash her dreams.

But he'd had dreams too, and they'd been quashed. It was simply a rite of passage that adults had to pass through before reality came crashing in.

So he would call in regularly and wait until she contravened the lease – there was no way she'd last thirty nights in that lonely cottage. And then he'd report it to his father, who would pat him on the back before razing everything in Sorrel Cove to the ground.

That was the way it was. That was business.

Nessa glanced up at him, probably surprised that he was sitting in his car, going nowhere.

She was very wrong about one thing, he realised. He *was* a total arse. But it was too late to change the entire direction of his life now. Nessa was trapped through financial insecurity and the responsibilities of single parenthood. His life was far more privileged but, in effect, he was trapped, too, by family expectations.

Turning away from the seascape, Gabriel started the car and drove off along the potholed road. He had work to do and his father was waiting for an update from the Ghost Village.

NINETEEN
NESSA

Nessa stretched her arms above her head and yawned. Pale light was streaming through the window and her watch showed it was almost seven o'clock. She'd survived another night in this strange, lonely place.

The first night here had been awful and she'd hardly slept a wink. Every creaking timber, sigh of wind and fox call outside had been terrifying. And the chill of the flagstones, seeping into her sleeping bag, had made her shiver.

The second and third nights had been almost as bad. But last night, her fourth in the Ghost Village, had been much better for two reasons: Rosie had brought her a camp bed from Drift-wood House, which was luxury compared to the floor; and she'd been so bone-weary last night that even all the ghosts of the village wailing in unison wouldn't have roused her from sleep.

Nessa pushed back her duvet and stepped onto the cold floor, before wrapping herself in her dressing gown.

'I've survived another night, Gran,' she said into the empty room, as she'd taken to doing every morning. 'I'm one day closer to saving your cottage and making a new home for Lily and me.'

There was no reply, of course. She'd have died of fright if

there had been. But speaking to her gran made Nessa feel less alone.

It was easy to feel terribly alone here, amongst the ruins. So much so, that even Gabriel's twice-daily visits were a welcome break from the solitude. Not that he stayed for long, and he never came into the cottage.

They'd developed a kind of routine already.

He'd knock on the door, on the dot of seven a.m. and ten p.m. She'd answer it, opening the door a crack so he couldn't see how far she'd got – not very – with renovating the cottage. As she'd expected, he never offered his practical help in any shape or form. Instead, he'd say, 'Hello' and she'd reply, 'Hello. I'm still here.' At which point, he'd nod, turn on his heel and leave.

It was a total waste of his time, but Nessa had to admire his dedication to work.

It must be wonderful to have a job that you loved, even if it did involve destroying people's dreams. Her hopes of a fulfilling career had vanished with her mum's illness that took her away from school. Not that she'd have done anything differently – the last few months she'd spent with her mum had been precious.

Nessa listened to the faint wash of the waves nearby and glanced again at her watch. Where was Gabriel this morning? Surely the King of Punctuality, who'd give Mr Scaglin a run for his money, hadn't overslept?

She looked out of the window. His car wasn't there. Perhaps he'd given up and gone back to London. Nessa felt a pang of disappointment, which was bizarre because she wanted him to go.

Spending too much time on her own was playing with her mind, she decided, suddenly catching sight of a lone figure sitting where the land met the sea.

It was Gabriel, staring across the water that was shimmering silver under the rising sun. What on earth was he doing?

Nessa threw off her dressing gown, pulled on her jeans and

jumper, and let herself out of the cottage. The grass was wet with dew under her bare feet as she padded towards him.

'Hello, I'm still here,' she said when she got closer.

'Good grief!' He jerked round. 'You frightened the life out of me, creeping up like that.'

'I wasn't creeping. Did you think I was a ghost?'

'Of course not,' he shot back.

Nessa couldn't help grinning because he was so obviously lying.

'This place can be a bit spooky.'

'Especially in the middle of the night, I imagine.'

'I wouldn't know because I'm fast asleep,' Nessa lied right back. 'Where's your car?'

'At Driftwood House. I woke up early so I walked over the headland.'

'It's beautiful up there first thing in the morning.'

'It's beautiful here.'

He went back to staring at the waves lapping the narrow strip of sand that appeared at low tide. There was something different about him this morning. Melancholy surrounded him like a shroud.

Nessa stood for a moment and then sat on the grass beside him. She'd regret it because the grass was wet, but he didn't seem bothered by the dampness that was already starting to seep through her jeans. He was wearing suit trousers as usual, but with the unexpected addition of a green waxed jacket.

'Nice coat,' she murmured.

'Hmm.' He ran his hand down the waterproof material. 'Ms Merchant—'

'Rosie,' Nessa interrupted.

'Rosie,' he said her name very deliberately, 'spotted me going out and insisted I wear it. The coat belongs to her boyfriend, I believe.'

'It suits you.'

The khaki jacket made him look less like a city hotshot and more like an outdoorsy local. He had nice cheekbones, Nessa realised. And nice pale grey eyes. He had a nice face when he wasn't sneering at her or looking exasperated.

'Why do you always wear a suit?' she asked, feeling bold in the pale morning light.

He glanced round at her. 'Why not?'

'I get that it's what you wear to work – a bit like a uniform. But surely you can ditch it when you're working in Devon in a heatwave?'

'My father insists that members of the management team always wear a suit.'

'Your father isn't here,' said Nessa quietly.

'Anyway' – he shrugged – 'that's all I brought with me. Ms Merchant... sorry, *Rosie* is letting me use the washing machine for my shirts.' He raised an eyebrow. 'I packed light, not realising I was going to be stuck in Heaven's Cove for so long.'

Nessa ignored the barbed comment. 'There's a good boutique in the village, down by the quay, that sells shorts and polo shirts.'

'Shorts?' A corner of Gabriel's mouth twitched upwards. 'My father would self-combust on the spot.'

'Well, I won't tell him your secret if you don't.' That sounded slightly flirtatious, Nessa realised. She wrapped her arms tightly around her body. 'So why are you sitting out here, rather than knocking on my door?'

'I'm admiring the view. I thought I'd give myself a treat, seeing as it's my birthday.'

Nessa blinked, surprised at Gabriel offering up personal information. No wonder he looked miserable, spending his birthday far from friends and family. She felt a twinge of guilt that he was still in Heaven's Cove because of her.

'Happy birthday,' she said, giving him a smile.

He ignored her, ducking as a gull swooped too close.

'How old are you?' she asked.

'Thirty-two.'

'Are you going to take the day off? Do something nice? Have some fun?'

He opened his mouth and closed it again.

'You know, fun?' persisted Nessa. 'You could go for a walk or have a swim or go shopping in Exeter. Whatever floats your boat. Or you could buy a pad from Stan's store in the village and do some sketching. You said you're good at art.'

'I didn't say I was good.'

'You must have talent to be offered a place at art college.'

'Maybe. But I don't have time to waste messing around with paints these days.'

He sounded so brisk and business-like, Nessa felt sorry for him. What kind of miserable life did he have if he couldn't spare an hour or two to do what made him happy? Not even on his birthday.

'My gran always said painting was therapy, not wasting time. She used to insist I have a go and she never told me I was dreadful, even though I was. Sadly, her talent bypassed my generation.'

He actually smiled at that. 'Did your grandmother paint Sorrel Cove?'

'No. She painted all the time. I've still got some of her pictures. But she'd never come back here, however hard I tried to persuade her. Too many traumatic memories, I suppose. She told me a few stories about the place and people, though.'

'Like what?'

'Like Ernie Jenkins, who came back from the war with only half an arm, and Minnie Brown, who used to sit outside her cottage making thread on an ancient spinning wheel, and the men who'd sing sea shanties together while they gutted their catch of fish.'

'It all sounds very... rural.'

He said 'rural' as if it was a bad smell under his nose.

'I think it sounds like an amazing community of decent people whose lives were shattered on the twentieth of March, 1946.'

Gabriel sucked his lip between his perfect white teeth. 'So what would your grandmother think of you living in Sorrel Cove, if she wouldn't set foot in the place?'

'She knew how much I loved it here and she wanted me to come back and live here for good.'

He shifted round until he was facing her. 'How do you know that? You found a lease, that's all. Did your grandmother actually tell you she wanted you to live in that derelict cottage?'

'In a way.'

When he frowned, not understanding, Nessa pictured her gran's writing from her box of treasures. *I was never brave enough to return. Maybe one day you will be.*

'As well as the lease, she left me a message from beyond the grave.'

'Is that right?' Gabriel frowned. 'I've never met anyone quite like you before. You're very strange.'

Was that insulting or a badge of honour? Nessa, who'd been called worse, couldn't decide.

'What do you mean by "strange"?' she said, trying to ignore the fact that her backside was so wet and cold, it was going numb.

His pale eyes met hers. 'A strange mixture. Unfriendly, vulnerable, quirky.'

Quirky, she'd take. Unfriendly was also fair enough. She hadn't been very nice to him, for good reason. But vulnerable? She tried so hard to hide her fears and cluelessness from everyone. What had he seen that others had missed?

'Well,' she said, feeling rattled. 'You're pretty strange yourself, actually.'

His eyebrows shot towards his hairline. 'Really? I'm a businessman chasing down a deal. I'm as normal as they come.'

'You're a normal, everyday businessman, who wears his suit like a coat of armour. Why? What are you hiding?'

Gabriel got to his feet, brushing off blades of grass. The slight thaw between them had vanished and corporate Gabriel was back.

'I'd better leave you to get on with your day. You have lots to do,' he said coldly. 'I'll be back at ten tonight.'

'Yeah, sure,' she answered, pulling her knees up under her chin. She watched him as he walked away.

She thought back to her last birthday, with cards from Lily and her gran, and a trip to The Smugglers Haunt in the village with her friends.

Gabriel Gantwich might be a successful businessman. He probably had a fancy house in London and enjoyed exotic holidays to places Nessa would never see. But, for all his money and privileges, he didn't seem to be having a very happy birthday.

* * *

What was *he* hiding? Nessa Paulson had a cheek, Gabriel fumed as he strode back towards Heaven's Cove.

There she was, messing up his life by pretending to be all tough and uncompromising. But he knew what she was really like. He'd glimpsed it in the flash of fear in her eyes and the wobble of her chin.

He knew it because he was an astute businessman trained to identify vulnerability in opponents. He knew it because she wasn't as good at concealing her demons as she thought.

He knew it, he admitted with a flash of clarity, because he recognised it in himself. Nessa acted as if she had life all worked out when, in fact, the truth was very different.

Gabriel stopped walking and leaned against the window of

the ice-cream parlour. He'd been walking so fast, he had a stitch that was catching at his ribs.

He rubbed a hand across his chest and looked into the shop. Tubs piled high with rainbow ice cream sat under chilled glass, ready for customers when the working day began.

He'd been in Heaven's Cove for over a week now, enduring, frankly, ridiculous temperatures, but he still hadn't enjoyed an ice cream. Licking at an ice cream cone in his suit felt far too frivolous.

Though maybe it was permissible on his birthday, seeing as he wasn't doing anything special with friends and family. Not that anyone ever made a big deal of his birthday. His father had been known to forget it entirely. At least Nessa had wished him a happy birthday, though that was ironic in the circumstances.

Gabriel sighed and read a notice that had been stuck to the plate-glass window. TWO-BED FURNISHED FLAT ABOVE SHOP AVAILABLE FOR LONG-TERM RENT. DEPOSIT AND REFERENCES REQUIRED. PLEASE ENQUIRE WITHIN.

Why couldn't Nessa and her child move somewhere like that, rather than a totally unsuitable cottage? If she wasn't so damned intransigent, he could be spending his birthday in London. He'd be in the office, no doubt, but at least he wouldn't be here.

His stitch easing off, Gabriel walked more slowly back towards Driftwood House and began to climb the path that wound its way up to the top of the cliff.

Flowers were splashes of colour amongst the grass, and the hue of the sea had deepened from silver to pale blue since he'd left Sorrel Cove. The scenery here was stunning.

Gabriel felt the beauty all around him starting to work its magic. He sat on a flat rock that was protruding from the earth, and stretched his legs out in front of him.

There were worse places to spend his birthday, he supposed, tilting his face towards the sun. It was certainly more picturesque than the glass and concrete he could see from his office window.

A bee buzzed lazily around his head as he began to sing under his breath, '*Happy birthday to me...*'

It sounded pathetically sad. And when he scuffed his feet in the dirt, a cloud of dust rose into the air and settled on the legs of his trousers. His suit trousers. His suit of armour.

Gabriel stopped singing and breathed out slowly, watching a red fishing boat moving from open water into the shelter of the quay.

The sooner Nessa's ludicrous venture failed and he could get back to his desk in London, the better. Heaven's Cove and an exasperating single mother were getting under his skin. His father would not be impressed.

Gabriel stood up wearily and walked on towards Driftwood House in the distance.

TWENTY

NESSA

An hour after Gabriel's abrupt departure, Nessa arrived at Valerie's to pick up Lily and take her to school.

Her head was still buzzing after her conversation with Gabriel. And she couldn't help feeling sad that he'd turned down art college in favour of destroying precious buildings. That didn't seem to be a life choice destined to promote contentment.

Plus, the tune to 'Happy Birthday' had become an earworm that was driving her mad. 'Stop,' Nessa said out loud as she stood outside Valerie's front door. 'Stop thinking about that man, for goodness' sake.'

She smoothed down her T-shirt, and wiped her mouth to get rid of any toothpaste traces. But there was nothing she could do about her hair, which was an unruly thick frizz. It turned out that washing your hair over a bucket wasn't ideal.

When Nessa pressed the bell, there was an immediate pounding of feet.

'Mummy!' squealed Lily, flinging open the door and throwing herself into Nessa's arms.

Nessa knelt down, squeezed Lily tight and took a deep

breath. She loved Lily's fresh, sweet smell and it was a welcome
change from the smell of old stone and fresh paint that perme-
ated the cottage.

'Mummy, look!'

Lily disentangled herself from the hug and pulled Nessa
into the hall. A pair of shiny pink ankle boots, scattered with
gold stars, were sitting at the foot of the stairs.

'Look at my new shoes. They're a present from Granny and
Grampy.'

'Wow.' Nessa stooped to look more closely at the boots.

She didn't like to imagine how much these bright creations
had cost. She could never have afforded them.

'That was very kind of Granny and Grampy,' she said,
straightening up.

'And this!' declared Lily, doing a twirl in her school
uniform. 'Look at my hair.'

When Nessa gently ran her fingers across her daughter's
head, she noticed a diamanté bee attached to a grip. It looked
pretty, holding Lily's thick hair back from her face.

'Was that from Granny too?' asked Nessa, ashamed by the
vague resentment she was feeling. Valerie was kind to shower
Lily with gifts, but it would all end when Lily came back to live
with her.

'Yes, Granny bought it for me in the gift shop.'

'Well, that's very nice of Granny,' said Nessa, vowing not to
be mean-spirited. It was wonderful that Lily had loving grandparents who could afford to spoil her.

On cue, Valerie came out of the kitchen, in black trousers
and full make-up.

'Oh, you're here already,' she said, giving Nessa a searching
glance. Nessa smoothed down her hair, hating that she felt
faintly intimidated. 'Lily slept well and has eaten lots of breakfast, haven't you, love?'

Lily nodded vigorously. 'I had chocolate cornflakes and fizzy orange. It was 'licious.'

Nessa's smile faltered. She tried to get some proper fruit into Lily at breakfast time, but she pulled back her shoulders and kept on smiling. Grandparents were renowned for spoiling their grandchildren. And Valerie was doing her a huge favour right now.

'Here's your lunch, sweetheart,' said Valerie, pushing what looked like a new lunchbox into Lily's school backpack.

'I can pick Lily up later and give her tea before bringing her back,' said Nessa, already looking forward to it.

'Oh, there's no need,' replied Valerie. 'Lily's going home with Clara for tea, and Clara's mum has kindly said she'll drop her back later. You could call in for a short while after that, if you like. As long as you don't get Lily too excited before bedtime. We wouldn't want that, would we?'

She smiled, but that didn't take the sting out of her words. Though Lily had only just moved in, Nessa was starting to feel surplus to requirements in her own child's life.

'Come on then, Lily,' said Valerie. 'You'd better get your new boots on or you'll be late.'

When Lily sat on the bottom stair and started pushing her feet into her new boots, Nessa caught Valerie's eye and said quietly:

'I think Lily had better save those for after school.'

'Why?' Valerie frowned. 'She wants to show them off to her friends, don't you, love?'

Lily nodded, her brow furrowed in concentration as she tied her laces.

'Of course she does, but the school is very firm on uniform and footwear. That's why Lily's school shoes are plain brown.'

'I'm sure they won't mind this once. Brown is *so* boring.'

'They will mind, I'm afraid. We had a letter home about it recently.'

Lily turned her face towards Nessa, her bottom lip pushed forward. 'I want to wear them at school today. Granny said I could.'

Valerie shrugged. 'I can't see the harm.'

'We've been specifically asked to stick to plain school shoes. They're more practical, and it's fairer to the kids whose parents can't afford pretty footwear.'

Parents like me, thought Nessa, willing Valerie to see sense and back her. But her ex mother-in-law drew her lips into a tight line and folded her arms.

'Mummy, please let me wear my boots,' pleaded Lily.

'I'm afraid it's not allowed.'

'Please, Mummy, please!'

'Why don't you take them to school in a bag and you can change before you go to Clara's,' Nessa suggested, trying to ward off a meltdown. Lily was mostly well behaved but she had her moments.

'I don't want to take them in a bag,' wailed Lily. 'I want to wear them now.'

'Of course you do, darling,' Valerie butted in, putting her arm around Lily's shoulders. 'I think you're being rather pedantic, Nessa, and look how upset you're making your daughter.'

'It's not me,' insisted Nessa, though she felt like a horrible mother when Lily began to cry. 'It's school rules. I'm trying to save Lily from getting into trouble. And it's just a pair of boots, for goodness' sake.'

Valerie pursed her lips, knelt down and began to untie Lily's laces. 'Come on, sweetheart. Mummy says you can't wear your boots today and Mummy's in charge. But I'll find a bag so you can still take them to Clara's.'

She grabbed Lily's hand and led her into the kitchen while Nessa tried to calm the fluttering in her stomach. Suddenly, she was the big bad wolf in Lily's eyes, the strict mother who didn't allow any fun – unlike Granny with her chocolate cornflakes and shiny boots and disregard for school rules.

Nessa was trying so hard to make a new home for Lily, but would her daughter want to come back at the end of a month living here? What could she offer, other than her undying love? That was important to a five-year-old, but so were the material comforts that Nessa couldn't provide.

'Here we are,' announced Valerie over-brightly, coming back into the hall. Lily, beside her, was carrying a canvas tote bag with the new boots stuffed inside. She put the bag down and pushed her feet into her school shoes, with a scowl.

'That's better. I know you're not happy about it, Lily, but it can't be helped.' Nessa smiled and held out her hand. 'Shall we go to school, then?'

'OK,' said Lily, before giving her grandmother a goodbye kiss.

But she walked all the way to school without taking hold of her mother's hand, which broke Nessa's heart.

TWENTY-ONE
NESSA

Nessa opened the door to Gabriel. 'Hello. I'm still here.' She flashed him a brief smile. 'Do you think you could come in for a moment?'

Gabriel squinted in the early morning light, suspicion etched across his face.

She couldn't blame him. She'd been in the cottage for a week now and hadn't let him over the threshold once. But something had shifted on his birthday.

'You want me to come in?' he asked in his quiet, deep voice.

'Yes, if you don't mind. I've got something to show you.'

Nessa groaned quietly. That didn't sound right. Actually, none of this felt right and she had a horrible feeling she was about to overstep the mark. But it was too late. Gabriel had walked into the cottage and was standing there with his arms folded.

'You've whitewashed the walls,' he said, looking around him.

'That's right.'

Nessa stepped over the paint pots in the middle of the floor. She'd also had the chimney swept so she could light a fire and

Sam from the village had kindly checked the roof and made a few repairs. But that wasn't why she'd invited Gabriel inside.

He walked to the mosaic above the fireplace and ran his fingers across it. 'Painting the walls has made your great-grandmother's artwork even more prominent.' He peered at it more closely. 'The small stones she's used are unusual. Do you know where she got them?'

'As far as I know, she used materials she found locally.'

'That's interesting.'

Gabriel leaned in for a better look while Nessa wandered over to a blanket-covered heap in the corner of the room.

'Actually, art is the reason why I invited you inside.'

When he looked up, she pulled away the blanket that was covering her gran's painting paraphernalia.

'What do you think?'

'Wow.' Gabriel walked over and stooped down. He began to leaf through the bare canvases and examine the oil paints, and the wooden easel that was splattered with rainbow splodges of colour. 'I didn't realise you had all of this.'

'It belonged to my gran and it seems a shame for it to stay shoved into boxes if it can be used.' Nessa swallowed. 'I thought maybe *you* might like to use it?'

When Gabriel glanced up at her, Nessa continued quickly. 'You don't have to, obviously. But you like painting – well, you've liked it in the past – and I'm sure you could find some time while you're stuck in Heaven's Cove. Think of it as a belated birthday present. Anyway, if it's a daft idea, just ignore it.'

She picked up a paint pot and put it on the windowsill, just for something to do, because Gabriel was still staring at her.

Why on earth had she said that about a belated birthday present? A terrible thought struck her. What if he assumed it was a bribe to make him change his mind about the Ghost Village?

Nessa went hot and cold before realising he was unlikely to assume any such thing. It would take more than a motley assortment of ancient paints and canvases to bribe a successful businessman.

He'll just think I'm being strange again and making a fool of myself, thought Nessa. Though that really didn't help.

'Don't worry about it,' she said, standing in the doorway and feeling the breeze from the sea on her back. 'It was a stupid idea.'

'No.' Gabriel got to his feet, frowning slightly. 'It wasn't stupid at all. In fact, it was really thoughtful.'

When his eyes locked on to Nessa's, she couldn't look away. Gabriel didn't seem so much like a fusty corporate businessman this morning. He was still wearing his stupid suit – minus his tie – but there was stubble on his chin and his dark fringe was flopping across his forehead. There was a definite hint of grunge going on.

The faint wash of the sea and the screeching of gulls faded away.

Nessa was the first to break eye contact. 'If you're interested in it, you can leave it here until you want to use it. I don't suppose Rosie wants it back, cluttering up Driftwood House. Anyway, that was all.'

She moved away from the door and, to her relief, he stepped past her, out into the fresh air. The last few minutes had been more awkward than she'd anticipated.

Gabriel walked a few steps towards his car, but then he turned and walked back.

'Why are you suddenly being nice to me?' he asked, his forehead creased in confusion.

Nessa paused, various answers running through her head.

Because you looked sad on your birthday. Because doing up the cottage is exhausting and I don't have the energy to sustain a feud. Because I want to see if you really can paint.

There was a grain of truth in all of them. But the real reason behind her magnanimous gesture was her grandmother.

She missed her gran so much. But being here in this cottage, surrounded by echoes of a long-gone community, made her feel that the old lady was still close. And Nessa knew one thing: Ruth Paulson, the gentlest of women, wouldn't approve of her granddaughter being unkind to anyone – with the possible exception of Jake.

And there was something about Gabriel that bothered her. A hidden sadness that sometimes bubbled to the surface. An absence of joy. A loneliness that, she guessed, had little to do with him being stuck here with her. Rosie would probably say she was overthinking things. But her gran would have understood.

'Well?' he asked, tilting his head to one side.

'I'm not being nice. It's only old stuff that would go to waste otherwise.'

'If you say so.'

'My gran wouldn't want her paints to sit in a box, unused.'

'Right.'

When he didn't move, Nessa breathed out slowly. Why was she letting this man get under her skin?

'Look,' she said, folding her arms. 'I think you're in the wrong. You're here, trying to destroy something precious purely for profit. But when I was lying awake this morning, thinking about you—'

He raised an eyebrow. 'You were lying awake thinking about me?'

'I was thinking about this cottage, actually. And I realised that you're just doing your job and I can achieve what I want simply by staying put for the next three weeks. So there's no need for us to be enemies all the time. Plus, my gran's stuff is already taking up enough space in Rosie's loft. OK?'

He stared at her for a moment. 'OK. But I'll still be calling in twice a day.'

'In the hope of catching me out.'

'That's right.' He turned his palms to the grey sky. 'As you said, I'm just doing my job as a property developer.'

'And I'm doing mine as a mother, trying to make a home for my child.'

He gave her the briefest of nods before turning and heading back towards his car.

They might no longer be enemies, thought Nessa as he drove away, but they were still at loggerheads and would be for the next three long weeks.

TWENTY-TWO
VALERIE

It was a beautiful spot, Valerie had to admit that. Sorrel Cove must have been an idyllic hamlet once upon a time, sheltered beneath rising ground with the sparkling sea so close.

But now the place was nothing more than ruins, with only one cottage still intact.

It had been years since Valerie had last visited Sorrel Cove and it had fallen into more disrepair since then. Large chunks of pale stone littered the site – stones that had once made up the walls of people's homes. If only the last remaining cottage had been engulfed by the sea as well.

Valerie felt a twinge of shame as she approached the building. Enough people had died here that night without her wishing for even more devastation.

But if only the storm surge had licked at the cottage walls or the howling gale had ripped off the roof. If that had happened, the building would have been too far gone by now for Nessa to even contemplate taking it on.

What kind of woman thinks she can save a building like this? thought Valerie, cursing loudly when she tripped over a stone and stumbled.

'Valerie! Is everything OK? Is Lily all right?'

Nessa had appeared around the side of the cottage and was firing questions at her. She was carrying what looked like a roll of grey vinyl flooring and her hair was tied up off her shoulders with a bright blue scarf.

'Lily's at school and fine, as far as I'm aware,' said Valerie, noticing Nessa's shoulders slump with relief.

Nessa placed the roll of flooring at her feet and brushed her palms together to clean them. 'So why are you here? You didn't say you were coming.'

Valerie sniffed. 'I thought I'd come and see where you're planning on bringing my granddaughter to live, if your...' She floundered about for the best way to describe Nessa's hare-brained scheme. There was no point in being rude for the sake of it. '... unconventional idea comes to fruition.'

'That's good of you,' said Nessa, though they both knew that goodness didn't come into it.

Valerie was here to see how appalling the cottage truly was and to pour cold water on Nessa's plans.

'You'd better come in,' said Nessa, picking up the roll of vinyl. She noticed Valerie looking at it. 'This is an offcut of flooring that Fred at the pub had left after doing up their kitchen, and he said I could have it. I thought it might make the kitchen here more welcoming if I can cut it to the right size, and Fred said he could help if I can't sort it out. People in the village have been so kind with donating things. Even Belinda, who doesn't approve of me at all, gave me some leftover paint.'

Et tu, Belinda, thought Valerie darkly, but she forced herself to smile. 'That *is* very kind of them,' she said, walking towards the cottage's front door.

She had to admit, from the outside the place didn't look half bad. The walls and roof seemed pretty solid and someone – Nessa or one of the many villagers who appeared to be supporting her – had filled and painted the window frames a brilliant white.

Inside, it wasn't so good. The walls, though whitewashed and clean, were bare, apart from some peculiar arty thing over the fireplace. And the flagstone floor would be bitterly cold on bare feet in winter.

'I'll need to get a few big rugs in here,' said Nessa, following Valerie's gaze. 'They'll cheer up the place.'

Valerie consciously un-pursed her lips. She'd never been much good at presenting a poker face. People often seemed to know exactly what she was thinking – apart from Alan, who remained oblivious to the dark thoughts that crossed Valerie's mind daily, which was probably just as well because many of them involved him.

'So, what work have you done here since you arrived?' she asked, poking her head into the tiny kitchen, which currently housed a camping stove, half a dozen mugs, a box of food and two thick pairs of socks draped over the back of a white plastic chair.

'Lots of filling and repairing and cleaning and making sure that the building is safe.'

'And is it?' asked Valerie, imagining her granddaughter picking her way through this trip hazard.

Nessa nodded. 'It is. Eddie in Heaven's Brook is a surveyor who knew my gran. He nipped over to give the place a once-over and he was surprised how solid the building is.'

'Me too,' murmured Valerie. 'So where are you sleeping?'

'I was sleeping down here, on a camp bed from Rosie. But now I know that upstairs is structurally safe, I've been sleeping in the bedroom that overlooks the sea.'

'And what about water and electricity?'

'I'm boiling water from the well until the results of the water tests come through. And there's no electricity so I'm using

candles and a couple of old oil lamps, but Phil has said he'll
have a look at the place for me.'

'Phil? The electrician who lives in Sheep Lane?'

'Yes, that Phil. And Rosie and Liam have been round to
lend me a hand. Like I said, people have been incredibly kind.'

Far too kind, thought Valerie. And far too keen to indulge
Nessa in this fantasy.

'Did you know that Magda's advertising an empty flat above
the ice-cream parlour?' she said as nonchalantly as she could. 'If
this doesn't work out, I mean.'

'I did hear that and Lily would love it. But I looked into it,
and I could never afford the deposit or the rent.'

'Surely you could, with all the support that Jacob provides.'

Nessa gave Valerie a straight stare. 'I'm afraid not. That's
why I'm working so hard on this property.'

When an awkward silence descended, Valerie pointed at a
pile of artist's materials in a corner of the room.

'What's this?' There were several blank canvases, an old
easel and a large wooden box. Valerie peeped inside. It was
filled with watercolour paint blocks in various shades and half-
squeezed tubes of oil paint. 'I didn't know you were an artist.'

Nessa smiled. 'I'm not, though I loved visiting art galleries
before I met Jake and… well, life changed. He's not that keen on
art, is he?'

Valerie felt her lips pursing again. It was true that Jake
wouldn't know his Rembrandt from his Vermeer, but it felt like
a criticism of her boy, by the woman who'd harried him out of
Heaven's Cove and Valerie's life.

'He's always been far too busy at work to have time for
hobbies. But if you're not the artist…' She waved a hand at the
painting paraphernalia. 'Who is?'

Suspiciously, Nessa's cheeks coloured when she answered.
'This belonged to my gran, who liked to paint. I fished it out of
some stuff that Rosie's storing for me at Driftwood House, in

case Gabriel wants to use it. He told me he enjoys painting. Well, he used to.'

'Gabriel? Is that the man from the property development company? The one I met briefly, who's staying at Driftwood House?'

'Mmm.' Nessa nodded.

'I heard he was checking up on you a couple of times a day.'

'That's right. He is. He calls round first thing in the morning and last thing at night to make sure I'm still here and haven't bunked off.'

'Because if you don't manage thirty consecutive nights here that would affect the lease, right?'

'Yeah, that's it,' said Nessa, her cheeks looking even more pink against the darkness of her hair.

Valerie felt a lurch in her stomach. Nessa was winning Gabriel round to get her own way, just as she'd done with Jacob. Which meant that Lily could end up living in this dreadful place when she should be living in Valerie's warm and cosy home instead.

It had been wonderful having Lily to stay for the last two weeks. Lily liked a cuddle with Granny when she woke up, and it meant the world to Valerie when she called for her. It gave her a reason to get out of bed. And the days didn't seem so interminably long if she knew that Lily would be returning from school mid-afternoon, full of chatter.

The thought of going back to a house with only taciturn Alan for company filled her with a cold dread that wrapped itself around her heart.

But Nessa would charm Gabriel, plans to raze Sorrel Cove and build luxury homes here would be scrapped – and Lily would leave Valerie for this health and safety nightmare.

'Are you OK?' asked Nessa gently, brushing her hand along Valerie's arm. Her bangle was cold against Valerie's skin. 'You don't seem quite yourself today.'

Valerie pulled herself together and stepped away from Nessa's touch. 'I'm perfectly fine, thank you. Tell me, how many nights have you slept here now?'

'Fourteen. It was hard at first but, as the cottage becomes more homely, it's getting easier all the time.'

I bet it is, thought Valerie, wondering if Gabriel was sleeping over. She could imagine the two of them here together, with darkness falling outside and Nessa whispering persuasively in his ear.

'I need to go,' said Valerie. 'Thank you for showing me the cottage, Nessa. You're doing a grand job of doing it up.'

'Thank you. I really appreciate that.' Nessa seemed genuinely pleased with the compliment and Valerie felt a pang of unease at her own duplicity. 'Also,' added Nessa, 'I know I've said it before but I appreciate you looking after Lily so well while I'm sorting all of this out.'

'That's no trouble at all,' said Valerie, feeling on steadier ground because she was speaking the truth.

She loved having Lily with her. She knew that for sure. What she wasn't so sure about was how far she was willing to go to ensure that Lily stayed with her for good.

But there had to be a way, and Valerie was determined to find it.

TWENTY-THREE
NESSA

Valerie had clearly come to the conclusion that her former daughter-in-law was deluded.

She hadn't said as much but then she didn't need to, thought Nessa, watching her Volvo disappear into the distance. Valerie could convey a whole raft of disapproval with the simple quiver of a lip or flaring of a nostril. And there had been a deluge of quivering and flaring from the moment she'd set foot inside the cottage.

Nessa sat on the wide stone windowsill and gazed through the glass.

She wasn't deluded. She'd been working her socks off but she was well aware of the scale of the task ahead. There was still loads to do before the cottage would be suitable for Lily, who seemed, at least, to have settled in well with her grandparents.

That wasn't surprising because Valerie was spoiling Lily. There was talk of new toys when Nessa took her to school, and excitement about a forthcoming trip to the cinema when they'd both gone to tea with Rosie at Driftwood House.

Valerie was also letting Lily eat chocolate, cake and biscuits every day, and Nessa, already indebted to her for having her daughter to stay, didn't feel able to challenge her nutritional choices.

But all of that could be sorted out when Lily came back. *If she comes back*, said the little voice in Nessa's head that seemed to have free rein in the silent cottage. *What if Lily would rather live with Valerie for good?*

Nessa sniffed. She wouldn't cry again. She felt all cried out these days.

Instead, she'd channel her anxiety into something useful, like cleaning the old outhouse at the back of the cottage. The spiders there would soon chase away any gloomy thoughts.

Half an hour later, all gloomy thoughts had been well and truly banished, by terror. Nessa was a country girl, well used to bugs, but she'd never seen spiders this big before. They lay waiting for her in dark corners, their black legs arched and their cobwebs a silvery hammock across the ceiling.

'Jeez!' yelled Nessa, running from the outhouse and frantically rubbing at her hair. 'Go away!'

'Really?' said a deep voice behind her. 'That's rude, even for you.'

When Nessa spun around, Gabriel was leaning against the wall of the cottage.

'No, I don't mean you,' she spluttered, still rubbing her head. 'A spider dropped on me, and they're enormous in there.' She wiped a hand across her face, realising too late that her hands were filthy. 'What are you doing here?'

She sounded sharp but Gabriel never arrived in the middle of the day.

He was still showing up first thing in the morning and last thing at night. And recently their brief interaction – 'Hello.' 'Hello, I'm still here.' – had expanded to take in the state of the weather.

'I thought...' Gabriel frowned. 'I thought I might take an hour off work to do some painting.'

'Gosh!'

Nessa had never used the exclamation 'gosh' in her life before, but it seemed fitting somehow. Her gran's art supplies hadn't been mentioned since she'd offered them to him a week ago, but here he was, ready to paint. Straight-laced, workaholic Gabriel was about to do something spontaneous.

'The painting supplies are still in the cottage, so... fill your boots.'

Gabriel smirked, and Nessa didn't blame him. She wasn't sure she'd ever said 'fill your boots' before either, but his sudden appearance had rattled her.

'I won't get in your way,' he said, leaning over and picking a piece of twig from her hair. 'I'll leave you to your spiders.'

Nessa smoothed down the hair he'd just touched. 'That's very kind of you.'

'That's me,' he replied, with what Nessa took to be an ironic eyebrow-raise. Then, good as his word, he left her to the perils of the dark, dank outhouse.

Two hours later, Nessa glanced through the window of the cottage. Gabriel had set up the easel a few feet from the sea and seemed absorbed in what he was doing.

Watching from a distance as his arm made great arcs across the canvas reminded Nessa of her grandmother. She would daub sweeps of colour and Nessa would watch in astonishment as the marks became recognisable as the landscape in front of them.

She'd tried to do the same but her attempts had ended up looking more like the pictures that Lily painted.

So far she'd resisted the temptation to see how Gabriel was doing but, summoning up her courage, she slipped out of the cottage and walked towards him.

He'd taken off his shoes and socks, she noticed, and had sunk his bare feet into the grass.

It was beautiful painting weather. The sun had vanished behind a hazy veil of thin white cloud so the temperature had dropped, but it was still pleasantly warm. The calm sea, lapping gently against the rocks, was a startling turquoise and, when Nessa got closer, she saw that he'd captured the shade perfectly.

Art critics might claim that the sea couldn't possibly be that colour. That the painter was taking artistic licence. But it was true to life. As were the scattered mounds of stone littering the land in the forefront of his picture.

The painting was all broad brushstrokes and there was a vibrancy to it that made the breath catch in Nessa's throat. He'd captured the spirit of the place.

Gabriel turned and looked over his shoulder as she approached, a wide streak of blue paint on his forehead where he'd wiped a hand across his brow.

'Don't look. I haven't finished and it's not very good.'

'I think you're being too modest.' Nessa studied the painting. It was even more impressive up close. 'You have a real talent.'

'I don't think so.'

'My gran would definitely think so, if she were here.'

Nessa had a sudden longing to see her beloved grandmother, whose ashes had been scattered only a few weeks ago over the same turquoise sea that Gabriel had just painted.

He put his paintbrush down on the easel. 'To be honest, I don't really care what my picture's like. It's very...' He hesitated, searching for the right word. '... freeing to sit and paint and to know that it doesn't matter how good or bad it is.'

'And it makes a change from working all the time,' said Nessa, batting away a fly that was buzzing around her neck.

Gabriel turned to her, his face flushed in the heat. 'I guess. Plus, at work, I always...' He shook his head. 'It doesn't matter.'

'What doesn't matter?'

'Do you always ask so many questions?'

'Do you always avoid answering questions by asking one back?'

Nessa waited, half expecting Corporate Gabriel to give her a steely glare. But instead, his shoulders dropped and he wiped his hands on the rag that her gran had used to mop up spills.

'At work, I always have a lot to prove.'

'It must help that it's a family firm.'

'Do you think? I'm the boss's son so people assume I'm only there through nepotism.'

'And are you?'

Nessa winced, wondering if she'd gone too far. But Gabriel answered straightaway.

'No. Not really. I work hard and I do a good job.' He gave her a sideways glance. 'Except when people make my life difficult.' He paused. Was he waiting for her to say sorry? He sniffed. 'And I'll take over the business one day, when my father retires.'

'That sounds very high-powered. Are you looking forward to being the big boss?'

'I don't know. I guess so. My father expects me to follow in his footsteps.'

'But it isn't always easy being what people expect.'

'Mmm.'

When Gabriel started packing up his paints and brushes, Nessa helped him without another word. He didn't want to talk about his life. All he wanted was for her to stop making his life difficult.

They'd almost reached the cottage when Gabriel came to a sudden halt. Nessa looked to see what he'd dropped but he still had the canvas in one hand and the easel under his arm.

'What do people expect of you?' he asked, shuffling his feet.

Nessa looked away, out to sea where fishing boats were smudges on the horizon.

'When my mum was very ill, a long time ago, people expected me to leave her with carers and go to school.'

'But you didn't?'

'I did, sometimes. But I was a serial truant in those days. I knew Mum didn't have long and I wanted to spend as much time with her as possible.'

'How old were you when she died?'

'Seventeen.'

Nessa found it hard to breathe as a wave of grief washed over her. Her mum had been gone a long time but the pain of her loss had never fully disappeared.

'I'm sorry,' said Gabriel gruffly.

'What about your mum? You've never mentioned her.'

'She and my father got divorced when I was a child and she left. She lives with a rich banker in a big house in the Cotswolds. I didn't see much of her growing up.'

So they both had mothers who had left them, in different ways. Nessa wrinkled her nose in sympathy. 'That must have been difficult.'

'I got used to it. That's all we can do, isn't it? Get used to things and get on with life.'

Thicker cloud was building up over the sea and Nessa shivered. The wind had picked up and bigger waves were rolling towards the land.

It felt as if there was a storm in the air and the ghosts at Sorrel Cove were stirring.

Gabriel seemed to feel the shift in atmosphere too. He glanced at his watch and started walking again, towards the cottage.

'I need to get back to Driftwood House and prepare for a Zoom meeting. Is it all right if I leave my painting here for now?'

'Of course. I'll leave it to dry.'

'Thanks.' He leaned the canvas and easel against the cottage wall. 'I'll see you at ten tonight.'

'I'll be here, making your life difficult.'

Gabriel stared at her for a moment, his eyes pale in his face that had caught the sun.

'I know,' was all he said before he turned and walked away.

TWENTY-FOUR
NESSA

Lily turned on the spot, round and round, until she fell to her knees, laughing.

Nessa, laughing too, bent down and wiped hair from her daughter's dark eyes.

'You'll make yourself feel sick if you keep whirling round like that.'

Lily giggled and sat back on her heels on the flagstones. 'When I was a baby, I sicked up on my teddy.'

Nessa agreed she had and smiled, even though the memory of looking after a poorly infant on her own still made her feel panicky. Lily's asthma had been a constant worry back then, before juggling different inhalers had improved her health.

Jake had missed all of that – sleeping on the floor by Lily's cot in case her breathing worsened, and ringing the doctor the moment the surgery opened for advice and reassurance.

He'd been busy, off somewhere else being a 'free spirit'. And now his mother was trying to step in and steal the daughter he had abandoned.

Nessa gave herself a mental shake. Sleeping here in this

isolated cottage was definitely playing tricks on her mind. Of course Valerie wasn't trying to steal Lily away.

She might not approve of Nessa, or like her, even. That much was clear. But where Lily was concerned, she was simply being an indulgent grandmother. And she was also helping Nessa out, which was exactly what Nessa had asked her to do.

'Mummy! Are you listening to me?'

Nessa dragged herself away from her destructive thoughts. 'What did you say, sweetheart?'

'I said, can we go now? I want to go on our picnic.'

'Yes, we can go *right* now. Just let me check I've packed all the food.'

Nessa pushed a bottle of water into the wicker basket she'd borrowed from Rosie and made sure she hadn't forgotten Lily's favourite flapjack. She was excited about a picnic on the beach too.

The storm that had threatened over a week ago hadn't materialised after all. Temperatures had dropped a little and the sky had been mainly overcast. But this morning the sun was shining and it was one of those glorious early July days when a heat haze shimmered in the distance. And she was going to spend time with Lily.

She missed her gorgeous girl so much and had to keep reminding herself that staying here in the cottage was for Lily's benefit in the long run. It was to gain a permanent home to call their own: a home with links to Lily's ancestors.

'What do you think of the cottage, Lils?' asked Nessa, buckling up the straps on the basket.

Lily tapped her nose, just like her grandfather did when he was considering something. 'It's a bit spooky. Archie in my class says ghosts live here and they do this.' She raised her arms and flapped them around.

'There aren't any spooky things here,' said Nessa, wanting

to give Archie's parents a shake. He'd presumably overheard them talking about the Ghost Village.

'But aren't you scared, being here at night?' Lily slipped her hand into Nessa's. 'Why don't you sleep at Granny's with me? Granny wouldn't mind.'

Granny would mind very much. But Nessa smiled and gently squeezed her daughter's fingers.

'It's only for a little while, like I explained, and then you and I will live together again.'

'Where?' asked Lily, her dark eyes huge in her perfect, sun-kissed face. 'At Auntie Rosie's?'

Now was the time to say that they'd be moving in here, together. In this cottage, by the sea, that was fast becoming more welcoming as Nessa's hard work over the last three weeks started to pay off. But something held her back.

Was it the thought of raising Lily's hopes for nothing, if Gabriel and his father won in the end? Or the fear that Lily, already spooked by the cottage's ghostly reputation, would refuse and beg to stay with Valerie for good?

Nessa hesitated and the moment passed when there was a loud knock at the front door. It swung open to reveal Gabriel standing there. He glanced between Nessa and Lily, a sheen of sweat on his forehead.

'Sorry. I've lost my phone and thought it might be here. It's in a black case and it has my whole life on it.' He wiped a hand across his brow. 'All I can think is, it fell out of my pocket this morning when I came round. I have to find it or—'

'It's here,' Nessa butted in.

Watching him stress out about his phone was painful. Though she supposed losing a top-of-the-range mobile packed with info about lucrative business deals was more angst-inducing than misplacing the cheap, pay-as-you-go phone she carried.

'Oh, thank God.' He breathed out slowly.

'I found it on the ground outside. It must have fallen out of your pocket. I rang Driftwood House and left a message to tell you.'

'I think Rosie's out. Thanks. I need it for work.'

'I thought as much. I did consider chucking it in the sea, but that seemed a bit mean.'

He gave her a straight stare but then the corner of his mouth twitched upwards. 'Very mean, I'd have said.' He switched his attention to Lily. 'Hello, there.'

'Hi.' Lily, startled by Gabriel's arrival, had moved close to her mother, with her arms round her waist. 'Do you live here with Mummy now?'

'No, not at all. I call in early morning – that's when I lost my phone – and late evening. That's all.'

'Why?' asked Lily, her cheek pressed against Nessa's stomach.

'Just to check,' said Gabriel, a faint pink washing across his cheeks.

'To check what?'

To check, heaven forbid, that your mother isn't bunking off to a comfortable bed for the night, thought Nessa. Gabriel looked embarrassed. She'd never seen him flustered before and there was something quite nice about it. Quite humanising. But she spared him any more cross-examination.

'Come on, Lily. Can you give Gabriel his phone? It's over there.'

'I can,' Lily declared. 'Mummy loses her phone all the time.'

'Does she?' Gabriel smiled. 'She has a lot on her mind.'

His eyes met Nessa's and she held his gaze for a moment before looking away.

'Here it is!' Lily picked up Gabriel's phone from the mantelpiece and waved it triumphantly. 'I found it.'

'You did.' Gabriel took the phone and put it in his pocket.

'Thank you for being so eagle-eyed.' He glanced at the picnic basket. 'Don't you have school today?'

'It's an insect day,' Lily informed him.

'An inset day,' corrected Nessa gently. 'No insects involved.'

'An *inset* day, so there's no school and we're going to the secret beach instead.'

'A secret beach? That sounds exciting. It's a perfect day for it.'

'It's not exactly secret. There's a tiny cove I know nearby so we're heading there,' said Nessa. 'Heaven's Cove beach is beautiful but it gets busy at this time of year.'

'I see. Well, that sounds lovely.' Gabriel undid a second button on his white shirt. He seemed to have ditched his tie for good these days. 'I hope you have fun, Lily.'

'Do you like having fun?' asked Lily, tilting her head to one side and regarding him thoughtfully.

'Yes, I suppose so. I don't have much of it.'

'That's sad,' said Lily, a furrow appearing between her eyebrows.

Uh-oh. Lily only frowned when she was having a Big Idea, and Nessa had a horrible feeling she knew where this idea was heading. She went to speak but Lily got there first.

'You can come too. Come to the beach with us. I can swim and you can watch me. It'll be fun.'

'I'm sure Gabriel is far too busy with work to come to the beach with us,' said Nessa, raising her eyebrows to convey *she doesn't understand how busy and important you are.*

But Lily wasn't to be dissuaded so easily. Sometimes she reminded Nessa of her grandmother. Lily ran over to Gabriel and looked up at him.

'Don't do silly work. Have a set day and paddle in the sea. Millie saw a dolphin at the beach the other day.'

Gabriel squatted down beside her daughter. 'A dolphin? Wow. Have you ever seen a dolphin before?'

Lily thought a moment before shaking her head. 'I've never seen a dolphin. But I have seen a seal. It swims in the harbour and head-butts the boats.'

Gabriel snorted with laughter. 'Does it really? I imagine that's a seal with a bad headache.'

Lily nodded seriously. 'I 'spect so. It's a bit silly. Come on, then.' She slipped her hand into his. 'Let's go to the beach.'

Gabriel got to his feet, his hand still in Lily's. Nessa watched carefully. Her daughter was often wary with strangers but she seemed to have taken to Gabriel very quickly.

'Sorry,' she said, picking up her basket. 'I know you've got work to do.'

'I always have work to do.' Gabriel glanced through the window at the sun glaring outside. 'Though a trip to the beach does sound tempting in a heatwave.'

'Please,' implored Lily, pouting at him. 'We'll see dolphins.'

'Lily, leave the poor man alone.'

'Why?' Lily demanded.

'He's busy.'

'Too busy to see a dolphin?' Lily spluttered.

Gabriel paused. 'OK, I'd love to come and see this hidden cove for myself, just for half an hour.' He glanced at Nessa and frowned. 'If you don't mind, that is. I don't want to intrude on your day out.'

When Lily turned her hopeful face towards her, Nessa felt well and truly boxed into a corner.

'No, that's fine,' she said, bending to pick up a bottle of sun cream and shoving it into the pocket of her shorts. 'The more, the merrier.'

But it wasn't fine. She didn't want to show Gabriel the hidden cove. What if he decided to build a load of posh houses there that local people couldn't afford?

She was worrying about nothing, she told herself as she led the way along the coast until they came to a path almost overgrown with high gorse. The cove was safe from Gabriel and his father – it was covered by the sea at high tide and surrounded by steep cliffs, so building there would be impossible. If only building on the Ghost Village was impossible too.

Squinting against the bright sun, she took hold of Lily's hand and picked her way down the narrow path and onto washed, golden sand.

TWENTY-FIVE
GABRIEL

Gabriel felt his shoes sinking into the sand and shaded his eyes with his hand. He should have brought his sunglasses but they were still in the glove compartment of his car – which would be like a sauna by the time he got back to it.

Part of him wished he'd resisted Lily's pleas. He'd been going to, until she'd declared that being too busy to see a dolphin was sad and he'd realised that she was right.

He was too busy to have any kind of life outside work. Too busy to meet friends, too busy to paint, too busy to fall in love. And he'd been alarmed by how panicky he'd got after losing his work phone this morning – though some of the panic had stemmed from the grief he was anticipating from his father.

So he'd said yes and highjacked Nessa's trip, which she obviously wasn't happy about. And here he was in this absolutely beautiful cove.

Nessa had brought him down a path he would never have noticed on his own. It was overgrown in places and narrow, but it led to a perfect beach that was invisible from the land above.

'It's amazing here,' he said, taking in the china-blue sea

lapping at the soft sand. He'd been on exotic Caribbean beaches that paled in comparison to this hidden gem.

'It's unspoiled because so few people know about it,' said Nessa, taking the basket from him that he'd carried down the path. 'The locals know about it, of course. But lots of them are working today, or they'll have headed for the beach at Heaven's Cove. This one isn't the easiest to reach and it disappears at high tide so this area isn't practical for development.'

Gabriel frowned. Did she really think he was going to poach this cove and build houses on shifting sand?

He took off his shoes and shook out what felt like half the beach.

'Are you keeping your socks on?' snorted Lily, already stripped down to the swimsuit she was wearing beneath her shorts. 'You look funny.'

He supposed he did look funny, standing on a beach in a heatwave, in his suit and socks. Nessa, beside him, was dressed far more appropriately in blue denim shorts, and a white, sleeveless top.

Lily had given up waiting for an answer about his socks and was running towards the sea, keen to splash in the water. She stopped and waved at Nessa, who smiled broadly and waved back.

Nessa and her daughter belonged here, and he did not. A rush of sorrow took Gabriel by surprise. He didn't belong here and yet he didn't really belong in London either. What was there in the city for him, apart from a 24/7 job, and persistent heartburn, which seemed to have vanished in Devon?

He was, he decided, as homeless, in his own way, as Nessa. And this trip to the beach wasn't proving to be as much fun as Lily had promised.

He sat down on the sand with a *whump*, took off his jacket and pulled off his socks. At least he wouldn't look quite so out of place with bare feet.

Nessa sat down beside him and pulled her knees up under her chin.

'Lily loves it here.'

'I can see why.' Gabriel squinted at Lily, who was running, squealing, into the sea, her hands sweeping through the waves that swelled against her knees. 'Can she swim?'

'Like a fish.'

'I suppose she would, being brought up on the coast.'

'Can you swim?' asked Nessa, looking across at him.

'I can, though I didn't learn until I was older than Lily. I was brought up in Wimbledon so it was the local baths for me, rather than the sea.'

He thought back to his one-on-one swimming lessons at the local swimming pool. He'd been frightened of the water at first but his father had insisted he go every week, even though the chlorine made his eyes sting and he had nightmares about sinking beneath the water.

He'd thought his father was being unkind at the time, but maybe he'd been right. Gabriel had learned to swim in the end, though he never went swimming now. Not even when he was in some flash resort with white sand and sea the colour of lapis lazuli.

'Penny for them,' said Nessa, pulling sunglasses from the basket and putting them on. Gabriel wished again that he'd brought his sunglasses, and a hat. It was so hot.

He undid another button on his shirt and Nessa smiled.

'You can go crazy and undo four buttons if you like. I won't tell anyone.'

She was making fun of him, but it was gentle and he didn't mind. When he undid another couple of buttons on his white shirt, Nessa glanced at his chest before looking away, out to sea where Lily was still whooping and splashing.

'Do you ever strip off?' she asked, then her cheeks flared red. 'I mean, in the sunshine. Do you ever ditch the suit completely?'

'I don't sleep in my suit,' said Gabriel, noticing how pretty Nessa looked when she blushed. 'I also own at least a handful of T-shirts at home and, when I went to Tobago, I wore a mankini.'

'Are you joking?' gasped Nessa.

'Fortunately for the people of Tobago, I am.'

It was a stupid joke but he wanted to show this woman that, whatever she thought of him, he wasn't just a sad, humourless arse with a destructive streak. He felt a glow of contentment when she grinned.

'As long as you didn't sit on the beach in Tobago in a suit.'

'I ditched my suit for the entirety of the holiday.'

'That must have been quite some holiday.'

'It was memorable,' he said, watching Lily splash in the waves without a care in world.

It was memorable, but for all the wrong reasons: arguments with Seraphina, her habit of flirting with the waiters, his habit of working even while they were away.

She'd been waiting for a proposal that holiday and he'd felt like a heel for disappointing her. But he hadn't loved her enough to make a life-long commitment. And she would have been just as unhappy as him if they had married.

You could have had affairs. Everyone does it.' That was what his father had said when he'd told him why he and Seraphina had broken up. But Gabriel didn't want to have multiple affairs. He wanted the real deal. A relationship for life. But maybe he was being ridiculous and a man like him was expecting too much.

'Gabriel!' Lily's high-pitched voice pierced his thoughts. She was waving to him from the sea. 'Come and paddle with me. There are lots of shells. I can show you.'

'I'm afraid there's no peace when my daughter's around,' laughed Nessa. 'But don't let her bully you into something you don't want to do.'

Gabriel waved back at Lily, who was still beckoning to him.

He could simply sit here on the sand, soaking up the sun. But it was getting hotter and it was hard to resist Lily.

'A quick paddle will be OK, I guess.'

He rolled up his trouser legs to above his knees – he must look like a right old fogey now – and stood up, shaking off the sand. Then he undid a couple more buttons on his shirt and pulled it out from his waistband before walking down to the shoreline. The breeze billowed the cotton and cooled his back.

'Hooray!' said Lily when he reached the waves gently whooshing onto the shore. 'The water's not cold.'

She was lying. Gabriel took a sharp intake of breath as a wave broke around his legs and eddied around his ankles.

'It's absolutely freezing, Lily,' he told her, and she gave a throaty giggle.

'I know.' She laughed again at his expression. 'Let's go and find the dolphins.'

The two of them began walking along the shoreline together, gazing out to sea.

* * *

Nessa lay back on her elbows in the soft sand and watched her daughter and Gabriel paddling through the surf. They had their heads bent together and seemed to be chatting about some shells that Gabriel had picked up.

He seemed like a different man down here on the beach. Less stuffy and formal. He'd even made a terrible joke. And he looked so different with his trousers rolled up and his shirt untucked and billowing around his body. His dark hair was being whipped around his eyes by the breeze.

He looked handsome. He looked like Mr Darcy, striding across the lawn at Pemberley after taking a dip in the lake.

An image of Gabriel standing at the window of Driftwood House in nothing but his pants flitted across Nessa's mind.

That, and an image of him in a mankini, which was less appealing.

She sank her hands into the sand and focused on the grains, letting them trickle through her fingers.

Gabriel's attractiveness had crept up on her. He was very different from Jake, but that had been a disaster anyway.

She brushed her hands together. There was no point in being attracted to Gabriel because she was merely an obstacle in the way of his plans. And no point in Lily getting attached to him either because he'd be gone soon enough. Just like Lily's father.

Nessa got to her feet when Gabriel's phone, abandoned on the sand, began to ring. It sounded urgent and wrong in this peaceful place.

'Hey!' She waved. 'Your phone's ringing. I think work needs you.'

Gabriel bent and spoke to Lily before walking back across the beach. His rolled-up trousers had dark patches where the waves had splashed him.

He took the phone that Nessa held out to him, and glanced at the screen. The ringing had stopped but he twisted his mouth.

'Damn. That was a client I need to speak to so I'd better go. I didn't think I'd be able to escape for long.' He rolled down his trouser legs and buttoned up his shirt. 'Will you explain to Lily and say goodbye from me?'

'Of course.'

'Thanks for letting me gate-crash your beach trip.'

'It was Lily's idea,' said Nessa, regretting her words immediately when his expression hardened. That sounded like she was sorry he'd joined them when, actually, he'd been fine, and Lily had enjoyed his company.

But it was too late to say something different because Gabriel was already walking to the back of the cove, where he sat on a boulder and put on his socks and shoes. Then he began to climb the cliff path and, when he reached the top, disappeared without looking back.

Nessa sat back down on the sand, feeling... She wasn't quite sure how she was feeling. Gabriel Gantwich often had that effect on her, she'd noticed.

It would be so much easier, so much less confusing, if she could simply hate him. She'd thought she did hate him when he first appeared in Heaven's Cove with his gung-ho plan for wiping out the Ghost Village – a heartless businessman who cared nothing for the area.

But now he seemed more of an enigma: still focused on destroying what she loved, corporate and uncompromising. And yet, there was a different side to him that she occasionally glimpsed. A gentler, more creative side, and a sadness that enveloped him like a cloud. As though he didn't want to be the man he was.

She'd spent more than three weeks in the cottage now – twenty-four long nights – so she was well on her way to meeting her goal and saving the precious place. But even if that didn't ultimately work, maybe there was a way to appeal to Gabriel's better nature? Or maybe she was deluding herself and this man would stamp over the only tangible ties she had left to her family.

Nessa deliberately put Gabriel out of her mind and focused on what was right in front of her. Whatever happened, the most important person in her life was Lily, and this morning the two of them were able to spend time together and have fun.

She walked towards the sea where her daughter, oblivious to all the different possibilities swirling around her life, was staring towards the horizon, wishing for dolphins.

TWENTY-SIX
GABRIEL

Gabriel stood in the sitting room at Driftwood House, staring out of the window at the sea. He ran a finger inside the collar of his new polo shirt.

The weather had turned today. A thick blanket of grey cloud had blocked out the sun and it was uncomfortably humid. The cooling breeze usually found on the clifftop had disappeared and the air was heavy and still.

The view from Driftwood House was still amazing, and far better than the cornucopia of concrete from his London apartment. But he was missing his air-conditioning.

At least no Zoom calls were planned for today – no work meetings at all, in fact. So he'd dressed down, more in keeping with the sultry weather.

After the trip to the beach four days ago, he'd visited the boutique near the quay and had bought a couple of polo shirts, new underwear, and a pair of jeans.

Nessa's month in the cottage was almost up – she only had three nights to go –and then he'd be heading back to London. But he'd determined to make his final few days here as comfortable as possible. He deserved as much because he knew what was waiting for him back at headquarters.

His father was furious that Nessa was still in situ and would take it out on him. Then, after he'd given his son a dressing-down, he'd bring in an expensive lawyer to take Nessa down. And he'd win. He'd have to spend time and money to do so, which would anger him even more, but he'd get the result he wanted in the end.

Gabriel shook his head. Perhaps it wouldn't come to that. There was still a slight chance that Nessa might change her mind about living there with Lily. Or slip up. That's why he was still knocking on her door at seven in the morning and ten at night.

He stared at the churning sea, which seemed to change colour every minute. Right now, it was a mossy green close to shore, with bands of grey stretching to the horizon.

It would make a wonderfully atmospheric painting, he thought, his fingers itching to sweep a brush across a canvas.

He was so deep in thought he didn't hear Rosie coming into the room and he jumped when she tapped him on the shoulder.

'Sorry.' She laughed. 'You were miles away. I did call to you from the door but you didn't hear me.'

Gabriel smiled, pleased to see her. In spite of the circum-stances, he was enjoying his stay in her isolated guesthouse above Heaven's Cove. His room was comfortable and spotlessly clean, and Rosie had gone out of her way to make him feel at home. And there was something else about being up here, on the clifftop... It made him feel freer somehow. Less weighed down by corporate responsibilities, in spite of his father's frequent terse texts.

'How can I help you?' he asked.

'It's not so much helping me,' she answered, biting her lip. 'I'm just heading off with a couple of friends to Sorrel Cove, and I thought you might like to come along.'

'Why?'

Rosie shrugged. 'I know you and Nessa aren't the best of friends but whatever happens in the end, she's had a tricky month and we want to offer her some support. So we're going to give her another hand with doing the place up.'

'You do realise it's a waste of time because the cottage is going to be pulled down? If she completes thirty days there, my father will simply contest the lease.'

He couldn't help wincing at how harsh that sounded. But there was no point in sugar-coating it.

'Maybe. But don't underestimate Nessa. People underestimated me when I started renovating Driftwood House after my mum died, but I proved them wrong.' Rosie smiled. 'Nessa's a fighter who's had a lot to cope with in her life, and if she thinks she can save the cottage and make a better life for her and Lily, I wouldn't put it past her.'

'You've obviously never met my father. I'm afraid Nessa is fighting a losing battle.'

He felt rather ashamed as he said that, but it was the truth, and there was no point in getting sentimental about it. He couldn't afford to feel sorry for Nessa or admit that she'd grown on him. Once you got past her pig-headedness, she was kind and vulnerable. And he already found himself thinking about her far more than was sensible.

'Maybe she is wasting her time but it's good to have a dream, don't you think?' said Rosie. 'Turning this place into a guesthouse was my dream and it came true. Anyway, I'm leaving in fifteen minutes if you'd like to join us.'

She'd reached the door before Gabriel asked: 'You and Nessa are good friends, so why don't you resent me for what I'm doing here?'

She regarded him with her warm brown eyes. 'I don't like it, but you're doing your job. I get that. You have your reasons for wanting to destroy the Ghost Village, and Nessa has her reasons for wanting to save it.'

'And you think that me seeing how hard Nessa is working to save it might change my mind?'

'Perhaps. But mostly I thought you might want to do something other than work. You've had hardly any time off since you arrived, and Heaven's Cove is very nice, you know.'

'A break would be nice,' Gabriel admitted. 'But it would be hypocritical of me to help Nessa out when I'm waiting for her to fail. Don't you think?'

'I don't think you lending a hand will be the deciding factor in whether Nessa succeeds or not. But you don't have to help. You don't have to do anything other than relax. And I thought you might like to meet some other people while you're here.'

'Are you worried that I'm lonely?' asked Gabriel, raising an eyebrow.

Rosie's cheeks flushed when she nodded. 'Maybe just a little. Anyway, I'll let you make up your mind.'

When she'd gone, Gabriel sat down heavily on the stone window ledge. To be honest, he *was* lonely here, in the depths of Devon on his own. But he felt ashamed that Rosie had noticed – as though he'd shown weakness and let himself down.

But he had been working solidly and he was tired. He didn't allow himself to think about how tired Nessa must be right now.

Before he could change his mind, he texted his father: *Will be offline for a few hours. Am going to check out situation at Sorrel Cove cottage.*

That was all true, as far as it went. It was probably best not to mention that he was going to be there with a gang of people doing renovation work. What his father didn't know wouldn't hurt him – or, in turn, Gabriel himself.

· · ·

Nessa swung round and her eyes opened wide when she saw Rosie and Liam coming into the cottage.

'What are you doing here? I thought you'd both be working.'

'We thought we'd bunk off for a bit to give you a hand,' said Liam, Rosie's farmer fiancé whom they'd made a detour into Heaven's Cove to pick up.

He and Rosie waved at a red-haired woman who was painting the ceiling with a roller attached to a pole, and she gave them a wide grin.

Liam dumped the armful of building supplies he'd brought with him onto the floor as Nessa's eyes slid past her two friends and met Gabriel's gaze. Her hand flew to her throat.

'Why are you here too?'

'Don't worry. He's here to help out, or not. Whatever he wants,' said Rosie, taking off her jacket, rolling it into a ball and throwing it into a corner. 'He's taking a break from work. Isn't that right?'

Gabriel nodded, wishing he'd stayed at Driftwood House with his laptop.

'What needs doing?' asked Rosie, grinning at the pinpricks of white paint that were scattered across the red-haired woman's shoulders, like dandruff. 'Gabriel, this is Lettie, by the way. Lettie, Gabriel.'

Lettie stopped pushing the roller across the ceiling and rubbed the back of her hand across her nose. 'You're the man who wants to knock down this cottage, even though it means so much to Nessa.'

'It's nothing personal. It's purely a business decision,' said Gabriel, spotting a dark-haired man through the window. 'Who's that outside?'

'That's Corey, my boyfriend,' said Lettie. 'He's repairing the back wall of the cottage.'

'Has he done the front yet?' asked Rosie and, when Nessa shook her head, she pushed a brush into Gabriel's hands.

'There you go. You can check out the condition of the front wall. It faces the sea so it cops the worst of the weather.'

Lettie went back to painting the ceiling. 'Corey's got cement to fill in any gaps in the stone,' she said, over her shoulder. 'Give him a shout when you get outside.'

When Gabriel didn't move, Liam picked up a trowel and handed it to him. 'You'd better get on with it, mate. If Rosie reckons you need to help, that's what's going to happen.'

He ducked and laughed as Rosie swiped him with the cloth she was carrying, and Gabriel envied them their easy familiarity.

It had never been that easy with Seraphina. If he teased her, she sulked for hours. He was happier without her, he knew that. But he still missed her physical presence in his bed at night.

He'd had plenty of offers of company since – it was amazing how attractive being a successful businessman made him. But one-night stands weren't his thing. He needed something more authentic. He needed... He glanced at Nessa, who was trying to prise the lid off a tin of varnish with a screwdriver.

Underneath your fusty exterior, you're just an old romantic trying to get out.

That's what Seraphina had said to him once, after he'd surprised her with a dozen pink roses. Shortly before she'd moaned that they weren't red so wouldn't look as good in the photograph that she'd immediately Instagrammed to the world.

He'd worried about the word 'fusty' for ages. Was he really an old fogey at such a young age? But it was what was expected at work: an old head on young shoulders.

Sometimes he felt like yelling 'That's not me at all!'. But it *was* him. Or he'd thought so, until he'd come to this strange place and met an infuriating single mother who knew what she wanted out of life.

He suddenly had a vision of tedious property deals stretching into his future and shook his head. No, right now, rather than think, he'd do something practical and help to repair this old cottage.

It wouldn't save the building. But it felt like sticking up two fingers to his father and to the family business and to the life he was living, if only for a little while.

Half an hour later, Gabriel stopped pushing filler into gaps in the stone and wiped a hand across his forehead. The sun was still blanketed in thick cloud but the temperature was rising.

He surveyed his handiwork. He'd checked a large area beneath one of the windows and had done what repairs he could with the cement provided by Corey.

Fisherman Corey had taken a day off work to help out Nessa. He was more friendly than his girlfriend and the two of them had had a decent chat before he'd returned to the back of the house to check out the stonework.

Gabriel wiped beads of sweat from his forehead and stepped back to look at the cottage. He had to admit that Nessa and her ragtag helpers had done a great job over the last twenty-eight days.

The cottage no longer looked derelict and sad. The front door and window frames were freshly painted, broken panes had been replaced and makeshift curtains installed, and the weeds twisting around the walls had been cleared away.

There was still a lot to do inside, but Nessa would manage it and turn this cottage into a decent home. He somehow felt sure of that. If only she had more time.

'What do you think?' Nessa's voice at his shoulder made him jump. She thrust a mug at him. 'Would you like some tea? Lettie brought a flask.'

'Does she know that you're giving some to me?'

'She won't mind.'

'Are you sure? I got the feeling I'm not her favourite person.'

'I'm sure. Lettie's lovely and usually very gentle. She's only sticking up for me.'

She waited while Gabriel took the mug and had a sip of tea before saying: 'I don't get it. Why are you here, helping me?'

Why, indeed? Gabriel breathed out slowly. 'It was either that or read through a twenty-page treatise on favourable methods of construction with regard to insulated concrete framework dwellings.'

'Eek.' Nessa smiled. 'That sounds tedious.'

'Very. And Rosie was persuasive. She said it was up to me whether or not I helped with the renovations when I got here,' he explained, raising an eyebrow. 'Though it turns out I didn't end up with much choice in the matter.'

'That sounds like Rosie. I like the new clothes, by the way.'

'Thanks.'

He suppressed a smile, feeling stupidly pleased that she'd noticed.

Nessa gazed out to sea, giving Gabriel the chance to look at her properly. He saw her twice a day but it was either first thing, when neither of them were at their best, or late at night when it was getting dark and he felt awkward being alone with her in such an isolated spot.

Now he could see that having a project to focus on – even a hopeless one like this – had done her good.

Her skin glowed as she brushed dark hair from her eyes, and when she suddenly turned to him and smiled, breath caught in his throat. She was beautiful.

He swallowed and stared at his feet. 'It's very peaceful here,' he said, just for something to say.

'It is now. It must have been so different on the night of the storm.'

'It must have been terrifying.' He imagined towering dark waves crashing over them, and shivered. 'But today it's still and brooding. Perfect to paint.'

'And yet you haven't been back since you painted the cove about two weeks ago.'

'I've been too busy,' Gabriel replied, though that wasn't the whole truth.

He'd avoided spending time with Nessa alone because she asked too many questions and he told her too much. There was something about her searching gaze that invited confidences.

'Why didn't you go to art school in the end?' she asked, confirming his reason for staying away.

'I focused on more useful subjects, like economics and business.'

'Useful, maybe, but I don't suppose they touched your soul in the same way that art did.'

Gabriel blinked. That was it exactly. Translating a changing landscape into a permanent work of art through the strokes of a paintbrush, or gazing with wonder at an artist's finished creation, seemed to nourish his soul. What was left of it.

'You seem to know a lot about art for someone who claims to have no talent.'

Nessa grinned. 'I can't draw for toffee, but I admire people who can, people who are creative. Though I guess you've channelled your creative streak into destroying and creating property instead.'

There was no bitterness in her tone, merely resignation that this was the way it was.

'How's Lily?' he asked, keen to change the subject. 'Has her dad been down to visit her?'

'No. He's too busy, apparently. You can see why I've given up on men.'

It seemed unfair to judge all men by the standards of her ex, but Gabriel let it go. She'd obviously been badly hurt.

Instead, he said: 'You must be missing Lily while you're living here.'

Nessa nodded. 'I miss her dreadfully but Valerie's taking good care of her.' She hesitated, as though she wanted to say more and he didn't fill the silence. 'I think...' she said at last, 'that is, I worry that Lily will want to move in permanently with her granny, rather than coming back to live here with me.'

She'll never want to live in this isolated spot with only ghosts for company. That's what he should say. Capitalise on her concerns and drive her from the cottage. But he didn't. He couldn't. Instead, he gave her a sympathetic smile.

'I expect her granny is spoiling her.'

'Horribly. New boots, new hair clips, late nights and chocolate cornflakes for breakfast.'

'Wow. I quite fancy moving in with Granny myself.'

Nessa burst out laughing at that. He hadn't heard her laugh before and the sound of it lifted his mood.

When she moved her hand to smooth down hair that was caught by the breeze, her golden bangle glowed against tanned skin. It was a snake, he realised, which was trying to eat its own tail.

'Your bracelet is very unusual.'

He resisted an urge to reach out and touch the metal, touch her.

'It was given to me by my gran and she was given it by her mother, who found it here, or so family folklore goes.'

'Found it where?'

'Buried deep in the mud when she was helping her father to dig a vegetable patch at the back of the cottage. They couldn't find its owner so she kept it.'

'And it became a family heirloom.'

'It means a lot to me.' Nessa ran her fingers along the bracelet. 'Oh, did you see that?' She pointed out to sea. 'There, again!'

As Gabriel stared at the horizon, lightning zigzagged into the water and there was a low grumble of thunder. The sky was tinged with yellow and Gabriel caught a faint hint of sulphur in the air.

'I think we're going to get that storm after all,' said Nessa.

'Or maybe, if we're lucky, it'll give us a miss and sweep farther out to sea.' She turned towards him. 'Look, I'd better get back to work inside. I know you think what you're doing out here is a waste of time, but thank you for doing it anyway.'

Gabriel sipped his tea when she went back into the cottage, a mix of emotions tumbling through him. It was a shame that he and Nessa had met like this because, in another life, they might have become friends.

Or more, said the little voice in his head. The same one that whispered to him that he was wasting his life, as he sat in his swanky office.

But the voice, his subconscious, whatever it was, was wrong because Nessa would want nothing to do with a fusty property developer like him, in this life or any other.

With a sigh, he went back to the totally pointless task of repairing a wall that would soon be reduced to rubble.

TWENTY-SEVEN
GABRIEL

It was a filthy night. The storm hadn't swept out to sea. It had settled on Heaven's Cove and was showing no signs of moving on.

Gabriel hammered on the front door of the cottage and peered through a rain-streaked window. It was ridiculous that he was out here while a storm was raging. It was ridiculous that Nessa was out here on her own.

The wind was howling and he could hear the sea pounding against the rocks nearby.

'Oh my goodness!' Nessa had pulled open the front door and was wincing as rain needled into her face. 'I didn't think you'd come out tonight. You must be soaked through. Come in.'

As another squall of rain hit the cottage, she grabbed hold of his coat, pulled him inside and slammed the door shut.

It was a relief to be out of the driving rain and, shivering, he stepped towards the fire flickering in the stone hearth. Above it, the mosaic crafted by Nessa's great-grandmother was catching the light and glowing bright on the dark wall.

The flames had warmed the room but they were throwing shadows that, together with the roar of the ocean and the wailing of the wind, made the cottage seem full of ghosts. The ghosts of those who'd lost their lives on a night like this.

Gabriel gave himself a mental shake because he needed to sort himself out. Nessa was the one liable to flights of fancy about the past, not him.

She was a stressed single parent with a dream of living here in this lonely place. Whereas he was a sensible, grown-up businessman – albeit one who was currently standing in an ancient cottage in the middle of a storm in a bid to prove himself to his father.

You're pathetic, he thought, as Nessa helped him out of Liam's waxed jacket.

'It's crazy coming out on a night like this,' she said, pulling a fold-up wooden chair in front of the fire and draping his wet coat across it.

'I've come out earlier than usual. It's only nine thirty.'

'It doesn't matter what time it is. Surely, you could have trusted me for one night, especially when the weather's like this? I'm so close to meeting the terms of the lease, I'm honestly not going anywhere.'

'I've realised that,' said Gabriel. 'But I wanted to...' When he hesitated, feeling awkward, Nessa leaned closer.

'You wanted to what?'

'I wanted to make sure you're OK out here on your own on such a dreadful night. After what happened to your great-grandmother and the other people who once lived here, I thought you might be anxious.'

Nessa's face softened in the flickering light. 'That was kind of you but I'm all right. I was about to have some food, actually. Would you like some, while your coat's drying? Lettie brought me some of her home-made stew but it's far too much for one person.'

Gabriel hesitated. He'd worked late to clear his inbox and

was planning on begging Rosie for a sandwich when he got back.

Nessa shrugged. 'Don't worry if you've already eaten.'

'No, I haven't.' He smiled, making up his mind. 'Thank you. That would be great, if you're sure you have enough.'

Nessa nodded and gestured for him to take a seat on the camping chair nearest the fire. Then she picked up a wooden spoon from the hearth and started stirring the contents of what appeared to be a cauldron hanging above the flames.

'What happened to the camping stove?'

'I broke a cardinal rule when staying in a derelict cottage way out in the sticks: make sure your gas cylinder doesn't run out. But there's a hook above the fire and I found this pot in a kitchen cupboard. It took some elbow grease to get it clean but it was worth it. It all feels very authentic, don't you think? A leap back in time.'

He watched while she stirred the food, her long, dark hair around her shoulders and her face lit by firelight. She looked like a witch, he thought. A young, sexy witch casting spells as the heavens opened above them.

He was jolted out of his reverie by thunder grumbling out to sea.

'It's quite a storm,' said Nessa, grabbing two bowls and ladling the steaming stew into them. 'I hope Lily isn't frightened.'

'Is she scared of thunder and lightning?' asked Gabriel, taking the bowl and spoon that Nessa offered.

'A bit, though I try to make a game out of storms like this. Counting how many seconds after the lightning that the thunder will crash. That kind of thing.'

She frowned and pushed her spoon into her bowl of stew.

'I'm sure Valerie will look after Lily,' he said, taking a mouthful. Lettie would probably choke at the thought of him enjoying her stew, but it was delicious.

'Do you think she will?' asked Nessa, as a draught snaking through the room made a candle in the windowsill splutter.

'She obviously loves her granddaughter and will want to do everything she can to make her feel safe.'

Nessa nodded. 'I know you're right, but she's not her mum, is she?' She put her bowl of food onto the hearth as lightning lit up the room. 'Sorry. You've caught me at a bad moment. But what am I doing here? I should be with my daughter on a night like tonight. What does it say about me as a mother?'

There was a clap of thunder overhead when she looked into the fire, tears glittering in her eyes.

'You're trying to do the best for your daughter,' Gabriel said gently.

Nessa gave a brittle laugh. 'By leaving her with her grandmother for nights on end and moving into a cottage that's falling down? I thought this could be a home for the two of us, but it's wild out here on a night like tonight and Lily would be scared. Maybe I'm just deluding myself about the whole thing.'

Gabriel closed his eyes. He could imagine his father standing beside him. *Now's the time to seed doubt in her mind. Of course the girl's deluded. Doesn't she know that I always win?*

When he opened his eyes, she was staring at him. And she looked so dejected, so done in, he couldn't put the boot in. She was a single parent, without his advantages, trying to do the best for her child.

'You're not deluding yourself. You're doing what you think is right but it's quite... ambitious.'

'Ambitious?' The corner of Nessa's mouth lifted. 'That's a kinder word for it. Basically, I've left my daughter and moved into a derelict cottage where I'm checked on twice daily by a man I hardly know.'

Gabriel smiled. 'It's an unconventional approach to motherhood, I'll give you that. But you don't strike me as the conventional type.'

'That's not what my ex used to say. Jake reckoned he was the free spirit in our relationship and I was boringly staid.'

'I imagine Lily needed stability rather than a—' Gabriel paused. He'd been about to say 'rather than a dickhead for a dad'. But he wasn't sure that was terribly appropriate.

Nessa gave a wry grin, as though she knew exactly what Gabriel had been about to say

'Anyway.' Gabriel gathered himself together. 'Like I said, you don't seem terribly conventional to me.'

'I'm less conventional than you, that's for sure.'

'Most people are,' he said, his words almost drowned out by a huge clap of thunder that came hot on the heels of a lightning flash.

Nessa winced and waited for the noise to die down. 'Did you go to a private school? Sorry. I know I'm being nosy, but I'm interested.'

He nodded. 'I went to a minor private school but managed to be a disappointment to my parents. What about you?'

'The local comprehensive. That's where I first met Rosie and Liam. Though, like I said, I missed a lot of schooling. That's why I'm finding it hard to get anything decent job-wise. It needs to fit round Lily too so it's even more complicated.'

'What happened to you after your mum died? And where was your dad?'

Nessa reached for her bowl of food, the bracelet on her arm glinting in the firelight.

'I moved in with my gran after Mum died, until I got married. My dad died when I was a kid. I don't remember him very well, which is sad. What about you? Tell me about your family.'

Gabriel took another mouthful of stew and stretched out his legs in the uncomfortable camping chair.

'I grew up in London, my parents divorced when I was eight and I stayed with my dad when my mum moved in with the banker. I work in the family business, as you know, along with my cousin, James. And that's it, really.'

'Have you ever been married? You've never mentioned a wife.'

She was doing what she always did. Drawing him out. Making him say more than he meant to. But what did it matter, here in the middle of nowhere, with a woman he'd soon be leaving behind?

'Nope. I was almost engaged, once, but the relationship didn't work out.'

'I'm sorry. So you've never had kids?'

Gabriel shook his head. 'God, no. I can't imagine me as a dad.'

'Why? Lily doesn't always take to new people but she likes you. You're good with her.'

Was he? Gabriel had felt increasingly comfortable with the five-year-old but he usually avoided children, much like his father, who'd never been much of a hands-on dad. He'd asked his mum once why she'd only had one child and her reply 'we only needed one' had reinforced the idea in his mind that the sole point of his existence was to take over the family firm.

'What about you?' he asked. 'How long were you and Lily's dad married?' He raised an eyebrow at Nessa's expression. 'You were the one who started asking personal questions.'

Nessa laughed. 'Fair enough. Jake and I were married for four years, much to Valerie's horror. Quite why he wanted to get married I don't know. He was brought up by a middle-class family, with lots of home comforts, but he likes to think of himself as a bit of a bad boy.'

Gabriel knew the type and they usually turned out to be idiots.

'I think I was attracted, initially, to the fact that he didn't care what anyone else thought,' said Nessa, almost to herself, gazing into the fire. 'That was so different from me at the time. But it turned out that being a free spirit and a hands-on dad didn't go together. He said a kid would tie him down.'

'That must have been hard. How long after Lily was born did you two split up?'

'She was fourteen months old. He had a one-night stand with a woman called Gemma, then he did a runner and he's been an intermittent father ever since.'

Definitely a dickhead, thought Gabriel, feeling his body tense. But he breathed out and spoke calmly. 'At least his mother's on your side.'

'Do you think so?' Nessa raked a hand through her hair. 'She reckons her son walks on water and I'm the evil woman who tried to ensnare him before banishing him to the frozen North. But she does love Lily and she's always wanted to be a part of her life. Alan, her husband, does too, though he doesn't get so involved. I guess I'm lucky really.'

Lucky? Gabriel admired Nessa's positivity in the face of the evidence. In reality, she was a single mum with a feckless ex-partner, no job and no home.

Nessa nudged a log that had fallen from the fireplace with her foot. 'I'm pretty sure Valerie wants Lily to live with her long term. She thinks it would be for the best.'

'Lily and you together?'

Nessa's pretty eyes opened wide. 'No! She only wants Lily. I don't think that Valerie and I in the same house would work.'

'You shouldn't give Lily up,' said Gabriel, raising his voice above the wind wailing outside.

'No, I shouldn't. Though sometimes, when things are going badly, I do wonder if she might be better off in Valerie's lovely home.' Nessa scrubbed at a tear that was trickling down her cheek.

'A lovely house isn't everything.'

'That's just as well if Lily does end up living here with me.'

Gabriel thought of the pristine house he grew up in. His father had employed a fierce housekeeper, along with the au pairs, and he'd been scared to play indoors in case something got broken. As for painting, that was definitely out of the question, with all the mess that it might entail.

'Wherever you end up living,' he told Nessa, 'if Lily's with you, she'll be happy.'

'Do you think so? That's kind of you to say.'

'I *can* be kind sometimes.'

'Even to people like me?' asked Nessa, pushing her hair behind her ears.

'Especially to people like you.'

Gabriel was suddenly aware of his heart beating in his chest. And when Nessa smiled at him, with tears in her eyes, he found it hard to breathe. He shouldn't be here, in this cottage full of ghosts, where the past and present seemed intertwined.

He was getting to his feet when a blast of wind blew the front door wide open. It crashed into the wall as debris from the storm swirled into the room and the candles spluttered out.

Nessa rushed from the fire to slam the door shut and almost stumbled on her way back to her chair. But Gabriel caught hold of her elbow and held her as she fell forward.

'Oof, sorry.' She'd ended up with her face against his chest. 'Thanks for that.'

She took a step back but he was still holding on to her arms. He didn't want to let her go.

'Nessa,' he said quietly, his voice unheard over the sound of heavy rain battering the windows.

She stood still, staring into his eyes. They were so close in this room, dark with shadows. He could kiss her. Did she want him to kiss her? She wasn't moving away.

The thoughts tumbling through his mind faded when he bent his head. Her upturned face was illuminated by a flash of lightning – her inquisitive eyes, her freckled skin, her full mouth. And a roar of thunder shook the foundations of the cottage as he kissed her warm lips.

She leaned against him as the kiss went on and windows began to rattle in the gale. It sounded like the world was ending outside but Gabriel didn't care. He pulled her into him, holding her close, and felt her arms loop around his neck.

His phone had started ringing, deep in the pocket of his drying coat, its shrill tone piercing the storm. He tightened his arms around Nessa's waist, determined to ignore it. But she pulled away from him, her face flushed.

'Do you need to get that?' she asked, biting her lip.

He shook his head and kissed the soft skin at the nape of her neck. The phone had stopped ringing but, as his lips strayed back to her mouth, it began again. Shrill. Distracting. If it was his father, he'd continue to call until Gabriel picked up.

'Sorry,' he said, when Nessa pulled away from him again. 'Ignore it.'

But she tensed in his arms when he pulled her back. And their kiss, as the phone stopped and began to ring again, felt different – less heat, more awkward.

He was the first to break apart this time. 'I guess I'd better—'

'Yes, of course,' said Nessa, not catching his eye.

She went to sit by the fire and stared into the dying flames while he fished the phone from his coat pocket.

'There you are. I thought you were avoiding me,' barked his father. Few people kept Billy Gantwich waiting.

'Not at all. I was busy.'

Nessa shot him a brief look before going back to staring into the fire.

'Where are you?'

'I'm in Sorrel Cove.'

'Checking up on that damn woman?'

'That's right,' said Gabriel tightly, wondering if Nessa could hear what his father was saying. He had a loud voice, and the storm had eased a little. The wind didn't sound like a wailing banshee any more.

'Is she still living there?'

'She is,' answered Gabriel, trying to keep his answers brief. He should have been braver and switched the phone off. But it was too late now.

'So how's it looking?' demanded his father. 'Any signs of her caving so we can get on with the project, or do we have to finish this ludicrous thirty-day charade first?'

'No change,' said Gabriel, trying to speak in code in front of Nessa.

'Then you'd better pull your finger out and do something about it, pronto. I'm very disappointed in you that it's gone this far, and I don't relish having to spend money and more time to get her out.' He paused for breath. 'Oh, and don't forget to call the Jacksons tomorrow about the Chelmsford deal. James has been doing a good job in your absence from the office, but they're used to dealing with you in person. So give them a call and schmooze them a little. "Everything's fine, your money's safe, I'm focusing on nothing but your project..." Yada, yada... You know the drill.'

'I'll call them first thing tomorrow.'

'Good. And if you can't get that woman out of the cottage permanently, I'll come down to Devon myself, or maybe I'll send James to do the job.'

'That won't be necessary,' said Gabriel stiffly, not sure which would be worse – his father arriving to bawl him out for not being up to the job, or James breezing in to show how it should be done. Neither of them would be sympathetic to Nessa's family situation.

'We'll see,' said his father, ending the call before Gabriel could reply.

'I presume that was your dad?' said Nessa.

'Yeah.' He dropped the phone back into his coat pocket. 'He was ringing for a catch-up. Not great timing.'

When Nessa said nothing, Gabriel stood silently, not sure what to do next. Had he instigated their kiss or had she? Would she like him to kiss her again or was she already regretting what had happened?

A horrible thought crossed his mind. Perhaps she'd been playing him, getting him to care about her so he'd let her win. Or maybe she thought he was playing her for the exact same reason.

Everything had been crystal clear when she was in his arms. He wanted her and she wanted him. But now, after his father's call, his head was buzzing with jumbled emotions.

'I guess I'd better be going,' he said, desperately hoping she'd ask him to stay. But she nodded in the firelight. She wanted him to leave.

The whole thing had become a sorry mess, thought Gabriel, pushing his arms into his coat. He wrenched open the front door but his jaw dropped at what was waiting for him outside. The thunder and lightning had moved off but rain was still falling and the black sea was roaring. Spray was blown into his face and he tasted salt on his lips.

Nessa had moved to stand beside him. 'You can't go out in this. You'll never get up the cliff road to Driftwood House.'

What was she going to suggest? Gabriel held his breath.

'I'm upstairs on the camp bed now but the sleeping bag and bed roll I used at first are still in the corner. You'd better sleep down here, if you don't mind roughing it for one night.'

Gabriel took another look outside, at the ground turned into a quagmire by the relentless rain and the white spray dancing in the wind. He didn't fancy his chances of reaching Driftwood House. But more than that, he couldn't leave Nessa alone in this isolated house on such a wild night. Not after what had happened here seventy-five years ago.

'I'm sure I can manage one night, seeing as you've managed twenty-seven so far.'

He closed the door and found the sleeping bag while Nessa busied herself tidying away bowls of half-eaten stew. She wouldn't look at him.

'I'm going to get an early night,' she said, pausing at the foot of the stairs with a hurricane lamp in her hand. 'Look, about what just happened...' She hesitated. 'I think we'd better forget all about it. I mean, we both know it didn't really mean anything. It can't mean anything because our lives are so different.'

'We got swept away, being marooned here in the middle of a storm.'

'Exactly! I knew you'd feel the same way.' Her face was ghostly in the glow of the flickering lamp. 'I hope you sleep well. I've left the fire to die down gradually so it should stay warm in here for a while.'

She began to climb the stairs and Gabriel heard the rafters creak above him when she walked into the bedroom.

Deciding to stay fully clothed for warmth, he climbed into the sleeping bag and zipped it up.

What would James and his father think of him, sleeping on the floor of a derelict cottage, in part to protect the woman they believed he should be trying to get rid of at every opportunity? The woman who obviously regretted kissing him. What on earth would they think if they found out about the kiss?

Gabriel closed his eyes, suddenly feeling bone-weary. So far he'd made an utter shambles of everything, including his relationship with Nessa, if you could call it that.

Basically, he was stuck in the middle, between a woman he had pointless feelings for and a father whom he loved in spite of his failings. And his reputation at work was about to nosedive when the Sorrel Cove project didn't go ahead as planned.

'Idiot,' he whispered, opening his eyes and staring at the

ceiling, dark with shadows cast by the dying fire. 'Why am I such an idiot?'

He would get back to London as soon as possible, he decided. That was the only way forward. He was stuck in Heaven's Cove for another couple of days, until Nessa had completed thirty nights in the cottage. But he'd keep his distance, as much as he could, and then get back to his ordered life. Away from a woman he wanted but could never have because their lives were too different and she didn't want him.

His father would blame Gabriel for Nessa's continuing hold on the cottage. That was inevitable. And he'd bring in the big guns to try to get her out. But maybe, just maybe, the lease would stand up and his father would lose.

Gabriel wasn't sure what he felt about that. He wasn't sure what he felt about anything any more, because the Ghost Village had seeped into his soul and messed with his mind. He berated himself for being fanciful. Ridiculous, even. But here, in this old, isolated cottage with a storm raging outside, that's how it felt.

He closed his eyes, determined to get some sleep. But he kept thinking about the kiss and hearing Nessa's words in his head: *It didn't really mean anything.*

TWENTY-EIGHT
VALERIE

Valerie sat at the side of Lily's bed, gently stroking her granddaughter's soft hair.

She'd had a bad dream, Valerie presumed. Something had woken her with a start in the middle of the night, even though she'd slept through the storm earlier.

Maybe it was because she had a cold and was finding it hard to breathe through her nose? Valerie leaned down and listened to her breathing, in and out. At least the asthma that had plagued her as an infant was under control these days.

Whatever had roused her from slumber had caused her to cry out for her mother. But her mother wasn't here. She was living in a run-down cottage in that spooky village, which would definitely give Lily nightmares.

But at least Valerie was here now. She'd always be here for her darling girl.

She glanced at the clock with its nightlight that was casting an amber glow around the bedroom. Almost two a.m. The dead of night.

Valerie shivered in spite of herself, as a cold draught snaked under the door and wound itself around her ankles.

Through the wall, she could hear the low rumble of Alan's snores. She'd be awake for hours, she realised, even after she was sure that Lily was fast asleep again. She'd never get back to sleep herself while Alan snorted and grunted next to her.

She'd asked him to go to the doctor about his snoring, which was getting worse. But he said his snoring wasn't a problem. Which it wasn't for him, clearly, since he was resistant to the gentle kicks that Valerie aimed at his shins to make him stop. Truth be told, the kicks weren't so gentle these days but he slept and snored on, regardless.

Valerie sighed and ran her finger gently down the bridge of Lily's perfect, bunged-up nose.

'Never marry a snorer,' she whispered into the semi darkness.

Or a man who'll abandon his own child.

The thought came out of nowhere, as it sometimes did these days, when she saw Lily growing and changing. How could Jacob bear to miss out on his daughter's life? What could be more important than family?

Valerie trampled down the traitorous thoughts until they slid back to where they came from. During the day, when life was busy, she could reason with herself over Jacob's choices: he was young; he was tricked into fatherhood; his work was important at this stage in his life.

But when she woke in the night, burning hot with her heart pounding, and the house was silent – apart from Alan's snores – she sometimes felt a rush of disappointment about her only child. Disappointment that he wasn't the man she'd hoped he would become. And an uncomfortable realisation that he was like his father in some ways.

Alan hadn't moved out when she'd had Jacob, but he had left all the childcare to her. Every nappy change. Every broken night. Every grazed knee. *But times were different back then, thirty years ago,* she reasoned with herself.

When Lily snuffled softly in her sleep, Valerie smiled and brushed hair from her granddaughter's eyes. At least she had this child who loved her.

But for how long? Cold fear lodged itself in Valerie's chest. Soon this child she loved so much would be back with Nessa, living in that dreadful cottage, and Valerie's home would go back to being quiet and oh so boring.

Nessa, for all her faults, seemed to be making a good job of staying in the cottage. She'd presumably stayed put during tonight's awful storm and, if she could manage that, nothing would faze her. The thirty days and nights would soon be up. And Lily would leave.

If only she could have her here for good. Valerie would give her everything that her mother couldn't. And Jacob would surely visit more if his daughter was living here all the time. He didn't come home for his mother. But he would come home for his child.

If only Nessa's plan would fail.

My life is filled with if onlys, thought Valerie sadly.

But it was true enough that Lily and Nessa couldn't stay at Driftwood House forever, and finding a decent new place to live wasn't easy with so many local properties now changed into holiday lets.

Tourists, according to Paula in the village, would pay top whack to stay in a pokey two-bed flat with a dodgy internet connection. That's what she'd bought as a holiday let with money from her late mother's estate, and she reckoned she was quids in.

There was the flat that had come up above the ice-cream parlour but Nessa had totally dismissed that idea, claiming she couldn't afford it. Surely she was being foolheaded?

Valerie huffed and stretched her neck from side to side. The top of her back was starting to ache from sitting hunched over Lily's bed.

If Lily lived here permanently, Valerie would turn this into her special bedroom, rather than a bland spare room for people who never came to visit anyway.

If only Nessa's plan to secure the cottage came to nothing.

An idea wormed its way into Valerie's head as she sat in the quiet room, watching Lily's chest rise and fall. An awful, unforgivable idea, which she tried to bat away.

But it kept coming back after she climbed into bed next to snorting Alan and tried to drift off. And after a sleepless hour, she'd come to a decision. Securing Lily's future was the most important thing in Valerie's life. And she would do that by any means necessary.

TWENTY-NINE
GABRIEL

The shrill ring of a mobile phone in the distance dragged Gabriel from sleep. For a moment, he thought he was at Driftwood House. But his aching back and cold feet soon reminded him of reality – he was sleeping on the floor in an old cottage on the Devon coast. And Nessa, the woman he'd kissed just a few hours earlier, was sleeping in the room above him.

It was pitch black and, when he fumbled for his phone, it lit up with a ghostly glow. It was three thirty in the morning and a mobile was ringing, but it wasn't his. Who on earth was calling Nessa at this time?

He unzipped his sleeping bag and was about to stand up in the cold room when he heard footsteps from the room above. Then, a torch beam shone down the stairs, growing brighter until Nessa appeared.

She was in a rush. She ran to the door, her body a dark shadow, and pushed her feet into her trainers.

'What's going on?' he asked, rubbing sleep from his eyes.

Nessa jumped violently. She'd obviously forgotten he was there. He'd lain awake for ages in his chilly sleeping bag, thinking of the woman sleeping only feet from him. But she'd forgotten all about him.

'Who was that on the phone?' he asked, his voice low and croaky.

'Valerie,' said Nessa tersely before cursing as she fumbled tying her laces. 'Lily's very poorly so I need to go.'

'Now?'

Nessa straightened up. 'Yes, now. I'm her mum and I should be with her. Valerie sounded really worried and said she's thinking of taking her to A&E if her breathing doesn't improve.'

'I'll come with you.'

Gabriel stood up and stretched out his legs. But Nessa shook her head.

'No. There's no need. Valerie will only freak out if I turn up in the middle of the night with you.'

'But how are you going to get there?'

'Rosie left her car here when you all walked home earlier. I'll use that.'

'That old rust bucket?' Gabriel dug into the pocket of his jeans. 'Here. Take my car.'

He held out his keys, which glinted in the glow from his phone.

'I'll be fine in Rosie's car,' said Nessa, shoving her arms into her coat and grabbing her handbag.

'No, you won't. The storm's died down but the roads will still be treacherous, and according to Rosie, her car's always breaking down. What if you break down in the middle of nowhere on the way to see Lily?'

'You don't want to lend me your car.'

'I do, so take it. You need to get to your daughter.'

Nessa hesitated for the briefest of moments before rushing across the room. She took the keys, her fingers brushing against his, and with a brief 'thank you' she was gone.

He heard the front door slam in the blackness and, a minute

or two later, the low growl of his car engine as it revved and disappeared into the distance.

Gabriel sat back down on his thin bedding roll and put his head in his hands. He hoped that Lily was all right. He hated to think of the child being unwell, and Nessa was right to go to her.

She'd gone, he realised, even though she was so close to completing the obligatory month in the cottage. Now, she hadn't met the terms of the lease. Which meant her efforts had been for nothing.

His father would win, as he always did, and this cottage would be razed to make way for luxury homes that people like Nessa could never afford.

But that was business. It wasn't always pretty and it wasn't always kind, but it was the way his world turned. And securing this deal would help prove to his father that he was worthy of taking over the family firm. For once, he wouldn't be a disappointment.

Around him, ghosts of the past seemed to crowd the darkness. Giving himself a mental shake for being so spooked, Gabriel wriggled back into his sleeping bag and zipped it up.

Losing this place would hit Nessa hard but she would survive, he told himself. She was the type of woman who would carry on fighting to do the best for her child.

He focused on the whoosh of the waves nearby and tried to sleep. But he was still staring at the ceiling, remembering their kiss, when beams of dawn light slid across the flagstones two hours later.

THIRTY
NESSA

Nessa cursed when a fox ran across the dark lane ahead of her, its eyes glittering in the car lights. She eased her foot off the accelerator. The storm had brought down branches and made the lanes slick with mud. And however desperate she was to reach Lily, ending up in a ditch wouldn't help.

It was only a few miles to Valerie's house on the edge of Heaven's Cove but the route seemed endless as worst-case scenarios played through her mind.

She wasn't normally one to panic. She'd dealt with lots over the years and had learned to cope with fear of the unknown. But the thought of anything happening to Lily made her throat tighten and a dark desperation wash through her. Valerie had sounded so worried.

Please come now, Nessa. I'm so concerned about Lily's breathing. She needs you.

Of course she needed her mother. Nessa berated herself for farming her daughter out to Valerie for thirty nights. Did she really think she could do up a derelict cottage and turn their lives around in just one month?

It had been a stupid dream, and one, she knew full well,

that was now over. She'd left the cottage in the middle of the night so the lease was null and void.

Though maybe Gabriel's father would never find out. Not if his son never told him.

Nessa's mind flitted back to the kiss she and Gabriel had shared only a few hours earlier. She could still feel his hands on her and she felt herself blush as she crunched down through the gears and took a corner on two wheels.

It had been wonderful, until his father rang and reality came crashing in. But while she was kissing Gabriel, her daughter was lying ill a few miles away. Seriously ill, if Valerie was right. Maybe Valerie was also right that Lily would be better off living with her forever.

'Stop thinking!' said Nessa out loud, slowing when she reached the outskirts of Heaven's Cove. She'd cause an accident if she raced through the narrow streets of the village.

Street lights were off and there were no lamps lit in the windows of the ancient cottages as Nessa drove, as quickly as she dared, to Valerie's house. She screeched to a halt outside, leaped out of the car and ran up the garden path.

She rang the doorbell once, twice, three times before Valerie opened the door, looking pale as a ghost without her make-up.

'You came, then,' she said, an emotion flitting across her face that Nessa didn't recognise.

'Of course I came.' Nessa stepped into the hall and closed the door behind her. 'Where is she? Is Lily all right?'

'She's in bed, and she seems a little better than when I rang you. I hope you didn't mind me calling but I was worried.'

'No, I'm glad you rang. I'll go up and see her.'

Nessa took the stairs two at a time and rushed into the spare room. Her precious daughter was asleep with the duvet pulled up to her chin.

Nessa knelt by the bed, tears in her eyes, and pressed the back of her hand to Lily's forehead. She was warm but didn't seem overly hot. Nessa leaned forward and put her ear close to Lily's mouth. She was snuffling in her sleep and there was a wheeze every time she breathed out. Nessa's body slumped with relief. The wheeze was almost inaudible and nothing that a puff or two of inhaler wouldn't ease.

Lily stirred when Nessa's hair brushed her face, and her eyes flickered open.

'Mummy,' she murmured sleepily, raising her hand to touch Nessa's cheek.

'Mummy's here, sweetheart.' Nessa kissed Lily's head. 'Are you feeling poorly?'

'Got a cold,' said Lily, giving a huge yawn. 'Granny gave me medicine. Why are you here?'

'I wanted to make sure you're all right.'

'I'm OK, Mummy.'

When she snuggled back under the duvet, after having a little more of her inhaler, Nessa sat back and tried to calm down. Lily didn't seem too bad, and she was always picking up colds. Her school was a germ factory.

Nessa sat with Lily for a while, inhaling her sweet, sleepy smell and stroking her soft hair until she was sure her daughter was asleep.

Valerie was peering out of the landing window when Nessa came out of the bedroom.

'Is everything all right?' she asked, twitching back the curtain.

'I think so,' answered Nessa quietly, making sure Lily's door was closed. 'She's not particularly hot and she seemed OK when she woke up briefly. She's a little wheezy. Did she have her brown inhaler before she went to bed?'

'Of course,' huffed Valerie, shuffling her bare feet through the thick pile of the carpet. 'I'm sorry if I disturbed you for nothing but I was so worried about her.'

'I'm just glad she's all right. You sounded so panicky when

you rang and I panicked when you said you were thinking of taking her to hospital.'

'I thought it might come to that because Lily seemed so unwell. But her temperature's gone down since I called you and her breathing's eased, thank goodness. It was awful earlier.'

'Really?' Nessa bit her lip as guilt and worry began to bubble up again.

'Really. She was crying out for you and upset that you weren't here.'

Nessa's stomach turned over. Her poorly child had called for her and she'd been miles away.

'I hope I did the right thing in calling you.'

'Yes, of course.' Nessa put her hand on Valerie's arm. 'Thank you. I'm glad you called and I was awake anyway, thinking of Lily.'

I'm a terrible mother, thought Nessa because she hadn't been lying there thinking of Lily at all. She'd been thinking of Gabriel and wondering if she had the courage to invite him to join her. The courage to risk her heart, for a few hours in the arms of a man who would soon be leaving Heaven's Cove. A man who planned to erase the Ghost Village.

Everything was so complicated. She'd lied and told him their kiss hadn't meant anything, and perhaps it hadn't to him. But feelings absent for so long had bubbled to the surface when he'd pressed his lips against hers – longing, desire, connection. She cared about the man she glimpsed beneath the business façade. She wanted to know that man better.

But then Valerie's call had upset her so much, she'd forgotten he was in the cottage at all when she went hurtling down the stairs.

'Will you stay?' asked Valerie, concern etched across her face. 'I'd rather you did in case Lily takes another turn for the worse. It'll cheer her up so much if you're here when she wakes up and you can have breakfast with her. I love looking after Lily but there are times when only a mother will do, don't you think?'

Nessa nodded, her bad-mother guilt rocketing off the scale. 'Definitely, and I'm so sorry you've had all this worry.'

'That's all right. Everything's sorted now.' Valerie smiled and opened the door to Jake's old bedroom. 'Here you go. You can stay in here. I always keep the bed made up in case Jacob pays us a flying visit.'

Chance would be a fine thing, thought Nessa, who, too wrung out to jib at sleeping in her ex's bed, let Valerie lead her into the room.

'How did you get here so quickly, by the way?' Valerie asked, smoothing the duvet cover. 'The car outside looks familiar but I can't quite place it.'

'It's Gabriel's,' said Nessa, who was also too tired to come up with a convincing lie. 'He called on me last night to check I was at the cottage and had to stay over because the storm was so bad.' When Valerie's eyebrows disappeared into her fringe, Nessa added: 'He slept downstairs in the sleeping bag.'

'I see. Well, how fortunate that he was there, in the circumstances.'

Without waiting for a reply, Valerie went out of the room, closing the door behind her.

Nessa put her hand into her jeans pocket and turned Gabriel's car keys over and over in her fingers.

She was lying on the bed, on top of the covers, but she couldn't sleep. Valerie probably wasn't sleeping either, not with Alan's deafening snores rumbling through the house. Though maybe she was used to them after thirty-five years together.

Nessa stared at the shadowy posters on the walls – Iron Maiden, Metallica, and a framed print of Che Guevara. Games figures from Jake's teenage years stood on a bookcase under the window.

This room was a shrine, thought Nessa, wondering where the prodigal son was right now. Not worrying about his daughter; that was for sure.

With sleep still refusing to come, Nessa went to the window and sat on the sill. Down the narrow lane, she could glimpse the sea in the distance. The sky was beginning to lighten from black to navy blue, and the horizon was glowing with the first rays of the rising sun. Everything was washed clean by the storm, and it would be a beautiful day in Heaven's Cove and the Ghost Village.

She pulled Gabriel's car keys from her pocket and ran her fingers across the cold metal.

At least Valerie's call had saved her heart, and her dignity. What if she'd invited Gabriel upstairs and he, after being reminded by his father of why he was there, had refused? Or worse, what if he'd accepted and had then left her, just as Jake had done?

She shivered. The drama of her dash through country lanes made their kiss last night seem unreal: a bizarre coming together that had never really happened.

Gabriel would soon be gone and he'd quickly forget her. Or perhaps she'd be remembered occasionally as the deluded woman who'd tried, unsuccessfully, to save the Ghost Village. Perhaps he'd rung his father already to report that her claim on the cottage was null and void: the difficult woman trying to ruin their plans hadn't stayed thirty days and nights in the cottage, after all. She'd fallen at the last hurdle.

Nessa picked up her phone and sent Gabriel a brief text message: *Lily's OK. Thanks for car. Shall I return it to Driftwood House?*

His reply came back almost immediately. *Relieved Lily's OK. Car at Driftwood is fine. Thanks.*

Nessa stared at her phone, feeling irrationally disappointed. What had she expected him to say? He'd made no reference to what had happened between them, but then neither had she. And the confusion she felt about the whole affair was beginning to make her head ache.

She could beg Gabriel not to let on that she'd broken the rules of the lease, if he hadn't already. But she wasn't the begging type. And he owed her nothing. The kiss, to him, had meant nothing.

Nessa put down the phone and closed her eyes as the first rays of the rising sun shone through the window. She was so very tired.

Her eyes jerked open when her phone beeped, and breath caught in her throat when she glanced at the screen. The kiss had meant something to him after all.

It was a text from Gabriel that simply said: *In case you were wondering, I won't tell.*

THIRTY-ONE
NESSA

Nessa rubbed at a mark on her dress. She'd given Lily orange juice with her breakfast this morning, and had managed to spray it everywhere when she opened the carton.

This was why she rarely got dressed up. Some people suited silk blouses and velvet trousers – grown-ups who could drink red wine without dribbling and eat spaghetti bolognaise without flicking sauce everywhere. She was not one of those people.

'There's stain remover in the cupboard under the sink,' said Rosie, walking past with an armful of freshly laundered towels.

'Thanks. You're the best.'

Rosie *was* the best, Nessa knew that without a doubt.

She'd invited her and Lily back to Driftwood House. And though Nessa didn't want to impose – again – the lure of a hot shower and soft bed for a few days had proved too much after her month-long stay in the Ghost Village.

It was a whole month, in the end. Nessa had managed only twenty-seven-and-a-half nights in the cottage before her mercy dash to Valerie's. But she'd gone back and stayed the following night and the two nights after that to ensure that she met the thirty days stipulated – albeit with a brief break.

Gabriel had promised to keep quiet about her few hours away, though she hadn't seen him in person since reading his text at Valerie's. He hadn't been around when she dropped the car back to Driftwood House, and he'd packed up and left for good that same morning.

Nessa had felt disappointed and relieved in equal measure about his flit – as well as worried that it meant he'd given up on her and was going to tell his father anyway.

But Rosie had reckoned otherwise when she'd dragged the whole sorry story out of Nessa.

'I *knew* Gabriel really liked you,' she'd said. 'I could tell by the way he'd started looking at you. And he helped with renovating the cottage. Why would he do that unless he secretly thought you were adorable? He's only disappeared without seeing out the thirty days because he's confused by his feelings now you've bewitched him. He'll be keeping his head down somewhere until he can go back to work and say you completed your task successfully.'

While Nessa was sure she'd never bewitched anyone, Rosie's explanation was comforting. Even though he hadn't texted her since, and she'd been too chicken to contact him either.

But, Nessa swallowed and smoothed down her orange-juiced dress, she was going to see him again this morning. And though it was pointless getting excited about that, she'd dressed up nonetheless.

Gabriel was back in his swish London life where he mixed with Seraphina types wearing designer labels. Her dress wasn't designer. She'd got it in a Primark sale. But it looked fine, and she wanted to show him that she wasn't just old trainers and combat trousers.

'You've scrubbed up nicely,' said Rosie, doubling back with the towels. 'Is that the dress you wore to your gran's funeral?'

'Yeah,' said Nessa, self-consciously tugging at her hair that she'd pulled into a smart ponytail. 'It's the only dress I own. Too black?'

'Not at all. It looks very sophisticated.' Rosie smiled. 'Are you dressing up for the benefit of Mr Gantwich Senior or Mr Gantwich Junior?'

'Neither,' replied Nessa, trying hard not to blush. 'But I thought I should look the part a bit more seeing as I'm meeting Billy Gantwich for the first time. It's probably best to look more grown-up and... and...'

'Desirable?' Rosie raised an eyebrow and laughed. 'It seems like *ages* since Gabriel left, even though it's less than a week, and you can't wait to see him again. Admit it.'

'I admit nothing of the sort,' said Nessa, being careful not to catch Rosie's eye because she, more than anyone, would know she was lying.

'Just be careful, Ness,' said Rosie, her expression suddenly serious. 'A quick snog round the back of the cottage is fine but remember he'll be going back to his life in London. Watch your heart.'

'There won't be any time for snogging. I'll be too busy ironing out the final details with Mr Gantwich Senior regarding me and Lily moving into the cottage permanently. Though I can hardly believe it's really going to happen.'

'Me neither. I'm surprised Billy Gantwich has backed down, though maybe Gabriel had something to do with it. What did Billy's text say again?'

Nessa pulled her phone from her pocket and brought up the text that had arrived out of the blue two days ago. She read it out to Rosie.

I'm contacting you in relation to the cottage at Sorrel Cove. I understand, following your stay in the property, that you have permission to live there permanently. I'll be in the area on Thursday and would be grateful if we could meet at the cottage at 10.30 a.m. to discuss how this will work going forward. My son will also be attending. Billy Gantwich

Nessa looked up from the screen. 'He says I have permission to live there permanently and he wants to discuss how it will work, so it sounds positive to me.'

'Hmm. Gabriel must have stepped in and changed his mind. But are you quite sure that you want to move into the cottage permanently, Ness? You can still back out. Lily didn't seem that keen on the idea.'

'She'll come around,' said Nessa, with more conviction than she felt.

She'd taken Lily to the cottage two days ago but the visit hadn't been a great success. Lily's bottom lip had wobbled when Nessa had mentioned moving in for good. And she'd had a nightmare that evening and had woken up crying.

But that was to be expected, Nessa told herself. The prospect of a new home was disconcerting when you'd had to adjust to so much already. She'd soon come round to it.

Valerie hadn't approved of Lily moving back into Driftwood House with Lily, even temporarily.

'She might as well stay here with us, until you both actually move into the cottage, to minimise the upheaval,' she'd said, patting Nessa's arm. And when Nessa, desperate to be back with her daughter, had hesitated, she'd added: 'We have to do what's best for Lily.'

But surely being with her mother *was* what was best for Lily? And now it looked like they had a cottage they could call their own. Once Nessa had sorted out a few final improvements there, they could move in together. Local electrician Phil had promised to help with restoring power to the property before the autumn chill set in, and maybe water from the well – now proven safe to use – could be piped into the cottage somehow.

Nessa thought more about Billy's visit during her drive to

the Ghost Village in Rosie's Mini. He'd probably still try to persuade her to give up the cottage so he could push ahead with his development plans, though surely he realised she was serious about living there after she'd spent thirty consecutive nights roughing it?

Twenty-seven-and-a-half consecutive nights, said the pedantic voice in her head. But she ignored it.

Nessa let herself into the cottage using the key from her grandmother's treasure box and looked around. She was proud of all the work that had been done over the last month. The cottage no longer felt empty and sad. It was cleaner and brighter and her great-grandmother's mosaic above the fireplace glowed in sunlight flooding through the window.

Nessa took a deep breath, not sure if she was more nervous about meeting Billy or seeing his son again.

She knew it was pointless but she couldn't stop thinking about Gabriel. She fantasised about him marching into Driftwood House, declaring she had bewitched him, and sweeping her off her feet.

Nessa shook her head and draped a blanket over the painting supplies Gabriel had left behind. When had she turned from a pragmatic single mother into someone whose head was filled with romantic nonsense?

Gabriel had his life and she had hers, and that was the way it would stay. They'd shared a kiss on a stormy night in an isolated cottage. And though it meant something to both of them, it didn't mean enough.

'Ms Paulson, I presume?'

A stout man in a dark grey suit was blocking the doorway. He walked towards her, his oxblood shoes slapping on the flag-stones. 'I've heard a great deal about you from my son. How wonderful to meet you at last.' He enveloped her hand in his and gave it a shake.

'You must be Mr Gantwich,' said Nessa, retrieving her hand.

'Billy, please. Let's not stand on ceremony. Can I call you Nessa?'

'Yes, of course.'

'That's grand.'

Nessa looked past Billy, disappointed that he was alone.

'I thought your son would be with you.'

Billy stared, his dark eyes boring into her. 'He'll be here shortly. I arrived yesterday actually, to have a look around Heaven's Cove, which is utterly charming. And it means I avoided the morning rush-hour in London. Gabriel's probably been caught in traffic.'

So she was here on her own with Billy Gantwich.

He was a big bear of a man, but less scary than she'd been expecting. Maybe it was the physical similarities between him and his son that took the edge off her nerves. Their noses were similar, and the way their hair curled where it hit their ears, though Billy's was steel-grey and Gabriel's dark brown.

Gabriel was more conventionally handsome than his father, but Billy had a presence that filled the room.

'So, I understand this cottage was once your family's home.'

'That's right. My family lived here until my great-grandmother was killed in a terrible storm seventy-five years ago.'

'Ah yes, what a tragedy that was.'

Nessa glanced at Billy. It was hard to tell from his tone if he was being sympathetic or flippant. 'And now you want to live here with your daughter, I'm told.'

'Yes. Lily's five.'

His lip curled. 'It's not the best place for a child, is it?'

'Not at the moment, but it will be when the work on it is finished.'

'Mmm.' Billy walked slowly round the room and stopped to

stare at the painting that Gabriel had done. Nessa had propped it up on the windowsill. The bright colours and thick brush-strokes cheered up the room. 'Are you an artist, Nessa?'

'No, not me. That picture was painted by your son, actually. It's great, don't you think? He's got a real eye for landscapes.'

Billy bent and peered at the canvas more closely. 'It's very...' He took a deep breath and, without finishing his sentence, stood up straight and looked out at the sea.

Nessa wished that Gabriel would arrive. His father was being polite – charming, even – but he made her uncomfortable. Waves of energy were bristling from him and shifting the atmosphere in the cottage.

He turned from the window. 'The view is magnificent here, with the sea ahead of you and the headland behind. This is the perfect setting for the development I have in mind, once this cottage has been demolished.'

'But your text said—'

'It doesn't matter what my text said. I wanted to make sure you turned up this morning.'

Nessa's stomach lurched. He hadn't accepted her moving in here at all. 'I'm sure there are lots of other places along the coast where you could build,' she said, trying to keep her voice level. 'Places without such a special history.'

'I'm sure there are but I've set my mind on this one.'

'Then I'm very sorry to disappoint you but my family has long-standing permission to live here.'

'Oh, I'm not disappointed, Ms Paulson.' When Billy stepped forward, Nessa fought an urge to back away from him. 'I'm afraid you're the one who will be disappointed because your lease on this cottage isn't worth the paper it's written on.'

'But I stayed here for a whole month as the lease stipulated.'

'A *whole* month? Are you sure?'

When Billy gave a cold smile, Nessa felt sick. He knew.

'The lease was very specific and included a rather peculiar clause,' he continued. 'Though, believe me, I've seen more peculiar in my many years in the property business. There was one that—' He paused. 'But I'm getting off the subject. The lease in question specified that you were obliged to spend thirty nights here. Thirty *unbroken* nights.'

'Which I did,' blustered Nessa.

Billy wrinkled his nose and made a 'tsk' noise through his teeth. 'Not really. I understand that you were absent from this cottage on the night of July the twelfth.'

Nessa felt her stomach sink into her sandals. The only way Billy could possibly know that she'd been away that night was if his son had told him.

'Not the whole night,' she said, her throat tight. 'My daughter was staying with her grandmother and I had a call in the early hours to say she was very ill. I had to go to her.'

'Of course. That's what any good mother would do. But the lease doesn't make an exception for family emergencies, I'm afraid.' He winced at a streak of dust on his trouser leg and brushed it off. 'Don't take it to heart, Ms Paulson. It's purely business. You contravened the lease criteria and therefore you have no right to this cottage, if indeed the lease would have stood up in court anyway.

'Don't get me wrong. I admire your pluck and resolve, I truly do. It's the kind of determination and bloody-mindedness that got me to where I am today. But on this occasion it wasn't enough and I'm afraid you've lost. I do hope you're a good loser.'

He breathed out a puff of air. 'You could challenge me in court, of course. But that would take money, which I doubt you have, and ultimately you would lose because the lease is in black and white and I have irrefutable evidence that you contravened a specific clause.'

Nessa felt completely blindsided. All of her efforts, and

those of her friends, had been in vain. All of the hard work and the sacrifice and the hopes and dreams. They'd all come to nothing. And Billy was right. She didn't have the financial clout to challenge him and, even if she did, she would lose. She had lost.

I'm sorry, Gran. She bit her lip to ward off the tears that were threatening to fall. She wouldn't cry in front of this man. She wouldn't give him the satisfaction.

No wonder Gabriel was untrustworthy after growing up with this cold, ruthless soul. No wonder he was still trying to earn some respect after all these years. No wonder he'd betrayed her to win a business deal.

'Who told you?' she asked quietly as the wind picked up outside and the open front door began to bang against its frame. 'Was it Gabriel?'

She still had a vestige of hope that Gabriel hadn't lied to her about keeping quiet.

But Billy fixed her with a hard stare. 'Who else?' He looked over her shoulder. 'Speak of the devil.'

When Nessa turned, Gabriel was standing behind her. He was clean-shaven and in his suit. The Gabriel she'd first met at Driftwood House a month ago.

'I thought we weren't meeting for another fifteen minutes.' He nodded at Nessa, his eyes meeting hers. 'Hello.'

She looked away. He'd told his father, even though he knew why she'd had to leave the cottage in the dead of night.

Families stick together. Wasn't that what people said? And Gabriel had chosen his father and his work over Nessa. Of course he had.

Nessa pushed past him without a word. She was bitterly disappointed that the cottage wasn't hers, and beyond upset that it and the Ghost Village would be razed to the ground. But she was also heartbroken that the man she'd started falling for had let her down so badly. He must have been laughing at her and her stupid dreams. Dreams didn't come true for people like her.

She marched up the path and climbed the slope towards Rosie's car. And she didn't turn once, not even when she heard Gabriel calling her name over and over from the cottage doorway.

THIRTY-TWO
GABRIEL

Nessa wouldn't look back. He kept calling but she kept on climbing the path, her ponytail swinging from side to side. What on earth had his father done now?

He should have known something was wrong when his father insisted on the two of them coming to meet Nessa. He should have realised that Billy wasn't about to give up without a fight. But he'd hoped that his father was going to do the right thing. He'd told Gabriel he was willing to discuss the situation with Nessa, to try and find a way forward that worked for all of them.

Gabriel ducked back into the cottage. His father was running his hand across the stone mantelpiece, standing where Gabriel had kissed Nessa during the storm.

'What did you say to her?' he demanded.

His father turned slowly to face him. 'The truth.'

'Which is?'

His father huffed as though he couldn't believe that Gabriel was even asking the question.

'She contravened the criteria of the lease and therefore must forfeit the cottage forthwith. I believe that's how my lawyers might word it, and will word it if she decides to pursue the matter. Though I doubt she has the finances to take it any further.' He smiled. 'She's certainly an impressive young woman. I almost felt sorry for her.'

'Almost?' Gabriel shook his head. 'She stayed here for a full month. How did she fail to meet the lease criteria?'

His father gave him his most intimidating stare. 'Why don't you tell me, Gabriel? Or more to the point, why *didn't* you tell me?'

Gabriel could feel his cheeks burning and hated himself for showing weakness. 'I don't know what you mean.'

Billy shook his head. 'You were never good at lying, Gabriel, even as a child. Of course you know what I mean. It appears that Ms Paulson was absent from this cottage on her twenty-eighth night here, for a number of hours. And I understand that you were here during that time.'

Gabriel nodded, the wind knocked out of his sails. 'I was.'

'You can't lie but you're taken in by a pretty face and a sob story.' His father sighed. 'Did you know that she'd left the cottage to go to her sick child?'

Gabriel pulled himself up tall. 'I did.'

'And yet you didn't tell me. You let me believe that she had fulfilled the obligations of the lease and therefore potentially had a legitimate claim to the cottage. You could have cost me a good deal of time and money.' He stepped forward until his face was inches from Gabriel's. 'Why was that?'

Gabriel could feel his heart hammering. He felt like a young child again, failing – always failing – to meet his father's expectations.

'It was an emergency and Nessa was here for most of the night. I didn't think it was relevant.'

'You didn't think it was relevant?' Billy shook his head. 'How can I trust you if you keep things from me? I can't imagine James doing the same.'

Gabriel blinked. His father was always pitching James against him. No wonder he and his cousin didn't get on. It wasn't fair. But his father wasn't fair when it came to family. He expected too much and gave little back in return, aside from a good salary. Money was important but, Gabriel realised, he'd trade every penny for a dad who loved him for who he was and not for who he expected him to be.

'I know you don't need this development,' said Gabriel. 'It's no skin off your nose because you can build farther along the coast. I've found some other sites which would do just as well. I told you that and I thought you were interested.'

'I don't want to build farther along the coast,' said his father, his voice quiet and low.

'Is that because this is the better plot or because this has become a battle that you have to win? Someone is challenging you and you don't like it.'

'I certainly don't like you talking to me like this.'

Gabriel had never spoken in this way before to his father. He could feel his throat tightening but the thought of Nessa walking away from him spurred him on.

'How did you find out that Nessa wasn't here the whole night?'

'She was seen. I have my spies, even in a nondescript place like this.'

'Who?'

'It doesn't matter who. I have it on good authority that the lease criteria weren't met.'

'And does Nessa think it was me who told you she wasn't here?'

His father shrugged. 'You'd know that you can't keep things from me if you weren't so befuddled by that woman.'

'What does that mean?'

'You were here with her that night, and I saw the way you looked at her. You've fallen for Ms Paulson, haven't you? All that time here together with the waves crashing outside. Oh, Gabriel.' He whistled through his teeth. 'I didn't think you'd be taken in by a woman like that.'

'A woman like what?' demanded Gabriel, experiencing a red-hot rush of anger.

'A single parent from the back end of beyond with a ludicrous dream to do up this place and live here happily ever after.'

'We all need dreams.'

'Exactly.' Billy spread his arms wide. 'And that's what we'll build here, together. Dream homes for tired executives who'll pay an arm and a leg for an amazing view.'

'Not everything comes down to money.'

His father's jaw dropped as if Gabriel had swung a punch at it. 'Don't be ridiculous,' he barked. 'Of course everything comes down to money.'

'Even when it means doing the wrong thing?'

His father shook his head. 'I sometimes wonder if you're really cut out to take over the business.'

'So do I,' said Gabriel quietly. He looked out of the window at the waves that rolled endlessly towards the shore. Was he really going to do it? Really going to say it? He took a deep breath. 'I don't think I fit with the business if this is how it operates.'

'It operates just fine and I won't be changing a thing.'

'Then perhaps it's time for me to move on.'

His father laughed. 'Move on? It's a family business, Gabriel, and you'll take over when I eventually retire. You'll benefit from my hard work that you find so distasteful.'

'But what if I don't want to take over when you retire?'

His father opened and closed his mouth.

'What if my heart isn't in property development and I'd rather be doing something else?'

'Something else like art?' Billy picked up his painting and waved it at him. 'Be realistic, for goodness' sake. Are you really going to become a starving artist, living in a Devon garret?'

'No, I'm not. I'm under no illusion that I can make a living from selling my art. It's a hobby. But what about displaying and selling other people's art?'

'A shop?' Billy snorted in disbelief. 'You want to give up the chance of running my property empire to run a shop?'

His father's derision was expected but it still hurt. Gabriel felt his shoulders drop. 'James is far more suited to the business. I know that and so do you.'

Billy continued, as though his son hadn't said a word. 'So what's the plan? You'll open a shop in Heaven's Cove and move in somewhere with Ms Paulson and her kid and become an instant happy family?'

Gabriel shook his head. 'She won't want me. You're going to destroy this cottage and lost community that means so much to her. And whatever I say, she'll think it was me who told you she left in the night. But spending time here in this isolated place, away from all the stresses of normal life, has given me time to think.'

'There's nothing so dangerous as thinking too much,' said his father, visibly angry now. 'You're tired after staying in this place for a month. You're not thinking straight.'

'Or perhaps I'm thinking straight for the first time in a long time.'

An emotion flitted across Billy's face. Was it fear? Gabriel had never known his father to be frightened of anything.

Billy carefully placed the painting back on the windowsill. Then he gave Gabriel a tight smile.

'I realise the past few weeks haven't been easy for you, being away from the office and stuck here. Why don't you take a week off? Go away and lie on a tropical beach somewhere to clear your head and come to your senses.'

'How I feel won't change.'

'We'll see,' said his father, patting his arm as though he was a difficult toddler. 'We'll see when you've had time to consider all that you've got to lose. I'll expect to see you back at work in a week's time.'

With that, he swept out of the cottage, banging the door behind him, and a couple of minutes later his car screeched off into the distance.

Gabriel walked to the sea and sat on the grass. This place was so peaceful but it would soon echo to the growl of diggers tearing up the land.

He closed his eyes and went over the conversation with his father. Was his father right, that being here had skewed his thinking, and life would get back to normal once he spent more time in London?

He rubbed his temples, trying to ward off a brewing headache. His father was a difficult man, but Gabriel didn't want to cause a family schism. And yet he felt a pull to this place and to Nessa, though she believed he'd betrayed her to his father. That hurt more than anything.

Gabriel didn't feel like the same man who'd pitched up at Driftwood House five weeks ago. Getting to know Nessa had changed him. He'd come to care about her deeply and had planned to talk to her today about their kiss. To see if it truly had meant nothing to her or if, like him, she'd been lying. He believed – he hoped – that she had been. But she'd want nothing to do with him now. His father had seen to that.

He opened his eyes and stared at the cottage that he'd helped Nessa to start renovating.

'Sorry,' he said out loud as a salt-laced breeze ruffled his hair.

He was sorry that this cottage and this Ghost Village and all of its history would be erased. And so very sorry that any possible future with Nessa had disappeared. Without her, he didn't have the courage to upend his whole life.

'All I have left are my work and my family,' he murmured, his words lost in the gentle whoosh of the waves. And leaving it all behind to sell art, to be with Nessa, was nothing but a dream.

So he'd take a week off to lick his wounds and then he'd go back to work and his real life. He'd throw himself into being the man his family wanted him to be. And his time in Heaven's Cove, and Nessa, would gradually lose their defined edges in his memory and become just one more dream that would fade away.

THIRTY-THREE

NESSA

'I want to see Gabriel from the beach,' demanded Lily, pushing out her bottom lip. 'He can help me look for dolphins.'

Nessa sighed. She wanted to see Gabriel too. Mostly to yell at him for telling tales to his father and ruining her life. She hadn't contacted him since her showdown with Billy three days ago. What was the point?

But, though she hated to admit it, a small part of her wanted to see him purely because she missed him – his penchant for wearing suits in a heatwave, and the way he daubed paint onto a canvas; his habit of shuffling his feet when asked personal questions, and the vulnerability on his face when he'd kissed her.

She kept looking up, expecting him to step through the doorway at Driftwood House, his tall rangy body filling the doorframe.

But he'd let her down and now he was gone, and good riddance, she told herself sternly.

She'd stop thinking about Gabriel because she had far more pressing matters on her mind – like securing a roof over her child's head.

This morning she'd gone to see a tiny flat that she could

afford, now she'd picked up a few intermittent shifts at the gift shop in Harbour Lane. But it had been awful, with black scars of mould in the bathroom and noisy neighbours. And it was a long way from Lily's school. She'd put up with it if it was just her – beggars couldn't be choosers – but she couldn't take Lily somewhere like that. Her daughter would be better off with Valerie.

Nessa suddenly felt weighed down with sadness. Perhaps she would have to let her daughter go in the end. She'd move into an awful bedsit and Lily would move in with her grandparents.

'Please,' said Lily, pushing her hand into Nessa's. 'Can we go and see Gabriel?'

'No, I'm afraid not.' Nessa wrapped her fingers around her daughter's. 'Gabriel has gone back to his life in the big city.'

'And he won't be coming back?'

'Probably not. His dad's business is doing some work round here. They're knocking down...' Nessa stopped and shook her head. 'It doesn't matter what they're doing, but I don't expect Gabriel will come here again. He won't need to.'

'I saw his daddy,' said Lily absent-mindedly, pulling her hand from Nessa's to nibble at a hangnail. 'Can we go to Magda's and have an ice lolly? Please, Mummy.'

'Yes, I suppose so,' said Nessa, mentally calculating that she could afford a trip to the ice-cream parlour if Lily had a lolly and she had nothing.

'Hooray!'

Lily turned her shining eyes towards her mother and Nessa marvelled anew at how quickly her daughter could move on from things that bothered her to things that brought her joy. If only she had the same ability.

She bent to buckle Lily's sandals. Something was niggling at the edge of her brain. Something that Lily had just said.

She straightened up. 'What do you mean, you saw Gabriel's daddy?'

'I did. I was in the garden but I saw him.'

'Which garden?'

'Granny's garden, of course.' Lily frowned at her mother for being so silly. 'After Granny picked me up from school and gave me tea, when you were speaking to that lady about your new job.'

'When I had my interview at the gift shop?'

'Yes. I was playing in the garden but I saw him.'

'How do you know it was Gabriel's daddy?' asked Nessa, finding it hard to breathe. Her daughter had to be mistaken.

'Grampy Alan said he was when he got cross with Granny Val.'

'He got cross with Granny?'

'He said—' She thought for a moment, her head to one side. 'Grampy said Granny was fearing, and his face went all red, like a tomato.' She giggled at the memory.

'Fearing?' Nessa frowned, then her jaw dropped. '*Inter*fering? Did Grampy say Granny was interfering?'

'Dunno,' said Lily, before grabbing hold of the bottom of Nessa's T-shirt and pulling her towards the front door of Drift-wood House. 'A lolly, Mummy. Can I have a lolly?'

'Yes, hold on a minute,' said Nessa, grabbing her purse. Her mind was whirling. 'What did Gabriel's daddy look like?'

'Um.' Lily narrowed her eyes. 'He was big and he had red shoes and grey hair that stuck up round his ears. It looked funny.'

That sounded like Billy, thought Nessa, but what was he doing at Valerie's house? Unless...

No. She shook her head. Valerie would never sabotage Nessa's future or, more importantly, her granddaughter's. Nessa bit her bottom lip. Not unless Valerie felt she knew what was best for Lily.

'Where are you two off to?' asked Rosie, coming into the hall with a steaming cup of coffee for the guest in the sitting room.

'The ice-cream parlour!' shouted Lily gleefully.

'Ooh, lucky you.' She glanced at Nessa. 'Are you OK, Ness? You look really pale.'

Nessa pulled herself together. 'Yes, I'm fine thanks. We won't be long and then I'll be back to help with the cleaning.'

It was crazy, she told herself as she and Lily walked hand in hand down the cliff path to the village. Lily had misheard Alan's words and got the wrong end of the stick. Billy Gantwich wouldn't have gone to Valerie's home, and there was no way that she'd have deliberately told tales to scupper Nessa's dreams. However much she wanted Lily to move in with her, that would be going too far.

They walked on with Heaven's Cove spread out before them. Pillows of grey cloud had hidden the sky and the sea was choppy.

Lily chattered all the way, about school and her friends, and whether she should have an orange or a strawberry lolly at the parlour.

But Nessa was only half listening. She was recalling all the sly digs from Valerie about her parenting skills and the way she was convinced that her precious son had only fled Heaven's Cove because of her.

She obviously didn't like Nessa but did she hate her enough to spoil her chances of having a proper home with Lily?

'Mummy, you're not listening to me again.'

Nessa pulled her thoughts back to the present and smiled down at her daughter.

'Sorry, Lils. Mummy was thinking about grown-up stuff. Now I'm all yours.'

But, she wondered, for how long would that be the case?

THIRTY-FOUR
VALERIE

Valerie pushed her bag back onto her shoulder – the stupid thing kept slipping off – and waved away a wasp close to her hot face.

Why on earth Nessa had suggested meeting in the woods on the headland, she had no idea. They could have gone to a café in town, if she wanted to chat about Lily and didn't want to come to the house.

Or they could have retired to The Smugglers Haunt, though the pub had gone downhill recently. It was always filled with sunburned tourists on days like this, at the height of the summer season.

In fact, the whole village was rammed with out-of-towners and it had taken Valerie longer than usual to make her way through the streets.

She pushed on through the trees that flanked the lower slopes of the headland, wishing she'd worn her flatter shoes.

But, she thought, her mood lifting, perhaps today was the day when Nessa would finally ask her to take on Lily full time.

She squinted into the distance. There, under a canopy of trees that formed a natural shade against the glaring sun, was

Nessa. She was sitting at a picnic bench, gazing into the distance. Though all she could possibly see from there were more trees, with a flash of blue sea between the tall trunks.

Valerie quickened her pace, suddenly feeling excited. Nessa had obviously seen sense at last and was going to let Lily move in with her permanently. Why else would she want a private meeting?

Alan would moan about having Lily in the house all the time. But seeing as he never lifted a finger when Lily stayed, it wouldn't change his life that much.

The thought of having Lily around cheered Valerie up immensely and she managed a smile when she reached the picnic bench.

'Hello there,' said Nessa, glancing round as Valerie approached.

The young woman had dark circles under her eyes, Valerie noticed, and she looked frail. Concern sparked inside her, but she did her best to ignore it. This was the woman who had hounded her son out of Heaven's Cove and left Valerie broken-hearted and lonely.

Alan was always home, apart from when he was playing golf, but she was still lonely. And she had been for quite some time.

'You found me then,' said Nessa flatly, shifting along the bench so Valerie could sit down. 'Sorry to drag you up here but I didn't want us to be overheard.'

'Alan and I used to bring Jacob here for picnics,' said Valerie, her mind slipping back to the past. They'd done things as a family then – trips to the beach and the zoo, and long week-ends in London.

But the trips had slowly petered out over the years. She suddenly remembered refusing Alan's requests to go for a walk together by the sea. She always had too much housework to do, even when there were only the two of them at home.

Perhaps she should have said yes to Alan more often and simply let the house get dusty. But he didn't ask any more, and it was too late now. Soon she'd have even more housework to do with Lily there full time.

Valerie wouldn't mind. She could feel herself sliding into late middle-age, and Lily would help to keep her young.

'How are you doing, Nessa?' she asked, to move things along. 'I assume Lily's fine?'

'Yes, she's spending the afternoon with her friend Clara.' Nessa shifted round until she was facing Valerie. She looked so young. 'I haven't seen you since I met up with Billy Gantwich so you won't know that I've lost the chance of moving into the cottage at Sorrel Cove. He found out that I was away from the house for a few hours that night that Lily was sick.'

Valerie worked hard to keep her expression neutral. 'No, I didn't know that. I'm so sorry. But Lily was ill and needed her mother.'

'Of course.' Nessa narrowed her eyes but said nothing more. She looked past Valerie at the tall oak trees swaying in the gentle breeze.

When she stayed silent, Valerie said: 'What will you do now, then? What about Lily? You can't stay at Driftwood House forever.'

'You mentioned a while back that you wouldn't mind having Lily to stay with you permanently.'

Valerie felt her heart quicken. 'That's right.'

She pushed down a bubbling sense of guilt. This was what she wanted. It would be better for Lily, and there was no point in feeling sorry for Nessa. She could always visit.

Nessa nodded. 'Lily mentioned something that happened when she was with you recently that I didn't quite understand.'

'Really?' said Valerie, unease prickling at the back of her neck. 'What was that?'

'She mentioned that Billy came to your house.'

'Did she?' Valerie gave a brittle laugh. 'She was mistaken.'

'That's what I thought, at first, but then she told me things about him that she wouldn't have known if she hadn't caught sight of him, talking to you. And suddenly everything fell into place.'

Valerie sighed. After reading the email she'd sent him, Billy Gantwich had rung up out of the blue and said he'd like to call round. All Alan had to do was keep Lily out of the way while he was there. But Alan couldn't even manage that. He'd taken Lily out for a walk – rather reluctantly, it must be said – but had come back too early and told her to play in the garden.

Even so, Valerie had assumed Lily wouldn't know what was going on. But she should have realised the child would cotton on because she was bright. She took after her father in that regard.

Nessa was staring at her, her eyes huge with disappointment.

'Why did you do it, Valerie? All I can think is that you exaggerated how poorly Lily was to get me to leave the house and then you told Billy all about it.'

Valerie opened her mouth to speak but didn't know what to say, so closed it again.

'So you're not going to deny it?'

'There's not much point, is there?'

'I know you don't rate me much as a mother but were you so desperate to take Lily away from me that you ruined a chance we had of making a better life together?'

Indignation began to smother the guilt that Valerie was feeling. 'A better life?' she spat out. 'You wanted to take my granddaughter to live in a derelict cottage and I couldn't let that happen.'

'I wanted to give Lily a permanent home that couldn't be taken away from us. And you hadn't seen the cottage for a while. It's so much better now than it was when you visited.'

'But she still didn't want to live there. She told me.'

'If she really didn't like it there, we'd have found somewhere else. Somewhere together. But I think she'd have come around to the cottage because it was starting to look good. I've had so much help from local people.'

'Including Mr Gantwich's son,' said Valerie, raising an eyebrow.

That news had been a catalyst for Valerie's increasingly desperate actions. Nessa had got her claws into Gabriel – giving him painting supplies and who knew what else – so he would, presumably, do her bidding when it came to the cottage. And Valerie couldn't allow that. He'd even slept over on the night of the storm but, as Valerie had suspected, hadn't told his father about Nessa's absence.

'Gabriel.' Nessa gave a sad smile. 'I thought he'd told his father about me being away from the house. But all the time it was you, someone I should have been able to trust. Tell me, Valerie, why do you hate me so much?'

Her direct question took Valerie's breath away.

'I don't hate you,' she managed, while leaves rustled around her, as though the trees were discussing her actions and didn't approve.

'Then why are you trying to scupper me at every turn? I know you've been telling people in the village that I'm a rubbish mother.' When Valerie went to speak, Nessa held up her hand to stop her. 'And I could cope with that. Words don't hurt me. Not really. But you told tales to Billy Gantwich and that's hurt me and my daughter. If you *really* cared about her, why have you never offered to help pay for a roof over her head? I don't want your money but that's not the point – you've never even offered.'

'You get quite enough from Jacob.'

Shock crossed Nessa's face. 'You really have no idea, do you? You don't know what your son is really like.'

This was too much. The gloves were finally off. Valerie hissed, 'I hate what you did to Jacob.'

'What I did to him?' Nessa shook her head. 'Your son abandoned me and our daughter after having a one-night stand. He moved hundreds of miles away when she was just a year old and he never comes back to see Lily. As a father, he's hopeless, and he doesn't even pay regular maintenance for her.'

'Of course he does,' stuttered Valerie.

'No, he doesn't. He flits from job to job and pleads poverty, though the flat he lives in looks nice enough and he's just bought a car. I see his Instagram. So he's not on the breadline. But I can never guarantee that a maintenance payment will arrive on time. How can I pay rent regularly when the money he agreed to provide to support his daughter is often late or sometimes doesn't turn up at all?'

'He's busy,' said Valerie, stung by Nessa's criticism.

'Oh, I know he's busy. Too busy to be a good parent or a good son.' Nessa paused and wiped her hand across her eyes. 'I know you love him, Valerie. Once upon a time, I loved him too. And I know he's your son and you'd do anything for him. That's how I feel about Lily. But your devotion has blinded you to how he treats people. How he treats me and Lily, and how he treats you and his father.'

'You drove him out of Heaven's Cove,' retorted Valerie, blindsided by Nessa's words. She wouldn't believe bad things about her son. She couldn't. Her boy wouldn't behave like that and abandon his daughter. She'd brought him up to be better than that.

'Exactly how did I drive him out of the village? Tell me that,' asked Nessa, her words soft and sad.

'You pushed him into a marriage that he didn't want, and tricked him into having a child.'

'I didn't trick him into anything. He said he wanted a child and promised to be a good father. And he was the one who persuaded me to get married, although I'd never expected that to happen, what with Jake being such a self-proclaimed...' She sighed. '... *free spirit*.'

'There's no need to be sarcastic,' said Valerie, pushing down memories of Jacob informing her he was too much of a free spirit to clean his bedroom, or pay rent when he lived at home. 'He's his own person. He's always been above average and too good for the people around here.'

Nessa laughed. She actually laughed. 'Do you mean too good for me? The woman who's stuck around to bring up his daughter, who drives through the night to her side when she's ill, who sleeps in a derelict cottage for a month to try and secure a roof over her head, who kept you and Alan stocked up with food when you both had flu? Who did all of those things? It certainly wasn't your perfect son.'

'He loves us,' spluttered Valerie. Her world was starting to spin off its axis.

Nessa's face softened and she grabbed hold of Valerie's hands.

'I'm sure he does love you. I guess he loves Lily too, in his own way. But he's not around to provide for her and to keep her safe and happy. That's been my job as her mother and I love her more than anything else in the world. Maybe the cottage was a stupid idea and was never going to work. But I was desperate, and I'm doing the best that I can. It's just not easy.'

When Nessa's bottom lip wobbled and a fat tear slid down her cheek, Valerie felt even more blindsided. She blamed Nessa. She'd blamed her for a long time, but the woman in front of her was vulnerable and in need of help.

Valerie wasn't a hard woman, or was she? Perhaps she'd become a hard woman over the years. Alan sometimes said she'd changed, but how could she stay the same when so much was different now? Her son was far away, she wasn't sure her husband still loved her, the job she enjoyed had ended, and even her body seemed alien to her these days – sometimes boiling hot, sometimes cold, with aches and pains that seemingly sprang from nowhere.

Thoughts and memories she'd locked away for so long began tumbling through her head: Alan adorably nervous on their wedding day; bringing their newborn son home from the hospital; a grown-up Jacob telling her he was going to be a father, his eyes shining with pride.

Then, when Lily was only one, Jacob informing them he had a new job two hundred miles away and was leaving Heaven's Cove. They'd seen him only a dozen times in the four years since. But he was busy carving out his career. And Valerie knew something Nessa evidently did not.

'Jacob *is* coming home this weekend, actually,' she said, resisting the urge to comfort Nessa but passing her a clean tissue all the same. 'He messaged out of the blue and said he'd like to stay on Saturday night, and on Sunday, Alan's birthday.' Catching sight of Nessa's face, Valerie added: 'He promised that he'd definitely be here, and he can't wait to see Lily.'

'Did he really say that?' asked Nessa, a hint of weariness in her voice.

'Of course,' said Valerie, trying to visualise the text message.

She was sure he'd mentioned Lily. He hadn't specifically mentioned Alan's birthday but the celebrations were obviously why he was coming back this particular weekend. Alan was going to be fifty-eight and Jacob wanted to wish his dad a happy birthday in person. Alan hadn't said much about his son's visit, but Valerie could tell he was pleased.

Nessa glanced at her watch. 'Look, I have to go. I'm working in Sally's gift shop for a few hours today. I know the last five minutes have been difficult but I had to clear the air between us.'

Was that what she'd done? To Valerie, it had felt more like a telling off, followed by a character assassination of her son. But at least they both knew where they stood – which was further apart than ever, it seemed.

Nessa got to her feet but didn't walk away. She cleared her throat but said nothing.

Valerie looked up. 'Was there something else you wanted to say?'

'Yes. I wasn't sure I could but...' She stopped, gathering herself together, then she said calmly, 'I can't find a job that fits round Lily and pays enough for me to give her the decent home that she deserves. But you and Alan can give her that. So, if your offer still stands, maybe she could move in with you? It wouldn't be forever,' she said, her bottom lip wobbling again. 'But it might be a while until I can get myself sorted out. I know it's an imposition, especially after our disagreement, and I still hate that you spoke to Gabriel's father, but—'

'It's fine,' said Valerie. 'Lily can stay for as long as she likes.'

'Thank you,' said Nessa, her voice tight. 'I'll give you a call after I've finished work so we can make some arrangements. If possible, I'd like her to stay with me at Driftwood House until the school holiday starts. So we have a little more time together.'

When Nessa walked off, Valerie watched until the young woman disappeared amongst the trees.

She sat back on the uncomfortable picnic bench and tried to enjoy the warmth of the sun on her face. In the distance, a horn sounded as the tiny ferry that ran from Heaven's Cove along the coast passed by.

Jacob was coming home for his father's birthday and Lily was coming to stay for who knew how long. The house would be full of life, and Valerie would have a purpose again. All was suddenly right in her world, so why did she feel so miserable?

THIRTY-FIVE
NESSA

Nessa stared at her mobile phone before shoving it back into her pocket. She couldn't do it, she thought, pacing back and forth across the clifftop. She couldn't ring him, not after how things had been left. It was all too complicated.

Complication number one: they'd kissed. She and Gabriel had kissed during the storm, and she had no idea how he felt about that. To be honest, she had little idea how she felt about it either.

She rather feared he regretted it now because she doubted she was his type. He preferred women with names like Seraphina who probably employed personal shoppers and never stepped outside the door without a full face of make-up.

Or perhaps he'd been trying to worm his way into her affections for nefarious business reasons, so he'd have more sway in persuading her to abandon her fight to save the cottage and the Ghost Village.

This possibility was more upsetting than him having subsequent doubts about spontaneously snogging her. And she found some comfort in the fact that his behaviour since then – keeping her absence from the cottage quiet from his father – shot holes in that argument.

Complication number two: since they'd met, she'd done nothing but make *his* life more complicated. The last few days of soul-searching had given her some perspective.

All Gabriel had wanted to do was get a building project underway to impress his scary father, and she'd been nothing but trouble from the start. True, it was a horrible project with upsetting consequences but he didn't have the same emotional attachment to the Ghost Village that she did, so why would he care? Why should he?

Complication number three: she hadn't heard from him between their kiss and the meeting with his father, or since. Surely, if he had proper feelings for her he'd have been in touch? She wasn't expecting him to ask her out, especially not now. But he could have texted, or rung, or sent a carrier pigeon, or something.

And complication number four, the biggie: she'd believed that he'd told his father she'd gone AWOL from the cottage, when it had been Valerie all along.

It turned out that Gabriel had kept quiet for Nessa's sake, which was noble in the extreme. But she'd automatically believed that he'd blabbed.

She hadn't given him the benefit of the doubt at all. She'd forgotten the man he was when he sat painting barefoot in the sunshine and had only remembered him as the aloof, suited and booted man he was on the day they'd met.

The whole thing had become a terrible mess and she couldn't believe that her grandmother would be very proud of her right now.

'Sorry, Gran,' she said out loud to the seagulls circling high above her, and then felt foolish. It wasn't her dead grandmother she needed to apologise to. It was Gabriel.

Grabbing her phone again, she scrolled through her

contacts and jabbed on 'Gabriel Gantwich' before she could lose her nerve.

Hopefully he wouldn't answer and she could leave a message. Or a text! Why wasn't she texting? That was a coward's way out but she was feeling cowardly today so an apologetic text would do just fine.

She was about to end the call when she heard Gabriel's low voice.

'Hello.'

When Nessa stared at the phone, rather than saying something... anything, he asked, 'Is that you, Nessa?'

'Mmm, yep, it's me. It's Nessa, just giving you a quick ring at work.' Nessa's shoulders slumped. She sounded like an idiot. 'Are you busy?'

'Not right now. Is everything all right?'

'Yeah, well, no, not really.' This conversation wasn't getting any easier. Nessa took a deep breath, trying to erase the image that had just popped into her head of Gabriel leaning towards her to kiss her, the cottage bright with lightning. 'Actually, I was ringing up to apologise, though maybe I should have texted instead.'

'No, ringing is fine.'

'Good.' Nessa paused, took a deep breath and said quickly, 'I've found out that you didn't tell your father about me leaving the cottage when Lily was sick so I wanted to say sorry for thinking it was you, and thank you for not telling him when you could have. I know family dynamics can be difficult and, even though I don't like what your family firm is doing to the Ghost Village, I hope you didn't get into trouble for not telling your dad because I wouldn't want that. Not at all.'

She stopped, partly because she was burbling on, but mostly because she'd run out of air. She waited for Gabriel to say something but there was nothing. Only silence. Had the phone signal dropped out? Had she made a heartfelt apology into thin air?

'Hello?' she said, her voice high-pitched. 'Are you still there?'

'Yes, I'm here,' said Gabriel. 'Sorry. I wasn't expecting you to call and I didn't know that you knew I didn't tell my father.'

'Why didn't you text to tell me it wasn't you who told him?'

'Would you have believed me?'

Nessa looked out across the sea and the blue sky that was streaked with the vapour trails of aircraft heading for places far away.

'Probably not,' she admitted. 'But now I've found out the truth.'

'So who was it? Who told my dad that you weren't at the cottage all that night?'

Nessa hesitated. Should she say? Oh, what did it matter? Gabriel wouldn't return to Heaven's Cove. He'd send his minions to do the work of demolishing the Ghost Village and putting up flash apartments in its place. She and Gabriel were unlikely to meet ever again.

'It was Valerie. Lily's grandmother. I found out she contacted your father and invited him round, and then she told him all about it,' she said, looking behind her for eavesdroppers, even though she was the only person on this windy clifftop.

'Your ex mother-in-law, Valerie? Good grief!' Gabriel whistled through his teeth. 'That is harsh. It did cross my mind that it could be her but I couldn't believe it. Do you think... I mean, was Lily ever ill at all?'

'She had a cold, but she wasn't as poorly as Valerie made out.'

'So do you think she planned it all from the start?'

'Maybe. She doesn't approve of me and she wants Lily to live with her full time. She never thought the cottage was a suitable home for her precious granddaughter and, actually...'

Nessa took a deep breath, about to admit something out loud that she'd only recently admitted to herself. 'She was right.

Even if I'd managed to make the cottage habitable enough for Lily, she'd be away from her friends, living in an isolated spot amongst the ghosts of the dead. It was never going to work but I was desperate.'

'And are you still desperate?' asked Gabriel, with such sympathy in his voice, it was almost too much.

Nessa dug her nails into the palm of her hand so she wouldn't cry. 'No. I've come to my senses. Lily is going to move in with Valerie and I'll find a cheap bedsit and a better job than the few hours per week I've picked up in a gift shop. I can do night shifts somewhere if Lily's living with her grandparents, and they pay more. So it'll be fine.' She tried to keep the wobble out of her voice when she added: 'And one day Lily will come back to me.'

'I hope so.'

Nessa swallowed. 'Could I ask a favour, if you get the chance?'

'What favour?'

'If there's any way of saving my great-grandmother's mosaic, when the cottage is demolished, I'd be grateful. It means a lot to me.'

'I know. I'll do my best.' He paused. 'So have you given up on all your dreams?'

'Dreams don't pay the bills and I need to be practical. Lily will be better off living in a decent house.'

'And what about Sorrel Cove, the Ghost Village?'

'It'll break my heart to see it disappear. I know you and your dad think I'm being overly sentimental. Perhaps I am, but it's a link to the family I've lost and a reminder of the terrible tragedy that happened there. But who am I to stand in the way of progress?'

Did that sound bitter? Nessa wasn't bitter. She was simply resigned. She tried again. 'What I mean is, your dad's won but, like you said, he always does. And that's OK. People like me never win. Not really. And I was daft to think I could. But it's not your fault, Gabriel, and thank you for not telling your father about me being away from the cottage. I'm ringing because I didn't want us to part on bad terms. And that's it. That's what I wanted to say.'

'OK.' Nessa heard voices in the background. 'Look, I'm about to go into a meeting but thank you for calling and I'm glad you know the truth.'

'I'd better go then, but Gabriel...'

'Yes?' The voices were getting louder.

'I hope your business career goes well, but most of all I hope you'll be happy. Don't forget to find time to paint. You're a really good artist, and it's good for your soul.'

'And we all need that. Take care, Nessa.'

'Bye, Gabriel.'

Nessa ended the call and walked as far as she dared to the edge of the cliff and looked down. The sea was roiling against rocks far below and throwing plumes of spray into the air. Farther along the coast, Nessa could see the pretty beach that gave Heaven's Cove its name and the headland, pushing out into the water, where she'd met Valerie yesterday.

She sat down on the grass and looked behind her at Driftwood House. Its white walls and russet roof were stark against the blue sky. The window where she'd seen Gabriel standing in his underpants was twinkling where sunbeams were hitting the glass.

A sense of loss, of missing him, crept over her. She and Gabriel were never going to work. Their lives and backgrounds were too different. But she'd grown accustomed to him being around over the last month and, in spite of her initial impression, she'd grown to care about him.

There were so many people she missed – her mum and dad, her grandmother, even Jake when Lily came home upset from school because she didn't have a father nearby. Gabriel would simply be added to the list.

Nessa lifted her wrist to her mouth and rolled her golden bangle across her lips. The feeling of the cold metal against her skin was strangely comforting, as was the beautiful view in front of her.

The sun would rise in the morning, the sea would rush towards the shore, and her little life would go on as it always did.

THIRTY-SIX
GABRIEL

Gabriel put his phone down in the shade of the parasol and sat up on the sun lounger. The noisy family heading for the beach bar was disappearing into the distance and everything was peaceful again.

He wiped a hand across his forehead. The heat was unrelenting and he'd been thinking of moving under the parasol himself, just before Nessa had called.

Why had he lied and implied he was at work? he wondered, squinting through the glare at white sand, and aquamarine water lapping gently at the shore.

Was it because he was thrown by her call? Or did he feel guilty that he was here, lounging in paradise while she was battling to put a roof over her child's head? A battle she'd won, it seemed, only by letting her daughter go.

Gabriel swallowed, imagining how hard that must be for Nessa, even though she was being brave about it.

She was being brave while he was lying here, having a holiday 'to clear his head' as his father had suggested, and already gearing up for getting back to work in a few days' time. Because work was all he had in his life.

But the hotter he got, under the Mediterranean sun, the more he thought of Sorrel Cove and its heatwave that was so often tempered by a cooling sea breeze. The gusty wind here was more like a blast from a hairdryer.

He closed his eyes and imagined that he was back in the Ghost Village. Back when Nessa was still living in the cottage, fighting off giant spiders and walking round with paint in her hair.

He could have spent longer with her, if he hadn't rushed off. He'd been planning to stay on, after her mercy dash to Lily's bedside. He'd planned to see the thirty days out and then tell his father she'd completed the task. But everything was so charged, so awkward after their kiss, he'd decided to leave instead. He was lying to his father anyway, so what did it matter?

The lie had backfired and the cottage would soon be gone. Yet all Nessa had asked of him in her phone call was that he do his best to save her great-grandmother's artwork. That amazing, intricate mosaic that glowed in the light. He pictured it in his mind – the complex pattern, the glowing colours, the shards of stone and glass.

It was worth saving because there was something very special about it. Something he'd seen before but couldn't quite put his finger on.

Gabriel's eyes snapped open and he swung his feet off the sun lounger. He moved into the shade, reached for his phone and began to research online. Twenty minutes later, as a headache began to pulse at his temples, he'd come across lots of interesting information and had found a particular name. Amelia Fulden.

Ms Fulden could be the key to him keeping his promise to Nessa, to try and save the mosaic. Or she could be the grenade that blew his life to smithereens.

Gabriel sat lost in thought, while holidaymakers nearby rubbed sun cream into hot skin and sipped cold drinks served by hotel staff. This was his privileged life and it could be his forever. If that was what he truly wanted.

He smiled as a bird flew past, a flash of yellow against the bright blue sky, and he remembered what Nessa had once told him: *Sometimes you have to do something crazy to change your life for the better.* He began to dial Ms Fulden's number.

Call completed, Gabriel pushed his phone into the pocket of his swim shorts and took a few deep breaths. His hands were shaking and his stomach felt as if he was on a rollercoaster. But he didn't regret what he'd just done. Not yet, at least.

Far out to sea, glass-bottomed boats were revealing the wonders of the deep, while closer to shore, parasailers towed by motorboats soared high into the air. But Gabriel wasn't interested in any of them.

He walked briskly across the baking hot beach until he reached the waves curling gently onto the sand. Bubbles eddied around his feet as he stood there alone, gazing out to sea, wishing for dolphins.

THIRTY-SEVEN
VALERIE

Valerie smiled, hardly able to believe that her beloved son was back in the family home. It had been a good few months since she'd last seen him and he looked leaner, like he'd been working out. Or not eating properly.

'It's so good to have you back, Jacob.'

She ruffled his hair as she went past the kitchen stool he was perched on.

'You know me, Mum,' he said, smoothing his hair down. 'I love coming back to visit.'

'Maybe you should do it more often, then.'

She bit her lip, cross with herself. She'd told herself she wouldn't spoil his visit by nagging, but he'd only been home for half an hour and she was already scolding him.

'What I mean is,' she added quickly, 'your dad and I miss you and of course Lily does too. Have you arranged with Nessa to see her?'

Jacob put down his mobile phone and reached for another chocolate digestive. 'Yeah, I'll sort something out with Ness.'

'Lily will be here for your dad's birthday tea, so you'll see her then too.'

Jacob paused, the biscuit halfway to his mouth. 'Birthday tea?'

'She's very excited about having tea with Grampy tomorrow on his special day. She's made him a card and bought him a present with her pocket money. Isn't that sweet?'

'Mmm.' Jacob took a large bite of biscuit and chewed for a while. 'I didn't know what to get Dad so I thought I'd give him a bit of cash, so he can get what he wants. And you know me, I'm not one for birthday cards. I don't agree with paying a fortune for a bit of cardboard. It's a capitalist rip-off.'

Valerie nodded and loaded plates from their lunch into the dishwasher. He'd forgotten his father's birthday. That was clear enough. But at least serendipity meant he'd missed his family enough to come home this weekend. It was a fortunate coincidence.

'What time is Dad's birthday tea tomorrow?' asked Jacob, running his fingers across Valerie's squeaky-clean granite worktop.

'Four o'clock.' When he grimaced, she asked, 'Is that a problem?'

'Four isn't great, to be honest. I'll be heading home by then. I don't want to leave it too late because you know what the trains are like. I would have driven, only the roads round here are terrible.'

Valerie straightened up from the dishwasher and stretched her aching back. 'Are you returning to Manchester tomorrow? I thought you were staying until Monday.'

'Yeah, I was thinking about making a long weekend of it but I need to get back for work. We've got a big project on right now and I'm an important part of it, so I can't stay.'

'That's a shame,' said Valerie calmly, going back to loading dishes.

'Yeah, but I'm sure Dad won't mind and maybe I can nip

LIZ EELES

round to see Lily tomorrow morning, so long as Ness doesn't have a mare about it. Are they still living with her gran?'

Valerie placed a smeared bowl on the worktop and turned to look at her son. 'No. Nessa's grandmother died a few weeks ago and they had to move out.'

'Oh yeah, of course. She did tell me about her gran but I forgot.' He picked up his phone and started scrolling through Instagram. 'So where have they moved to?'

'They've been living at Driftwood House for a few weeks, apart from when Lily stayed here with us for a month. Didn't she tell you that too?'

'Probably. I zone out a bit when Ness sends a long email.' He closed down his social media and reached for another biscuit. 'Driftwood House, eh? I heard Rosie's making a great success of the place. I wouldn't have thought she'd have enough room in the summer season for Ness and Lily to move in.'

'She doesn't. It's been a stop-gap while Nessa's looking for somewhere else suitable for her and her child to live. It hasn't proved easy.'

Valerie was about to tell him all about Nessa's crackpot plan to house his daughter in a derelict building, and to reassure him that his daughter would, in fact, be moving in permanently with her and Alan in two days' time, but what was the point? she wondered. What was the point when her son didn't even know that his daughter had been living in a seaside guesthouse? And he didn't seem particularly interested.

He hadn't mentioned Lily's living arrangements during the brief phone calls he'd made to them over the last month, and she'd assumed he was so worried sick he didn't want to talk about it. She'd gone along with that, not wanting to add to his stress and spoil their precious chats. But it seemed he hadn't been worried at all. He'd been oblivious.

Valerie deliberately relaxed her shoulders, which were heading towards her ears. 'Maybe we could switch Dad's tea tomorrow to a birthday meal this evening. Lily might be able to come round for a couple of hours if I text Nessa. I'm cooking roast lamb because it's your favourite.'

Jacob swung his legs off the stool, stood up and stretched.

'I'd love to, Mum, but I'm due at Karl's at six thirty for pre-loading before we meet the gang in The Smugglers. And we'll grab a curry later.'

'I... I didn't realise you'd be out this evening,' said Valerie, her heart sinking. Not only had she bought lamb, she'd also made bread pudding because she knew how much her son loved it. She'd end up comfort-eating the whole lot and putting on even more weight.

'It's Karl's thirtieth and there's a big celebration. I thought I'd told you.'

'No,' said Valerie, feeling stiff and wooden. 'I'd have remembered if you had.'

She'd certainly have remembered that he was coming home for the first time in months for his friend's birthday, rather than his father's. He'd obviously rather spend time with his friends than his parents. Or his daughter, for that matter.

How on earth did Nessa put up with him for so long? The thought slid into Valerie's mind and took her breath away. She looked again at her son, feeling as if she was seeing him for the first time.

Jacob was dressed in what looked like new clothes, with an expensive haircut and branded trainers, while Nessa was scraping together hand-me-downs for herself and worrying about putting a roof over their daughter's head.

She *was* a good mother who cared about her child, thought Valerie, picking up a plate and scraping salad into the bin. In fact, Nessa cared so selflessly about Lily, she was willing to give her up. She'd agreed that Lily could move in with Valerie, even though Valerie could see that it would break her heart.

'Do you pay maintenance for Lily?' she asked, letting the lid close with a bang.

Jacob pouted. 'Where did that come from? Of course I do, and it's a fortune. Nessa really screwed me on that one.'

'How much? And do you pay regularly?'

'As regularly as I can. I might be a bit late sometimes.'

'And even miss the occasional payment?'

Jacob's face clouded over. 'What's Nessa been saying? It's a private arrangement between the two of us and I can't give her money I haven't got. Has she been dissing me to everyone?'

Valerie shook her head. 'No. She rarely says anything about you at all.'

And what she had said, Valerie had dismissed as untrue. But, she realised with a sickening lurch, Nessa was probably right. Jacob was only here this weekend to see his friends. He wasn't bothered about catching up with his family, or seeing his daughter. So why would he bother about being on time with money to support his child?

'It's just as well Ness isn't talking about me,' said Jacob with a laugh that went right through her. 'She can be a bit of a moaner.'

'I wouldn't blame her if she was. It's not easy being a single mother, you know.'

'I don't need a lecture, Mum. I send money when I can. All right?' countered Jacob, an unpleasant whine in his voice.

'But "when you can" doesn't pay the bills or the rent, does it?'

Jacob stared at his mother for a moment, as though deliberating whether to argue or not. Then he glanced at his watch, a new one by the look of it. Valerie hadn't seen it before.

'I'd better unpack and ring Karl to finalise plans for this evening. I'll see you later, Mum.' He walked over and kissed her on the head. 'You worry too much, you know.'

He walked out of the kitchen, leaving Valerie standing by

the sink. She looked out of the window, at the grass blowing in the breeze and the white-tipped waves in the distance on the grey sea.

She was such a fool. Her eyes filled with tears and she grabbed hold of the sink to steady herself. She loved Jacob. He was her son. But he wasn't the perfect person she'd built him up to be. He could be, in Nessa's words, a bit hopeless at times.

'Poor Lily,' said Valerie softly. Her father might not care enough about her, but at least she had a mother who cared enough for both parents.

And, thought Valerie, wiping her eyes with the back of her hand, Lily had a grandmother who would always do what was truly best for her precious grandchild.

THIRTY-EIGHT
NESSA

This was awkward. Nessa sat on the edge of the sofa, crossed her ankles and sipped the glass of Prosecco that Valerie had thrust into her hand the minute she'd arrived.

Sitting opposite her, Jake swallowed and rubbed his temples with his fingers. Valerie had told her he'd woken up with a headache. A hangover, more like, thought Nessa, recognising the signs. His skin was pale and his eyelids heavy, but at least he was spending time with Lily.

'Daddy, come into the garden,' she implored, bouncing up and down on her toes in front of him. 'Come and watch me go down the slide. And I can stand on my hands.'

'Wow!' said Jake unconvincingly. 'You go on into the garden. I can watch you through the glass from here.'

'But it would be much better if you went outside with her, don't you think?' said Valerie in a tone that brooked no argument.

Jake got to his feet with a scowl and swayed slightly, before following his excited daughter through the French windows.

What had she ever seen in him? wondered Nessa, watching him drop into a garden chair. He'd seemed so vibrant and full of endless possibilities when they'd first met. Now, he just seemed selfish and jaded.

'Thank you for changing your plans and dropping Lily off for a birthday lunch,' said Valerie, breaking into her thoughts.

'It wasn't a problem. You decided not to have a birthday tea, then?'

Valerie's face froze. 'Jacob has to get back to Manchester,' she said, her lips hardly moving. 'He's very busy, apparently.'

'Right.'

Nessa shifted on the sofa. She'd planned to drop Lily off and run and had been surprised when Valerie had insisted she come in. So surprised in fact, following their difficult conversation on the headland, that she'd meekly followed her indoors.

'I'm glad Lily's seeing her dad and we both wanted to wish Alan a happy birthday,' said Nessa, taking a huge gulp of wine.

Alan gave a grateful grunt. He was sitting in the corner, reading his Sunday newspaper, with a cardboard hat made by Lily perched on his head. He took a sip from the mug Lily had bought him that had *World's Best Grandad* plastered across it.

The mug was inexpensive and tacky but Nessa had been touched by how choked up Alan had seemed when he'd unwrapped it. Never a particularly tactile man, he'd pulled Lily in for a hug and had kissed her on the cheek.

It had filled Nessa with hope – hope that he wouldn't mind too much when Lily moved in with them on a more permanent basis. Though even thinking about that made Nessa's heart hurt.

She stood up and smoothed down her jeans. 'I'd better be going. Thank you for arranging for Lily to see Jake, and have a lovely birthday lunch, Alan. I'll come and pick up Lily later, and then...' She swallowed. 'I'll bring her round again tomorrow as planned.'

Lily could have moved in with her grandparents today, but

Nessa wanted one more night at Driftwood House with her daughter.

'I'll show you out,' said Valerie. She gave her husband a nod and he nodded back.

Nessa went into the kitchen and put her wine glass on the drainer next to the sink. Through the window, she could see Lily talking nineteen to the dozen at her father, who was still slumped in the garden chair, paler than ever.

'Jacob had a curry last night and I don't think it agreed with him.' Valerie had come to stand beside her and was looking at her son. 'It's a shame, when he doesn't see Lily very often.'

'It is,' agreed Nessa, biting down all the other things she could say about Valerie's son.

She'd said quite enough to Valerie the other day and, really, there was no point. It was better to accept things in life, rather than pointlessly rail against them. That's what Gabriel reckoned, and Nessa was so worn out with constantly striving, she was beginning to think he was right.

She'd railed against her mother dying so young, but her mum had died anyway. She'd fought to save the Ghost Village and the cottage from obliteration, but they would soon be demolished. And she'd fought to keep her daughter with her – even spending a month in a derelict cottage in the deluded hope that might prove to be the answer. But she had to let her go. And who knew if Lily would ever come back to live with her again?

Nessa glanced around Valerie's beautiful, clean kitchen. A five-year-old would never have wanted to live in a crumbling, isolated cottage. And she wouldn't choose to live in some damp bedsit miles from Heaven's Cove, either. Not when she could live here instead.

'I have something for you,' said Valerie quietly, pushing her fingers into an earthenware storage jar. She pulled out two silver keys, which she placed on the worktop in front of Nessa.

'What's this?'

'It's the keys to the flat above the ice-cream parlour. You told me that Lily would love to live there.'

'I don't understand,' said Nessa, distracted by Lily screaming with delight as she hurtled down the slide. 'I've heard it's lovely, but I can't afford the deposit on that place.'

'No, but we can. We save a little money every month for Lily, to go to her when she's older and needs it. But I had a talk with Alan about it yesterday afternoon. We properly talked. Like we used to.' Valerie's cheeks flushed pink. 'And he agreed with me that Lily needs it now. She needs a decent home with her mother. So I went and saw Magda this morning and had a look at the flat, which is perfect for the two of you. I've paid the deposit and sorted everything out. You and Lily can move in next week.'

Nessa held her breath, hardly able to believe what she was hearing. From Valerie, the woman who blamed her for driving away her precious son. The woman who wanted to claim Lily as her own.

'I don't understand,' she began. 'You want Lily to move in here with you and Alan.'

Valerie's smile was unbearably sad. 'I'd have loved that but it wasn't only for Lily's sake, it was for mine, too. I get... I get...' She took a deep breath. 'The truth is, I get lonely here and feel that life is passing me by. I miss my job and my son and my youth and my life with Alan, how it used to be. And having Lily here makes everything better. She doesn't judge me or upset me or find me a great disappointment.'

'She loves you, Valerie,' said Nessa, touched by her words. 'What's brought all this on? Is it because I upset you when we talked in the wood the other day? Maybe I shouldn't—'

Valerie silenced her with the wave of a hand. 'It had to be said. It was time I listened. And I'd told tales to Mr Gantwich, which I regret now.'

She looked out of the window at Jake, who was pushing Lily on the swing but paying her scant attention. He was too busy staring at the mobile phone in his other hand.

'He really hasn't turned out the way I thought he would, you know. I couldn't see it, but now...' She sighed. 'His behaviour as a father is disappointing but I still love him, and I dare say I'm a disappointment to him as a mother. I certainly was as a mother-in-law.' She turned to face Nessa and swallowed. 'I apologise for that. Being a single parent can't be easy and my attitude hasn't helped.'

She sniffed, her eyes bright with tears.

'You are such a huge help to me,' said Nessa, grabbing hold of Valerie's hands. 'Lily loves you and Alan. You're the only family she has – the only family who are around to give her the love she needs now that my gran's gone.' She sniffed back tears herself. 'Honestly, Valerie, I couldn't cope without you picking up Lily from school and giving her tea and taking her out on trips and having her to stay. You're a fantastic grandmother and I appreciate you and Alan so much. Lily and I both do.'

'That's very kind of you to say.' Valerie gently pulled her hands away. 'But we need to do more because Jacob isn't reliable. That's what Alan and I agreed and that's why the flat is yours, if you want it. I'd love Lily to live here with me but I've realised that's better for me, not for her. She needs to be with you.

'And if Jacob messes up with his maintenance money again and payments are late, let me know and we'll do our best to plug the gap. He's pleaded poverty to you in the past and I know he's moved from job to job over the last few years, and has been out of work occasionally, so that might be right.' She pulled her lips tight, as though it was hard to speak. 'But I think right now he's in a steady job and has more money than he's letting on. So we could support you with challenging him and setting up something more official. Anyway, that's for the future. The new flat is for now.'

Nessa's head was reeling. 'Thank you, Valerie. I appreciate everything you've said,' she spluttered, 'but I can't take your money.'

She left the keys to the flat on the worktop. They were the answer to a huge problem that kept her awake at nights, but she couldn't accept them.

'Yes you can, for Lily's sake. And in a way, it's not our money anyway. It was always meant for our beautiful grand-daughter. I mean it,' she added when Nessa looked doubtful. 'We want you and Lily to have the flat in the village. But I hope Lily can still come to stay sometimes.'

'Lots of times,' said Nessa, doing something she'd never thought she would in a million years. She stepped closer to Valerie and put her arms around her.

When Valerie stiffened, Nessa wondered if she'd gone too far. But then the older woman softened and put her arms around Nessa too. And as Nessa stood there, her cheek against Valerie's shoulder, she remembered how it had felt to be held close by her own mum, half a lifetime ago.

'Thank you,' she mumbled.

Valerie said nothing but squeezed her more tightly.

'What the hell's going on in here?' demanded Jake, bowling into the kitchen. He winced when the back door hit the wall with a thud. 'Has someone died or something?'

'My gran did, seven weeks ago,' said Nessa, not moving from Valerie's embrace.

'I know that.' Jake blinked as though he was finding it hard to focus.

Lily ran into the kitchen behind him and, with a giggle, ran to her mum and grandmother and threw her arms around the both of them.

'All right, sweetheart?' asked Valerie, reaching down to stroke her hair. 'Are you having fun with Daddy?'

'Daddy feels sick so he has to come in,' mumbled Lily into Nessa's waist. 'Silly Daddy.'

Silly Daddy indeed, thought Nessa as Jake stood in the corner of the kitchen, watching the group hug but not a part of it. He didn't know what he could have. He didn't know what he was missing.

THIRTY-NINE
GABRIEL

She's here. Gabriel felt his heartbeat quicken at the sight of Nessa.

He'd sent her a text yesterday: *Work starts at Ghost Village tomorrow. Please be there at ten. G*

It was brief but he'd spent five minutes composing it, all the same. Adding and subtracting words, wondering if he should tell her why he wanted her to be there.

Her phone call the other day had sounded like a line in the sand. *I've apologised to ease my conscience and now I'm moving on.*

She was through with men from London who arrived out of the blue to turn her life upside down. Men so out of touch with their emotions, they didn't have a clue about what was truly important in life.

But he wanted her here. So he'd sent his text and she'd read it and sent back just five words: *If I can make it.*

She hadn't railed against the work starting or asked why she should be there, and that made him sad. Nessa had been so worn down by disappointment and loss in her short life, she seemed resigned to more.

She was here to say a last goodbye to the Ghost Village that she loved. Or perhaps she hoped he'd found a way to save her great-grandmother's mosaic from the wrecking ball.

Either way, she was here, and he was grateful to see her one last time.

She was sitting on the grass above Sorrel Cove, her knees pulled up under her chin. Her long dark hair was flying in the breeze blowing off the sea.

Nessa, staring out across the sparkling blue water, didn't notice him approaching until he'd almost reached her.

'Where did you come from?' she demanded, scrambling to her feet. Her cheeks flushed adorably pink as she pushed hair from her eyes.

'I parked in Heaven's Cove and walked over the headland,' he told her, noticing the gold snake bracelet bright against her suntanned skin.

It might help that Nessa was here when Amelia Fulden arrived. Amelia, the woman he'd rung from his Mediterranean beach, might just change everything.

He checked his watch and squinted into the distance. She should be here soon.

He hadn't told Nessa anything about Amelia or about his plan, such as it was. He worried that she'd be disappointed in him all over again when it failed. *If* it failed, he told himself, trying to stay positive.

'Well, you shouldn't creep up on people like that. You frightened the life out of me,' said Nessa.

'Sorry.' He gave her what he hoped was a wry grin. 'So you came, then.'

'I did. I was glad to get your text.'

'Why?' he asked, holding his breath. Had she been thinking about him? Missing him, perhaps?

'I wanted to say goodbye to the Ghost Village and I wasn't sure what was happening when.'

He breathed out slowly, disappointment blooming. She hadn't thought about seeing him at all. She was only interested in the cottage and the ruined village that was about to be obliterated.

'So what *will* happen?' she asked. 'Will diggers arrive and start demolishing everything?'

He nodded, hating the flash of sorrow in her eyes. 'I think so. I've been out of the office for the last week so I haven't been involved in the arrangements. I did wonder if you were going to come along with a placard or lie down in front of the diggers,' he said, trying to lift her mood.

Nessa smiled. 'I thought about it but when I mentioned placards to Rosie, she gave me a good talking to, about letting things go. Accepting life rather than railing against it. I think someone else told me that once.' She gave him a sideways glance. 'Anyway, here I am, placard-less. Just as well because I need to pick Lily up from school later and I can't do that if I'm in a police cell for obstruction. Your dad seems the type to press charges.'

'You're probably right.'

Gabriel glanced at Sorrel Cove to make sure his father was here. He hadn't seen him since their disagreement at the cottage, but he knew Billy liked to be on site on the first day of a project. The thrill of the chase was over, the deal was done, and work was about to begin.

There he was, kitted out in a high-vis jacket, talking to his site foreman amid the ruins of the Ghost Village.

Gabriel glanced at his watch again. The first diggers could arrive at any moment so he had to move fast. Where on earth was Amelia? She'd said she'd be here by now.

Nessa, standing beside him, cleared her throat.

'I know I said it on the phone but I'm sorry I thought you'd told your dad about me leaving the cottage that night.'

'I think my father might have implied it was me.'

'He did, but I shouldn't have believed him so easily. Not after we... I mean...'

She trailed off, pressing her lips together. The lips that Gabriel had kissed. Was he staring at her mouth? He was definitely staring at her mouth.

'It's all right,' he said gruffly, dragging his gaze away and focusing on the dust coating his shoes. Anything to divert his attention away from Nessa because he desperately wanted to sweep her into his arms and kiss away the worry lines on her forehead.

But he had a plan to carry out, and a conversation to have with his father, and his feelings for Nessa were nothing but a ridiculous notion.

Her impression of him might have gone up a notch since she'd found out he hadn't told tales to his father. But every time she saw luxury apartments where the Ghost Village had once been, she'd think of him as an interfering out-of-towner who'd stamped on her hopes and dreams.

What she didn't realise was that she'd ignited hopes and dreams in *him* that were buried beneath years of corporate responsibility. Was he brave enough to stand up and see them through?

'Is that them?' asked Nessa, pointing at two lorries that had turned onto the narrow, pot-holed road that led to Sorrel Cove.

'Yes.'

Gabriel's heart started pounding. His plan was going wrong from the start. In fact, it wouldn't get off the ground at all if Amelia let him down.

'That's it, then,' said Nessa, her shoulders slumped. 'Do you think you can save the mosaic at least?'

'I'm not sure,' said Gabriel, his mind jumping ahead.

What could he do if Amelia let him down? He could always lie down in front of the diggers. His father wouldn't have him arrested... would he? Probably not. But he'd ship him off to some 'spa' instead, for psychological assessment.

Nessa was shifting from foot to foot. 'I'm afraid I can't watch this. I thought I'd be OK but I'm not. I need to leave.'

'Please don't,' said Gabriel, his hand shooting out and grabbing her arm before he could think it through. Her smooth skin was warm beneath his fingers, and he didn't want to let go.

'Gabriel, is that you?'

His father's shout reverberated through the air as the growl of the lorries carrying the diggers got closer.

Gabriel let go of Nessa. It was all too late. Too late for the Ghost Village and the cottage that Nessa loved. Too late for him to have a different life.

'Who's that?' asked Nessa, squinting into the distance.

A car was approaching, through a cloud of dust. It stopped next to the lorries, which had parked and switched off their engines.

A short woman with grey hair stepped from the car and walked briskly towards him. 'Mr Gantwich? Apologies for my late arrival but I got caught in traffic. It's wonderful living in Devon but the world and his wife want to visit us in summer.' She thrust out her hand.

'Please call me Gabriel, and thank you for coming.'

Gabriel shook her hand, not sure if the butterflies in his chest were nerves or excitement. He couldn't back down now. And whatever happened in the next ten minutes, his life was about to change irrevocably. His father would never forgive him, whatever the outcome.

'What's going on?' asked Nessa, looking between Amelia and Gabriel.

He stared into her eyes, keen to get this over with. 'Just trust me. Please.'

Would she trust him? Nessa didn't say a word but she

followed him and Amelia when they walked into the heart of the ruined village, towards his father.

Billy ended the call he was on and gave a self-satisfied grin. 'I knew you'd be back, Gabriel, after you'd had a chance to calm down.' He glanced over his son's shoulder and his face clouded over. 'What's *she* doing here, and who's this?'

Gabriel took a deep breath. 'This is Amelia Fulden, who's here because I invited her. She's an archaeologist.'

'An archaeologist? Why is...' His father trailed off, understanding dawning in his eyes. He turned to Gabriel. 'Really?'

'Yes, really. I thought she should see the mosaic in the cottage before the building's demolished.'

'That bizarre thing on the wall? Why?' Billy turned to Amelia and gave her a broad smile. 'I'm sure Ms Fulden has more pressing matters to attend to. Proper work, rather than looking at questionable art by a woman long dead.'

But Amelia Fulden was obviously not a woman to be put off by the likes of Billy Gantwich. She smiled back, a hint of steel in her blue eyes. 'It's no problem at all. It'll only take a couple of minutes.'

'Follow me,' said Gabriel, leading the way to the cottage and feeling his father's eyes boring into his back the entire way.

'Gosh, you've done a good job with starting to renovate this place,' said Amelia, stepping over the threshold into the cottage. 'What a shame it's due to be demolished. Now, let's see this mosaic you called me about, Gabriel?'

Nessa sidled up to Gabriel as Amelia stood close to the mosaic, her nose almost touching the brightly coloured stones and smooth pebbles of glass.

'What are you doing?' she whispered.

'I'm following a hunch,' he answered out of the corner of his mouth.

'What kind of a hunch?'

Amelia was still standing nose-to-stone with the mosaic.

Gabriel pulled Nessa into the kitchen.

'Your grandmother said her mum would use whatever she found to make her art, and when you asked me to try and save the mosaic it got me thinking. I've had a week off work so I was able to do some research. The artwork looks so old and unusual.'

'It is old. My great-grandmother would have been well over a hundred if she was still alive.'

'No, much older than that. And, the more I thought about it, the more I wondered if she'd found the stones and the glass here, in the Ghost Village.'

Nessa opened her mouth and then shut it again, confusion in her eyes. 'So what are you thinking? Do you—'

She didn't get a chance to finish her sentence because Amelia suddenly proclaimed loudly: 'Well, I never! That *is* surprising.'

Gabriel and Nessa scurried out of the kitchen.

'Surprising in a good way?' asked Gabriel, hearing the heavy tread of his father coming into the cottage behind him.

'Oh yes, definitely in a good way. I thought you must be mistaken when you rang and invited me here. But at first glance, I'd say the materials used by... was it your great-grandmother?' she asked Nessa, who nodded. 'Many of the materials she's used appear, at first glance, to be fragments of tesserae. That is, stone and glass used by the Romans to construct mosaics at their grand houses. Did you know that the Romans settled in Devon during the first century? Exeter was a walled town.'

'So what does that mean, if there are fragments of tesserae?' asked Nessa, her voice wobbly.

Amelia clapped her hands together. 'It means there could be something hidden here, beneath the soil, which is potentially very exciting. Isn't that wonderful? We didn't think there was anything of significance in this area but it appears we may have been mistaken.' She turned to Billy, who was listening in. 'What exactly have you got planned here?'

'Housing. Luxury apartments. Have you seen where we are? People will pay through the nose for that view.'

Amelia raised an eyebrow. 'Do you have planning permission?'

'Not yet,' bristled Billy. 'But I've been told unofficially that it'll definitely get the green light. Similar housing is being put up all along the coast.'

'Well, in light of what I've just seen, I'd insist on a comprehensive survey before any permission was granted, to ensure there's nothing of value beneath the soil.'

'Which means delays,' huffed Billy, his cheeks turning purple. 'All for a few bits of old stone that might not have come from here anyway.'

'My great-grandmother didn't travel far,' said Nessa, stepping forward. 'She used what materials she could find around here to do her art.'

'Damn artists,' huffed Billy, staring at Gabriel, who tried not to flinch under his father's hostile glare. 'If you don't know where the materials came from, I don't see that I should change my plans for a few bits of old stone and glass.'

'What's that on your arm?' asked Amelia abruptly, staring at Nessa.

The archaeologist's face was very peculiar. Her cheeks had turned bright red and her eyes were open wide. She looked like she was about to explode.

When she rushed across the room, almost stumbling in her haste, Nessa took a step towards Gabriel. But Amelia grabbed hold of her arm and pulled it towards her.

'Where did you get this?' she demanded, staring at the bangle that encircled Nessa's wrist. The golden snake was glinting in light streaming through the window.

'It was a gift from my late grandmother. She was given it by her mother.'

'The same woman who made this exquisite mosaic? And

where did *she* get it?' asked Amelia, carefully slipping the bangle over Nessa's fingers.

'I'm not exactly sure. She found it.'

'*Where* did she find it?' demanded Amelia, cradling the bracelet in her palm as if it were her first-born.

'My gran always believed her mum found the bracelet when she was digging the garden.'

'And where was this garden?' asked Amelia, not taking her eyes from the golden snake in her hands.

'Here. They had a garden at the back of the cottage, where it's sheltered by the headland from the worst of the winds.'

'In that case we'll definitely be doing a survey of this area, Mr Gantwich, because...' Amelia swallowed, the blush on her cheeks even brighter. 'If I'm right, this is a rare Roman bracelet from around the first century A.D. I've only ever seen anything like it in books.' She looked up at Nessa, her eyes shining. 'Did you have any idea of what you were wearing around your wrist?'

'No, I mean, that is...' Nessa paused, stunned by Amelia's revelation. 'I've always loved the bracelet but my family thought it was a piece of inexpensive jewellery, dropped and forgotten by someone who'd lived here before them. A little while before them, that is. Not two thousand years before them. My gran told me it was gold-plated brass.'

'Your grandmother was wrong about that,' said Amelia. 'I believe this bracelet is solid gold and precious historically as well as in monetary terms. It's quite remarkable.' She turned the bracelet over in her palm. 'Would you allow me to let an expert in Roman jewellery examine the bracelet?'

'Of course you can examine it. I'd love to know more because it meant so much to my gran.'

'Yes, that's all fine and dandy,' Billy butted in. 'But where does that leave me? I've got diggers here and men ready to start work.'

Amelia turned to him, her expression hardening. 'I would advise you very strongly to hold off from any work on this site until we've discovered more about the significance of what I've seen today.'

'And if I don't?'

Amelia reached into her handbag and brought out an identity card, which she flashed at Billy. 'As you can see, I'm a professor of archaeology, and I occasionally advise the local authority on planning matters. It could cause you and your business all sorts of difficulties if it transpires there's a site of national significance beneath our feet and your diggers cause damage to it.' She put her hands on her hips. 'The publicity alone would be dreadful, don't you think?'

Amelia Fulden meant business, thought Gabriel, and his father knew it.

Billy turned his back on Amelia and spoke directly to his son, his voice dangerously low and quiet. 'I'd like to have a word with you in private, Gabriel. Perhaps Ms Fulden and Ms Paulson could leave us?'

'Of course,' said Amelia. 'I'm keen to talk more with this young lady about her great-grandmother and the provenance of the bracelet. I trust you won't be starting any work, Mr Gantwich?'

Billy's head twitched as though the words were being forced from him but he replied, 'It appears that my hands are tied so there will be no work, for the time being.'

'Would you like me to stay?' whispered Nessa to Gabriel as Amelia left the cottage.

He shook his head. 'No, you go and speak to Amelia and I'll join you in a minute.'

When the front door banged shut behind them, the room was plunged into semi-gloom.

'Well, Gabriel.' Billy walked to the window ledge and ran his finger along the stone. 'I appear to have underestimated you.'

'You've always underestimated me,' said Gabriel quietly.

'Perhaps. You certainly showed some backbone inviting that archaeologist along today. You must have known how it would end, whatever she thought of that absurd artwork on the wall.'

'Yes,' said Gabriel sadly. 'Think of it as my letter of resignation.'

Billy paused and rubbed stone dust from his finger. Then he turned to his son.

'Your resignation? All of this for a ruined village and a girl who isn't worth it?'

'But she *is* worth it,' said Gabriel. 'She has more integrity than anyone I've ever known, and more determination. But I'm not doing this for her, not completely. I'm doing this for me.'

'Don't tell me,' Billy snorted, 'you're going to...' He formed air quotes with his fingers. '... "find yourself".'

'If you like,' said Gabriel, surprised by the calm that had crept over him. This was hard but it was the right thing to do. He knew that down to his bones. 'I've never wanted to disappoint you, Dad, but I have and I'll continue to do so because I'm not cut out for your world. But James is. He's your successor, not me. Deep down, surely you must know that?'

Billy stared at his son for a moment, then he sat with a *whump* on the window ledge, all of the fight gone out of him.

'So you're leaving. It looks like you've won, after all.'

'It's not about winning and losing. But if I stay with the family firm, we both lose anyway. I'll be discontented and you'll be disappointed. But if I go, I hope I can carve out a happier life for myself doing something that I'm better at and maybe one day you won't be disappointed in me any longer.'

'Good grief.' Billy's face suddenly crumpled and he wiped a hand across his eyes. 'Have I been such a terrible father to you?'

'God, no.' Gabriel went to his side and awkwardly put his hand on his father's shoulder. 'You brought me up after Mum left and gave me the chance of a life like yours – a comfortable and privileged life. But I'm a different person from you and it's not the kind of life I want.'

'You were all right before you came to this godforsaken place and met that woman.'

'No, I wasn't. I was trying hard to fit in and hating myself for being discontented when I had so much. But being here in this beautiful place and seeing how Nessa lives her life made me realise why I was so unhappy. It made me believe that maybe I can have something different. Be someone different.' He raked a hand through his hair. 'Can you understand that? This isn't about you. This is about me.'

That was the kind of crass thing people said when they broke up, and Gabriel steeled himself for his father's derision. But Billy merely nodded and sniffed. He pulled a white handkerchief from his pocket and rubbed it across his nose.

'So you're going, then,' he said gruffly. 'Will you stay in London?'

Gabriel shook his head. 'I don't think so. I'll sell up and move away. I need to make a fresh start.'

'A fresh start away from your family.'

'Away from my family business, not away from my family. We can still see each other. If that's what you'd like.'

'Will you stay in Heaven's Cove?'

'No, I don't think so. It would be too hard... I mean, with Nessa... She doesn't care...' Gabriel stopped speaking and pulled himself together before carrying on. 'Anyway, I hope you'll come and see me wherever I end up.'

Billy swung round and looked out of the window, at the piles of stone where people's homes had once stood, before the sea had ripped away their dreams.

'She does care,' he said quietly.

'What did you say?' Gabriel stepped closer.

His father turned back to him. 'I said, that girl does care about you. I might not be in touch with my emotions, or whatever people say these days, but I've seen the way she looks at you. There was a time when your mother looked at me like that.'

Gabriel swallowed, his head fizzing with more emotion than he could handle. Could his father be right? His distant, emotionless father – who was showing a side of himself right now that Gabriel had never seen before.

'Will you build here?' asked Gabriel, changing the subject because he wasn't sure what else to say.

Billy shook his head. 'I doubt it. Your archaeology woman will put a delay on everything, and my heart has rather gone out of the project. I'll move on and build somewhere else.'

'I've spotted a new site that's perfect, a few miles along the coast. It's got views to die for and no sitting tenants to complicate matters,' said Gabriel, twisting his mouth into a grin.

'Is that right? Perhaps you should stay and see that project through?'

Gabriel shook his head. 'No, I don't think so. But I'll email you all the particulars so you and James can swoop in and make a killing.'

Billy stared at his feet. 'Things won't be the same without you, Gabriel. I've only ever wanted the best for you.'

'I know. But it'll be better in the long run for both of us, you'll see.'

He put out his hand for his father to shake. For a fleeting moment, he thought his dad might pull him in for a hug. But some things never changed. Billy curled his fingers around his son's and shook his hand.

'Well,' he said gruffly. 'You'd better go and see that girl and then tell the lorry drivers to return to base with the diggers. I'll stay in here for a bit longer.'

Gabriel hesitated. Should he say anything more? But his father had turned his back and was staring out of the window at the flotsam being pushed by grey waves towards the shore.

FORTY
NESSA

Nessa paced between the stones, out of sight of the cottage. She didn't want Billy to think she was spying on him. Even though he'd got his son to spy on her.

He had! He'd got his son to keep tabs on her, day and night, so she was totally within her rights to see what he was up to now. And she hated the thought of Gabriel facing his father's wrath on his own.

She could hardly believe what Gabriel had done. She stroked the bracelet on her wrist. He'd put his job and his relationship with his father on the line. His father would be furious with him, and she was going to find out what was going on. Even if that meant listening at the back door.

Nessa had started circling round to the back of the cottage when the front door opened and Gabriel strode out.

He looked shell-shocked, his face pale and his eyes tired. He walked straight to the edge of the land and gazed out across the ocean.

Did he want to be alone? Nessa stood still, not sure what to do. But he cut such a lonely figure, outlined against the swell of the sea. So lonely, she couldn't bear it.

'Are you all right?' she asked, walking over and standing beside him, the breeze coming in off the sea lifting her hair.

Gabriel nodded, his eyes still fixed on the horizon. 'I will be.'

'Was it awful with your dad?'

'Not really. I thought he'd be furious but actually he was sad. And that was harder to bear.'

When Gabriel turned to look at her, Nessa's heart broke. Vulnerability was etched across the face of this incomprehensible man. He'd driven her to distraction. He thought she was ridiculous. And yet he'd kissed her. And today he'd wrecked everything that mattered in his life to save what mattered in hers.

'What's happening about your job?'

'I've left the family firm by mutual consent with immediate effect.'

Nessa's breath caught in her throat. 'He sacked you?'

'No, I resigned. In effect, I resigned the moment I rang Amelia and told her about my suspicions.'

'I can't believe you did that.' Nessa moved a little closer until her arm grazed his. '*Why* did you do that?'

'Because of this place, because I didn't want something beautiful under the soil to be destroyed, because it was time for me to move on and make a different life. Because of...' He stopped talking and turned his face back towards the sea.

'So what will you do now?'

'I'm not sure. Something to do with art. Somewhere away from London. I can sell my flat, which will give me a financial cushion for a while.'

'I'm sorry.'

'Why are *you* sorry?'

'I'm sorry that standing up for me and the Ghost Village has cost you so much.'

Gabriel shrugged. 'It was time to make a change. And you

helped me with that.' He scuffed his feet into the grass. 'So what about you? I see you're still wearing the Roman bracelet.'

Nessa grinned. 'Amelia's sending some security firm to pick it up and transport it to her Roman jewellery expert. She had kittens that I'm still wearing it, but I've promised not to let it out of my sight. She was reassured by the fact I've kept it safe for this long. So I'd better not drop it in the sea by accident.'

Gabriel snorted. 'I think Amelia would literally kill you.'

'Probably. She's quite scary. My gran would never believe that the bracelet she loved was two thousand years old. I can hardly believe it myself.'

'Me neither. That was the icing on the cake.'

'Did you know what my great-grandmother's mosaic really was?'

'No. But I had a feeling about it.'

'A hunch?'

His mouth twitched. 'Definitely a hunch. I was dragged round dozens of museums as a child by a succession of bored au pairs, so maybe all that enforced culture finally paid off. The research I did, during my time off, seemed to confirm my suspicions. But I wasn't sure until Amelia got excited.'

'Boy, did she get excited!'

'Mmm.' Gabriel nodded. 'How's Lily doing?'

'She's fine. She misses you.'

'Really?'

When he smiled at her, Nessa felt her heart flip. She would miss this man, too.

'She's happy because Valerie's come up trumps and has helped me and her to get a decent flat in the middle of Heaven's Cove.'

He beamed. 'Wow, that's great. Was it a guilty conscience on Valerie's part after consorting with my dad?'

'Maybe.' Nessa remembered the hug in Valerie's kitchen, as Jake stood by. 'I think she's finally realised that the sun doesn't shine out of Jake's backside. Anyway, she's being kind to me, just like you.'

Gabriel raised an eyebrow. 'I wasn't always kind to you.'

'I think we were unkind to each other, to begin with. But you've certainly redeemed yourself. I'm not sure that I have.'

He paused, his face more serious. 'You've changed my whole life, Nessa.'

'That's what I mean. Before you met me, you had a posh job and amazing prospects. Now you have neither.' Guilt and shame coursed through her. 'I was so single-minded about doing what was best for me and Lily, I didn't give you enough thought. I'm sorry.'

His eyes met hers. 'You really need to stop apologising. I'm a grown-up, Nessa, and I made my decisions knowing the consequences. And it felt good to make decisions about my life, rather than have decisions made for me.'

'So what happens to the cottage and the Ghost Village now?'

'Nothing. Whatever Amelia does, my dad has lost interest in the project and is moving on.'

'So you've saved this place?' Nessa was talking too loudly, almost shouting. But she didn't care. Gabriel had done something wonderful. 'I can't believe what you've done, Gabriel. You're amazing.'

Without thinking, she threw her arms around his neck and hugged him, her cheek against his collarbone and her lips close to the bare skin at the hollow of his neck.

I could kiss that skin, she thought. But he was leaving Heaven's Cove and she had to be careful with her heart.

She went to move away but his arms slid around her waist.

'Nessa,' he said gruffly, his chin resting against her hair. 'I can't stop thinking about you. You drove me crazy when we first met, and you're doing the same now but for very different reasons. I know I'm not your type. But you kissed me and I have to know if you regret that, before I leave for good. I need to know how you feel about me.'

Nessa breathed out slowly, savouring the heat of Gabriel's skin against her cheek. Then she looked up into his eyes. 'I feel... I feel...' There were no words to describe the maelstrom of emotions inside her. So she kissed him instead.

Gabriel's lips were warm and she felt his fingers lace through her hair.

They kissed as seagulls wheeled overhead and sunlight burst through the sea spray, shattering the droplets into tiny rainbows.

At last, they pulled apart.

'That's how I feel,' said Nessa simply.

When she leaned her head against his shoulder, he pulled her close and they stood looking out to sea.

The water, pale blue at the horizon, was translucent closer to shore, and Nessa watched fish dart among slabs of stone that had once formed people's homes. Before the storm came and the sea rose up and her family's fortunes were changed forever.

But today the waves were gentle and the Ghost Village was calm and she felt at peace as she stood here, with Gabriel's arm around her.

'Do you think you might consider staying in Heaven's Cove?' she asked after a while.

'There's nowhere I'd rather be,' said Gabriel, and then he bent his head and kissed her again.

EPILOGUE

NESSA, FOUR MONTHS LATER

'There you go,' said Nessa, securing the brown-paper wrapping with a piece of sticky tape. 'That should get your painting home safe and sound. Have you got far to go?'

'Far enough,' said the woman, frowning at her two children who were squabbling in a corner of the shop. 'We're travelling back to Leicester this afternoon but this...' She picked up the large wrapped picture and put it under her arm. 'This will remind me of our stay here in Heaven's Cove.'

'You've been fortunate to have some winter sunshine during your visit.'

'We've been very lucky,' said the woman, shepherding her boys through the shop door. The air was filled with the peal of bells from the village church, calling people to Sunday morning service. The woman closed the door and gave a wave before chasing her boys along the road.

Behind her, Nessa heard the back door to the shop open and Gabriel's familiar tread. Two arms snaked around her waist and he planted a kiss on the side of her neck.

'Hello, gorgeous,' he said in his low voice.

She twisted round in his arms until they were face to face and planted a kiss on his mouth. 'Wow, you're all painty.'

'Sorry.' He grimaced at his white T-shirt that was splattered with pinpricks of colour, and released her from his embrace. 'I was finishing off my picture of the castle. I can't get the light right, but I'm almost there.'

'Talking of paintings, I have some good news. Guess which painting I just sold.'

Gabriel scanned the walls of the shop that displayed paintings of all sizes. Bright splodges of wildflowers, muted seascapes, swathes of Dartmoor fading into a purple horizon, and pastel pictures of quaint cottages.

He noticed a gap on the wall, towards the back of the store, and his mouth fell open.

'You're kidding me!'

'Nope.' Nessa linked her arm through his, for the simple reason that she liked to be as close to him as possible. 'I wouldn't joke about something like that.'

'Who bought it?'

'A woman from Leicester. She said she thought it was powerful and beautiful and it would remind her of this place.'

'I can't believe she chose it from amongst all of these.'

Gabriel waved his arm at the other paintings, all done by talented Devon artists. Then he gave Nessa a beaming smile that made her tingle right down to her toes.

Being a part-time business owner and a part-time painter suited Gabriel. He'd grown his hair longer, ditched his suits in favour of jeans and sweatshirts, and he was more relaxed. 'More myself' was how he liked to describe it to Nessa, when she marvelled at his transformation.

But he'd also proved himself a canny businessman since taking over the premises of Shelley's and turning the former hardware store into an art shop-cum-gallery.

It was hard work – the shop was open all week, including

Sunday mornings. But his first excellent action on opening the business had been to hire Nessa and, with her help, he was hosting exhibitions, running viewing evenings and organising painting workshops.

He'd become a part of Heaven's Cove already and Nessa couldn't imagine her life without him.

'I think we should go out to celebrate,' he said, picking Nessa up and twirling her round until she begged him to put her down.

She laughed, her head against his chest. 'What about Lily?'

'She can come too, or maybe Valerie would like to have her round for Sunday lunch? We could drop her over when the shop closes later. What do you reckon? Can you text her?'

'You can ask her yourself,' said Nessa, as the shop door opened and Valerie walked in. She smiled at the two of them, entwined behind the counter.

'What are you two up to?'

'Celebrating,' said Nessa. 'One of Gabriel's paintings has sold this morning.'

'Well, that's excellent news. Which one?'

'The painting of Sorrel Cove, with the cottage in the background,' said Nessa proudly before Gabriel could answer. 'The one that showed a storm rolling in across the sea.'

'I'm not surprised,' said Valerie, smiling broadly. 'It was very atmospheric.'

Valerie smiled a lot more these days. She said that was due to working part time in the art shop, which gave her a new focus, and Alan getting up off his backside, following a frank chat with his wife, and helping more about the house.

Nessa felt her change in mood was also helped by the shed-load of hormones she'd started taking after being persuaded, finally, to speak to her GP.

'I wanted to nip in to let you know that Jacob's coming to stay next weekend,' said Valerie, peering at the latest addition to the shop – a vibrant painting of narrow Devon lanes edged by high hedges. 'Gosh, I didn't realise there were so many different shades of green.'

'Lily will be pleased to see her dad,' said Nessa, though she wouldn't believe her ex was coming to Heaven's Cove until she saw him in person.

Jake was still a flaky father to Lily but Gabriel had started to fill the gap in her life. Lily adored him and the two of them were thick as thieves.

At first Nessa had worried about it, concerned that Gabriel's burgeoning relationship with Lily might upset Valerie. She doubted that Jake would much care.

But when she'd tentatively mentioned her concerns, Valerie had simply said, 'Lily needs a father figure, and it's Jacob's loss. He'll be sorry one day.' She'd looked sad for a while, until Lily had raced over, given her a hug and assured her she was the 'bestest granny in the whole wide world'. That had cheered her up.

'I'm about to collect Lily from Olive's. She's been over to play this morning,' said Nessa, pushing her arms into her winter coat, 'and I wondered, well, we wondered actually—'

'If there was any chance of her coming round to yours for Sunday lunch?' said Gabriel, butting in.

He gave Valerie his best hangdog expression and she laughed, unable to resist him. 'I'm always happy to see Lily and I just happen to be cooking chicken, which is her favourite. I'd love to have her round, and maybe...?' She glanced at Nessa. 'If Lily wants to, maybe she could stay over and I'll take her to school in the morning?'

'I'll ask her, but I'm sure she'd love to,' answered Nessa, already planning to take advantage of Lily's absence and stay over at Gabriel's tonight.

He lived alone above the shop, and Nessa and Lily were happily settled in the flat that Valerie had secured for them. But he and Nessa seemed to spend a lot of nights at each other's places.

Sometimes in the dead of night, when the wind whistled through Heaven's Cove, Nessa would lie awake next to Gabriel, remembering how she used to feel about him, back when he was spying on her in the Ghost Village. Before he changed his whole life, and hers too.

And she'd snuggle up to him, with her head on his chest, and thank her lucky stars that he was her type after all, and she was his.

An hour after dropping Lily off with Valerie, Nessa stopped at the top of the track that led down to the Ghost Village. She pulled her scarf tighter around her neck. It was a bright day but the salty air was cold in her lungs.

'Do you think they've found anything else?' she asked, pushing her arm through Gabriel's. 'They still seem to be excavating over there.'

She pointed at a trench that ran from the side of her great-grandmother's cottage towards the rise of the land.

So far, the scanning and excavation had been a great success and a beautiful mosaic floor had appeared from beneath the ground at the back of the cottage. The soil covering it had been carefully brushed away by a host of archaeology students.

Amelia had been beside herself when she'd seen the floor completely uncovered. She'd invited Nessa and Gabriel to view it and had cried as she'd explained just how historically important it was. She'd cried, too, when delivering the news to Nessa that her bracelet was indeed a prized piece of Roman jewellery.

It had pride of place, now, in the museum in Exeter, where it glinted under the lighting in its display case. A sign next to it read: ON LOAN. GRATEFUL THANKS TO NESSA, RUTH AND MARIANA PAULSON OF SORREL COVE. Nessa was happy for the museum to have it on permanent loan, but had insisted on the wording.

'Look, there's Amelia,' said Gabriel, giving her a wave.

Amelia, Nessa had realised, was one of those people whose toughness hid an emotional core. Just like Gabriel, who, after years of steeling himself to be hard and corporate, was slowly revealing his soft centre.

She felt softer these days, too, after years of building up a tough shell around herself. Gabriel's love for her was smoothing off her rough edges. Her grandmother would approve.

Amelia caught sight of them and waved back, a trowel in her hand.

'I'm pretty sure she's moved into the cottage for a while because she hates being away from the site,' said Gabriel.

Nessa noticed smoke drifting from the chimney and smiled. 'I do hope so. It's nice to think there's someone living there.'

'What are the chances that she'll go home to her cosy bed before too long though?'

'Pretty high, I'd have thought,' said Nessa, trying to give Gabriel's arm a pinch but failing to penetrate the thick wool of his pea coat. 'Only an idiot would contemplate living there long term.'

'Yep. Only an adorable idiot.' Gabriel leaned down and kissed the tip of her cold nose.

Nessa grinned. 'I know it's only a building at the end of the day.'

'Really?' Gabriel raised his eyebrows.

'Yes, I can see things more clearly now. Now life isn't so...' She searched for the right word. 'Awful. But I'm still glad that it's not going to be smashed into rubble.'

Amelia hoped the site would either be opened up to the public to view the Roman remains, in which case the cottage could double as a visitor centre, or, if that proved impractical, that the mosaic floor would be documented and covered again in soil, to protect it from the elements.

Either would be fine, but Nessa rather hoped that the intricate mosaic would once more return to the land. She liked the thought of it sitting undisturbed, an echo of people long gone. Just as the tumbled-down stones on the surface, and her great-grandmother's beautiful artwork on the cottage wall, told of a more recent civilisation that had disappeared.

'Oh, I've got some news,' said Gabriel. 'My dad emailed just before we came out. He said he's down this way on business next week and he'd like to call into the shop, if we don't mind.'

Nessa glanced at Gabriel, whose cheeks were pink with cold. 'Do *you* mind?'

'No, I don't think so. He's coming round to the idea that I have a different life now, and he tells me that James is doing well. I'd like to show him what I've done and what I have.' He planted another kiss on Nessa's nose. 'He also sent something for you.'

'For me?'

'There's an attachment, look.'

Nessa took Gabriel's phone and skimmed through his father's email. It was brief to the point of brusqueness, but Nessa noticed an X after he'd signed off 'Dad'. Billy had sent his son a kiss. It was a start.

A postscript to the email said: *The attached is for that infuriating woman.*

'Nice,' said Nessa, raising an eyebrow. 'I'm not sure your father's coming round to the idea of me.'

But when she opened the attachment and read the document that Gabriel's father had sent, she put her hand to her mouth.

'What is it? I knew I should have read it first. What's he done now?'

'Something wonderful,' she spluttered, passing the phone

back to Gabriel. 'He's donated the land here to Amelia's archae-
ological trust.'

'Donated? For free?' Gabriel read through the document,
his brow furrowed, then he grinned. 'Well, who'd have thought
it? The old man does have a heart after all. Though, thinking
about it, he can probably offset the donation against tax or something similar. I bet his accountant—'

'It doesn't matter,' said Nessa quickly. 'I don't care why he's
done it, only that he has.'

Nessa gazed at the Ghost Village, nestling on the edge of
the land. She could hardly believe it. This precious place was
now safeguarded forever. She pushed her hand into Gabriel's
and felt his fingers tighten around hers.

The wind picked up and began to swirl around them,
bringing with it a whisper of the past.

'We did it,' she murmured to the ghosts of Sorrel Cove.
'Sleep well.'

Dear reader

Thank you so much for reading *The Key to the Last House Before the Sea*. I loved bringing Nessa and Gabriel together – and saving the Ghost Village, of course – and hope you enjoyed the book.

If you did, you can find out about my new releases by signing up at the following link. Your email address will never be shared (so you don't need to worry about spam) and you can unsubscribe at any time.

www.bookouture.com/liz-eeles

Can I ask a favour? I'd love it if you'd write a review of *The Key to the Last House Before the Sea* – short or long, whichever most suits what you'd like to say. I'd like to know what you think, and reviews are so helpful when new readers are deciding whether or not to dip into the Heaven's Cove series.

Talking of the series, if this is your first visit to Driftwood House, there are another three Heaven's Cove novels you might like to read: *Secrets at the Last House Before the Sea, A Letter to the Last House Before the Sea* and *The Girl at the Last House Before the Sea*. They're all standalone stories, full of mystery and romance, featuring a host of new characters, along with some familiar ones you might recognise.

I'm often on social media – sometimes when I should be

writing – if you have time to say hello. There are links below for my Facebook, Twitter and Instagram accounts, and for my website. I look forward to hearing from you.

Liz x

www.lizeeles.com

facebook.com/lizeelesauthor
twitter.com/lizeelesauthor
instagram.com/lizeelesauthor

ACKNOWLEDGEMENTS

There's so much more involved in bringing out a new book than simply writing it. Thank you to everyone at Bookouture who's worked so hard to bring this book to publication. And extra-special thanks go to my wonderful editor, Ellen Gleeson, whose expertise and encouragement make all the difference. I'm also grateful for the support shown by my family and friends, and by everyone who picks up one of my books and reads what I write.

Made in the USA
Columbia, SC
30 June 2023

19726218R00178